1994

Harold Arwin

(1994

BEFORE
THE
WALL

ALSO BY GEORGE CLARE

Last Waltz in Vienna

GEORGE CLARE

BEFORE THE WALL

Berlin Days   1946–1948

A WILLIAM ABRAHAMS BOOK

DUTTON   NEW YORK

DUTTON

Published by the Penguin Group

Penguin Books USA Inc., 375 Hudson Street,
New York, New York 10014, U.S.A.

Penguin Books Ltd, 27 Wrights Lane,
London W8 5TZ, England

Penguin Books Australia Ltd, Ringwood,
Victoria, Australia

Penguin Books Canada Ltd, 2801 John Street,
Markham, Ontario, Canada L3R 1B4

Penguin Books (N.Z.) Ltd, 182–190 Wairau Road,
Auckland 10, New Zealand

Penguin Books Ltd, Registered Offices:
Harmondsworth, Middlesex, England

First published in the United States in 1990 by Dutton,
an imprint of New American Library, a division of Penguin Books USA Inc.
Distributed in Canada by McClelland & Stewart Inc.
Originally published in Great Britain under the title *Berlin Days*.

REGISTERED TRADEMARK—MARCA REGISTRADA

Library of Congress Cataloging-in-Publication Data

Clare, George, 1920–
[Berlin days]
Before the Wall : Berlin days, 1946–1948 / George Clare.
p. cm.
"A William Abrahams book."
Originally published in Great Britain under title: Berlin days.
Bibliography included in "Recommended reading": p.
ISBN 0-525-24896-X
1. Berlin (Germany)—History—Allied occupation, 1945– 2. Clare, George,
1920–   . 3. Intelligence officers—Great Britain—
Biography. I. Title.
DD881.C53   1990
943.1'550874—dc20   90-2797
                                              CIP

Printed in the United States of America
Set in Trump Medieval
Designed by Earl Tidwell

For Christel—my best of Berlin

As there shall be a search for the guilty, so there shall be a search for the innocent, who, if he be in need, shall be given help. The hand which metes out justice and punishes shall also be the hand that succors; because only thus does justice become a whole. The hand which succors shall also be the hand which metes out justice and punishes; because only thus does help become a whole. Both together then form the totality of rectitude.

Leo Baeck, Chief Rabbi of Berlin (Born Lissa [Posen], May 23, 1873; deported to Theresienstadt Ghetto 1942; died London, November 2, 1956)

Contents

✠   x   ✠

BEFORE
THE
WALL

Prologue

In early January 1946 I arrived in what was then the most harrowing and yet most fascinating place on earth—Berlin.

Harrowing, because all around me I saw the terrible aftermath of the corruption of a once great and formative European culture and civilization; fascinating, because in Berlin, and only in Berlin, Russians, Britons, Frenchmen, and Americans every day and every night rubbed shoulders—if nothing else—with the men and women of defeated Germany and also with each other. Fascinating too as a unique seismograph that, sensing every quiver between East and West, gave one early warning of the coming quakes of world politics. And, last but not least, because for me—a Royal Artillery bombardier attached as interpreter to the Control Commission for Germany (British Element)—the German capital was the focal point in my search for a solution to the German enigma.

During those two years, 1946 and 1947, Berlin inscribed

itself on my memory as firmly as Vienna, the city of my birth, childhood, and youth. However my acquaintance with Berlin began not in 1946, but eight years earlier when I, my feelings a mixture of eagerness and fear, looked out through the window of my sleeper compartment on the Vienna–Berlin overnight express and watched our train weave over the points, directing its final approach to Anhalter Bahnhof. I had longed to see Berlin ever since I was a little boy when my parents, after a journey through the Germany of the Weimar Republic, told me how scintillating a city it was. Yet September 2, 1938, was hardly the best of times for me, a seventeen-year-old Viennese Jew, to be aboard a Deutsche Reichsbahn coach steaming into the principal city of Hitler's Third Reich.

I had never been to Germany and had met few of its citizens until March 12, 1938, when thousands of them—Hitler's Wehrmacht soldiers—marched into Austria, having to brave nothing but the flower bombardment with which my jubilant compatriots welcomed them.

My first encounter with the might and men of Germany had painful consequences: I lost my home, my youth, and, ultimately, my much-loved parents. Yet in spite of this—or perhaps because of it?—a lifelong involvement with Germans and with Germany followed. Destiny? Yes, if one accepts, as I do, that our destinies are not merely the whims of the gods but are formed—consciously or unconsciously—by what formed us, by what we are.

By my origins I am a second-generation Viennese Jew, born into an enlightened and assimilated bourgeois family that wore its Jewish descent and traditions lightly. First and foremost we considered ourselves Viennese and Austrians. My parents' and their circle's spiritual and intellectual home was not Judaism but the world of the great thinkers and writers of the German tongue. Indeed,

Jews of our kind were not merely passive devotees but active protagonists of Austro-German culture. My father worshiped, never at a synagogue, but almost daily at the altar of German literature. By profession and with his brain he was a banker, but his heart belonged to the German classics, most of all their poetry. His daytime reading was the balance sheet, but in the evening he refreshed himself with Goethe, Schiller, Heine, Eichendorff, Rilke. He knew many of their poems by heart and, when reciting, occasionally slipped in one of his own, some genuinely moving, particularly those he wrote as a young Austrian Army officer during World War I. This love for German culture was paired with respect, not much short of admiration, for Germany and her achievements. In those days many Austrians, including Jewish ones, did not see in the Germany of the liberal Weimar Republic our country's "big" but its "great" brother.

My parents visited Germany in the late spring of 1929. Father had never been there, but my mother, who had spent her late childhood and teenage years in Hamburg, knew the country well. They went to the Hanseatic city first and then to Berlin, where some of my mother's relatives lived. In 1929, the most glistening year of Berlin's Golden Twenties, it was the most exhilarating, most creative, and also naughtiest of cities. The brilliance of its theaters, the satirical wit of its cabarets, its palatial cinemas, luxurious restaurants, the daring paintings in its avant-garde galleries, the vast scale of the place with its raucous streets and teeming crowds, overwhelmed my parents. I was only eight then, but their stories gave me the image of a bubbling, throbbing town full of vitality. And when I overheard my father—he had not noticed that I was in the next room—talking about Berlin's nightlife to his brother, I sensed from their voices that something a bit wicked but rather delicious was being discussed.

In brief, the atmosphere in which I grew up was one full of illusions about Austria and Germany, and the hopes we assimilated Jews based on them were as high—and as firm—as the clouds.

Until the awakening! In Vienna and Austria it was sudden and shattering. The tidal wave of anti-Semitism that swept over us, this Jew-baiting and Jew-beating festival with which the Viennese mob celebrated the Anschluss, was a violent explosion of race hatred the like of which even the Jews of Germany, who had already endured five years of Nazi rule, had not experienced. This was our perverse good fortune. It saved us from the tragic error of so many German Jews who, instead of fleeing, stayed on in their beloved fatherland, hoping some form of bearable existence might still be possible. We knew at once that there was only one way for us to go—*out*.

But where to? What country would grant us refuge? We were luckier than most and quickly found one: the then Irish Free State. My father's many business connections included some influential men there. In August 1938, only five months after the Anschluss, they cabled that our immigration permits had been granted and that our visas were ready for collection at the Irish Legation in Berlin. It was perhaps a bit "Irish" that our escape route from Hitler should lead right through his lion's den.

Our flat closed down, our furniture in storage, tearful farewells said, we boarded that overnight express to Berlin, which, having slowed to walking pace, now slid to a halt at the platform of Berlin's biggest railway terminal. Vienna's railway stations were not exactly cemeteries either, but at Anhalter Bahnhof one knew instantly that one was in a city of different temperament and dimensions. Noise, movement, travelers rushing, porters (who unlike their Viennese colleagues had never heard of lethargy) speedily following with the luggage; soldiers entraining or detraining at the double; shouting, whistling; bells ringing; embraces, kisses, tears, hurry, hurry, *schnell, schnell*; tremendous, cacophonous, enjoyed and enjoyable hullabaloo. It was so exciting I forgot my fears and felt regret that our stay in Berlin was to be so short; just two days to pick up our visas, book our passage to London—the first lap of the journey to Dublin—brief farewell visits to mother's Berlin cousins, and off.

That was the intention. But we knew hardly anything about Ireland, and none of us had ever heard of Murphy's Law. Well, we soon started to learn about both at the Irish Legation in the Tiergarten district when we went there the morning after our arrival in Berlin.

We went in with our heads held high. We had made it; we felt practically as good as Irish already. We knocked at the frosted glass door marked VISA SECTION. A woman's voice answered, "Come in!" We did and said—no, proclaimed—we were the Klaars from Vienna; our self-assured tone implying that we were who she had been waiting for.

"Yes?" she said, an audible question mark in her voice.

We had come to collect our visas.

"What visas?" she asked, her question mark now in italics.

Surely, she knew about us?

"No," she replied.

"B-but . . . ?"

"One moment," she said, "let me look through my files." She did. Then she shrugged her shoulders.

My father showed her the telegram from his business friend in Dublin saying "Permits granted" and his subsequent letter confirming that our visa applications had been approved by the Irish Foreign Ministry.

She read the documents, went to her filing cabinet again, and looked through it for a second time.

"I'm so sorry," she said, "but there's nothing about

you from Dublin. Not a word." She was German, not Irish, but her face expressed sympathy. She was a nice German.

What were we to do? What would she advise?

"Send a telegram to your Dublin contact immediately," she suggested, adding that she would also write to the Foreign Ministry.

How long would all that take?

Again she shrugged her shoulders. She knew Murphy's Law!

We left with faces as long as our shadows drawn on the pavement by the late summer sun.

Now I had all the time in the world, ten endless weeks as it turned out, to become not just acquainted but pretty familiar with Berlin. The city was, of course, no longer the one that had so entranced my parents nine years earlier. But some of its cosmopolitan spirit, though dampened by the stark but nebulous philosophy of its present masters, survived. Berliners still had spunk, irreverence, and their typical dry, impudent, and often sarcastic humor. The city, so to speak, wore its brown shirt sloppily, unbuttoned, and with collar open; unlike Vienna, which having slipped into it so eagerly, now preened itself in the pseudo-glamour of the new uniform.

Walking through the streets I lost my way now and then and had to ask for directions. I was a bit hesitant at first. I do not look like one of Hitler's copybook "Aryans," but nobody was ever rude to me. Even policemen were helpful. My Viennese accent may have helped. Knowing that it sounded a bit humorous but also rather charming to North Germans, I exaggerated it. What struck me most, though, was the absence, with one or two exceptions, of the "Jews not wanted here" notices that were on practically every shop, every coffeehouse, and place of entertainment in Vienna. My parents and I ate in restaurants and went to the cinema or the the-

ater—impossible in Nazi Vienna. And not once did anyone complain loudly in our hearing about the foul smell
of Jew polluting the air, the sort of joke much favored
by Vienna's Nazi "ecologists." We did not feel free in
Berlin, but freer than we had at home.

I knew that our situation was serious, but at not yet
eighteen one possesses—to echo Milan Kundera—"a
lightness of being" that enables one to dance, and with
some élan, even over such thin ice as our existence in
Berlin. I enjoyed observing Berlin's pulsating life, not
least its *Fräuleinwunder*, a phenomenon the world
would discover some two decades later. My Viennese
prejudice about German women was that they came in
two patterns: fat, frumpish *Hausfrau* or lumpy Hitler
maiden with straw-blonde plaits wound around the head.
Not in Berlin, or at least not in that part of the city
where I did most of my exploring, the Kurfürstendamm
and the area around it. There the girls were pretty and
smart, the women well turned out, even elegant, and the
Nazi ordinance that the true German *Frau* shun cosmet-
ics and nicotine was clearly honored more in the breach
than in the observance.

I loved Kurfürstendamm, Berlin's Fifth Avenue or
Knightsbridge. Its wide tree-lined pavements were always crowded with strollers. I could sit by the window
of a coffeehouse or *Konditorei* for hours and watch the
world and its girls go by. Wherever you looked, at people,
at shop windows, at the dense traffic, you saw the signs
of prosperity. In the early autumn of 1938 life in Germany—unless one either was a Jew or valued justice,
liberty, individuality—was pleasant. Most Germans
thought the jackboot had hit the jackpot.

I, however, was a Jew. As week followed week and still
no visa came, the ice under my feet began to feel very
brittle. Then, after six weeks in Berlin, out of a miraculous blue, a letter arrived from the managing director of

the French bank for whose Austrian subsidiary my father had worked for thirty years. He was offered a position at the bank's Paris head office for 3,333 French francs per month. An odd sum I never forgot. Father felt uneasy about leaving mother and me. We insisted that he had to accept. There was nothing he could do for us in Germany, but once he was in France he could move heaven and earth to obtain permission for us to follow. We no longer believed those Irish visas would ever come through. Father telephoned his acceptance, and forty-eight hours later, the French visa in his passport, he was on the train to Paris. The Banque des Pays de l'Europe Centrale was influential.

It was the right decision, the only possible one, and also the worst decision, the fatal one.

From then on Father beat his head against the cotton wool of French bureaucracy, which kept on inventing new excuses why his wife and son could not yet join him. On November 9, 1938, the day of the Reichskristallnacht pogrom, we were still in Berlin in the Jewish Pension Lurie on the Kurfürstendamm. With the other guests we sat in fearful silence in the lounge listening to the howls of the organized mob smashing the windows of Jewish shops. We all had but one thought. When would the SS come and take us away? Nothing happened, no one came. Why we were spared while Jews were arrested all over Germany in their thousands I never could explain. It seemed a miracle, but an even greater one occurred next morning while my mother and I were having breakfast in the dining room. The phone rang. It was for us. That nice German secretary from the Irish Legation was at the other end announcing with jubilance that our visas had been granted.

Even though the Lufthansa plane to London was airborne, I had no feeling of relief. Not yet. What if the captain was ordered to return to Tempelhof airport and hand us over to the Gestapo? I could not believe the nightmare was truly over until the evening of that day, November 11, 1938—the luckiest of my life—when, from our boardinghouse in Greencroft Gardens, I more skipped than walked along Finchley Road to Swiss Cottage and then down the whole of Wellington Road and back, singing softly with every step: "I'm free, I'm free, I'm free!"

Austria and Vienna, Berlin and Germany belonged to my past. Forever, I thought.

1

Beyond Hate
or Pity

The war in Europe was over, Hitler had gone wherever it is that Hitlers go, a new world was about to be born—and where was I? Stuck in the battery office of 137 Battery, 117 Field Regiment RA, in the middle of nowhere, the woods of the National Forestry Commission at Thetford in Norfolk. Inhaling ozone by the ton was wholesome to excess, but the air I wanted to breathe was the fetid and polluted one of bombed and burned-out Germany. I needed to know why—to quote the single sentence in which the Austrian satirist Karl Kraus summed up the history of Germany from 1848 to 1945—the country of the *"Dichter und Denker,"* the poets and thinkers, had turned into the land of the *"Richter und Henker,"* the blood-judges and hangmen, that had murdered my parents. Was there an answer? If so, then it was certainly not to be found in all the salubrious greenery around me. I had to wangle a transfer to Germany. But how?

My battery commander, Major Sugden, solved that problem for me when he came into the battery office one morning, put a new Army Council circular on my desk, and said, "You, Clare, might care to go in for this. You're the sort of intellectual type they want." The circular asked for volunteers willing to undergo a six-month intensive Russian course at Cambridge and serve afterward as sergeant-interpreters for British officers on liaison duty with the Red Army in Germany. I filled in the application form, Major Sugden endorsed it, and four weeks later I was told to report to the Control Commission for Germany offices in Prince's Gardens in Knightsbridge.

Walking up the staircase to the reception desk I immediately recognized the lance corporal sitting behind it, my old Viennese school chum Oppenheimer. We had been ships passing each other in the long night of our scholastic careers as we sailed from school to school. Whenever I was kicked out of one of Vienna's *Gymnasia* and moved to the next, Oppenheimer was already there. Never for long, though. Soon they would throw him out again, and when, a few months later, I suffered the same fate and changed to yet another school, who would be sitting there—a broad grin spreading over his face as he saw me walk into the classroom—why, Oppenheimer, of course!

He came straight to the point in three famous first words. "You are nuts," he said.

"Why?"

"You want to go to that Russian course in Cambridge, don't you?"

"Yes, what's wrong with that?"

"Nothing, except they'll make you sign on for another two years. When did you join up?"

"June 1941."

"Same time I did. We're the same age, so we're in the same demob group. You'll be out round about September

'46. You go on that course and you'll be in until the end of '48. Is that what you want?"

No, I said, but how else was I to get away from Thetford and to Germany?

"So, what's the problem?" he replied. "You speak German, don't you?"

"Ha-ha, very funny," I said. "But what use is that? I'm here for the Russian thing."

"Who d'you think cares? D'you think anybody here knows what's going on? I'll take your papers from the Russian bunch and put them on top of the German pile. That's it. Nobody'll have a clue, believe me."

The nonexisting old school ties of the various Viennese educational establishments we had jointly disgraced worked just as well as an Old Etonian one. I was transferred to the Control Commission, promoted to bombardier, attended a pretty useless interpreters' course at Prince's Gardens, and at 6:30 on the morning of Monday, January 7, 1946, found myself once again looking out at Berlin through a train window. This time it was the overnight British military train from Rhine Army HQ in Bad Oeynhausen steaming into Charlottenburg station, the rail terminal in the British Sector of the former capital of the former Grossdeutsche Reich. The dark of the winter night outside was fading, but there was not much to see. A blanket of foggy, freezing gray overlay the suburban housescape.

The train stopped. Three Rail Transport NCOs and a shabbily uniformed German policeman were the only people on the arrival platform. Grayness, deadness, emptiness. What a contrast to the rumbustious sounds of Anhalter Bahnhof echoing in my memory! We got up, stretched our weary bones, slipped into our greatcoats, and buttoned them up to our necks. Then we helped each other with our webbing equipment and finally—

belts with ammunition pouches, haversacks, and water bottles buckled up, shoulder straps untwisted, the packs with the steel helmets on our backs, our Lee-Enfield Mark IVs in our right hands (perfect attire, I thought, for my return to Berlin)—we moved down the narrow coach corridor. As we disembarked the station public address system crackled alive and twanged: "Attention. Your transport is downstairs outside the station. Watch it when you go down, there's black ice on the steps."

"Got your skates?" Jock MacDonald, my new friend from Edinburgh, joked. It was just as well they had warned us. Tired, hungry, sweaty, dirty, and balancing heavy kit bags on our shoulders, we were none too steady on our feet.

"Careful, dear boy, don't break anything," a familiar voice said from behind me. "Oh shut up, Sely, you patronizing twerp," I thought, as that high and mighty captain passed me, followed by a German driver carrying his two elegant leather grips to the waiting staff car. What still rankled was that he had rebuked Joanna, one of the lady interpreters from our Prince's Gardens course, for going to the army cinema in Bünde with a mere NCO—me.

Our transport was a tarpaulin-covered army lorry. An RTO corporal stood by its tailboard. Our names? Jock told him. He looked down the list on his clipboard.

" 'Aven't got no Clare or MacDonald 'ere," he said. "Where's your movement orders?"

We gave them to him.

"Bleedin' interpreters' pool. I should 'ave known," was his comment. "The most shambolic outfit in this place. Right, get on the lorry. The driver'll take you there after he's dropped the others at Kaiserdamm."

"Where do they 'ang out?" the driver asked.

"Uhlandstrasse. Number 17, I think."

"Where's that?"

"When the other shower's got off, you turn around on Kaiserdamm. Go down it, then turn into Wilmersdorfer. You know where that is?" The driver nodded.

"Stay on it till you see Kantstrasse . . ."

A burst of hilarity from those already in the lorry, followed by shouts of "That's what we all want, Corp!" No wonder; the corporal did not pronounce the philosopher's name the English way with a long *a* as in "can't," but with a short, sharp *a* as the Germans do.

"Oh shut it," he shouted back, "you'll get plenty of that in this town anyway! You turn left into Kant," he grinned, obviously enjoying saying it, "and Uhland runs across, just before you get to Bahnhof Zoo. Throw them two out at the corner. They can walk from there. Right, off you go."

We had a bit of a problem finding the building. Its number plate was hidden behind one of the two ample sculpted Valkyries that flanked the top of the stairs leading to the entrance. It was half-past seven when we got there, but the door was already open; it was marvelous to get out of the biting cold. Walking down the long ground-floor corridor we found a door marked INTERPRETERS' POOL CCG (BE). To our amazement it opened when we tried the handle. Just about anybody could walk into this British office building and go where he liked. We thought it incredible negligence in a city that had been Hitler's capital eight months earlier. We went in, dumped our things, walked through the rooms, and struck what to us was sheer good fortune, a washbasin with running hot water in the loo next to the office of the commanding officer, one Lieutenant Colonel E. F. Garrett, MC.

Washed and shaved, we felt almost like human beings again. Then Jock had a brainwave. "Let's teach that lot a lesson in security and proper military discipline. Let's mount a guard," he suggested. Steel helmets on our heads, rifles in our fists, we took up position outside the door of the Interpreters' Pool, two self-important Berlin greenhorns with not a round of live ammunition between them, ready to defend the files and dictionaries of the interpreters against SS or SA thugs, or fanatical Hitler Youth werewolves. They, apparently, were otherwise engaged that morning. The Germans who did arrive were harmless clerks and secretaries. Startled by our martial display, they scuttled into their offices.

After playing soldiers for over an hour, we spotted a British officer coming in our direction. Smartly rapping our rifle butts on the stone floor, we sprang to attention. At this he did a double take, as if wondering whether we were real or a hallucination of the kind owners of bibulous red-and-blue-veined noses like his were prone to.

"Great Scot," he exclaimed, having stared at us two rigid figures for quite a few seconds, "who's put sentries on my place?"

"Sir, we found the door unlocked, so we thought we'd better make sure the place was safe," Jock said.

"Of course it is. How d'you expect the cleaners to get in? Oh, for God's sake stand easy. Who are you, anyway, and who's sent you?"

"Corporal MacDonald and Bombardier Clare, sir. We're new interpreters," I reported.

"New interpreters? I don't need any. I haven't asked for you."

"They told us we were urgently needed in Berlin."

"Who did? Never mind. Come in and get rid of your warpaint first. You're making a ridiculous spectacle of yourselves. The war's over. I dare say you've heard. I'm Colonel Garrett. When you're ready, come into my office and explain who sent you here and why."

The "who" was easy, but the "why" neither of us knew.

You see, Jock and I first met on the army train that

took us from Ostend to Bünde, a Westphalian country town a few miles from Lübbecke, the Administration HQ for the Control Commission's interpreters. I liked him from the moment he opened the door of the compartment I shared with three other non–British-born NCOs from my interpreters' course and asked in his endearing Edinburgh accent whether he could join us. We talked a lot during the long train journey. I found him intelligent, well educated, thoughtful, and refreshingly chipless—in contrast to us Central European Jews who still carried loads of them on our ex-refugee shoulders. He was tall, slim, tough, proudly and fiercely Scottish, in spite—or perhaps just because—of his German mother. She came from Münster, the Catholic town and see in Westphalia, where Jock, spending most of his prewar holidays with his grandparents, had learned his flawless German. The old people had survived the war. Jock wanted to get a posting to Münster so that he could look after them. There and then, in the first flush of our new friendship, I decided to stay with him. If he wanted Münster I would go there too. Was that really my true motive? I sometimes wonder. I knew full well that Berlin, not provincial Münster, was the place where I ought to be. Was I acting on impulse, as I thought then, or subconsciously grasping this chance of not having to face Berlin with its many memories of my parents? I do have a tendency to avoid painful confrontations.

In Bünde they left us to kick our heels. Literally. What else was there to do in that boring little town but go for boring walks and discuss what stratagems we could use to get us to Münster? On the fourth morning there we were told to report to Lübbecke for an interview. Was it about our postings? Yes. Would we be given a choice? Of course, that was what it was all about.

My name beginning with *C*, the Lübbecke captain who was to assign us to our destinations saw me first. Nodding his head understandingly he listened to the reasons that Jock and I wanted Münster. When I had finished he gave me a kindly smile and said, "That's fine, Bombardier. You and your friend can stay together. Not in Münster, but in Berlin. Berlin is screaming for more interpreters. No good arguing. Actually there's no need for me to see Corporal MacDonald as well. You just tell him how it is. He can try for a compassionate posting later. Your railway warrants for Berlin are in the sergeant major's office, signed and ready to be picked up. Thank you, Bombardier."

That was all we could tell Garrett. "Oh well," he said, "I'll find you something to do." He signed a requisition form for our accommodation at Kaiserdamm barracks, bade his sergeant organize transport, and told us to take the rest of the day off to settle in.

The so-called barracks were four German apartment blocks, their perimeter surrounded by a high chicken-wire fence. The sentry box by the entrance had no sentry and the billeting office inside was empty as well. We went on into the stairwell and after we had yelled "Shop!" several times a lance corporal appeared on the second-floor landing. "Shut up and come up," he shouted. We showed him the form with Garrett's signature. "Oh, all right," he grumbled. "Come with me."

"Where can we get some food?" we asked him, after he had shown us into one of four large interconnecting rooms furnished with army beds, trestle tables, and a few requisitioned German chairs.

"Put your things on your beds," he said, "and when you've done that go out, cross Kaiserdamm, turn right, and at the first intersection, Königin Elisabeth Strasse, you'll see our tram shuttle at the corner. It'll take you to the mess."

Five minutes later we were at the former Nazi storm-trooper drill hall, which was now the British soldiers' mess. A spread-winged eagle sculpted in stone, holding a laurel-wreathed swastika in its claws, still loomed over the entrance. It was half-past ten, but we were by no means the last ones to sit down to a late breakfast. German waitresses brought us porridge, bacon and eggs, big mugs of tea, and toast; on each table were two soup plates, one with marmalade, the other with Golden Syrup. The younger and prettier waitresses spoke fairly fluent English, their German accent interestingly laced with British local idioms, ranging from Glaswegian to cockney; only very private lessons—never a Berlitz school—could have produced such linguistic curiosities. When we had finished and smoked our cigarettes, Jock said he was going back to the billets for a nap. I was much too keyed up for that and glad to be on my own. I wanted to walk to the house at the north corner of Wilmersdorferstrasse and Kurfürstendamm where the Jewish Pension Lurie had been in 1938, the last place my parents and I had lived together as a family.

Warmed through by our super-calorific breakfast, all tiredness gone, I stepped out into the street. It was still cold, but a late and wintry sun had sponged the gray off the sky and turned it into a sparkling icy blue. It felt good to walk in the uniform of the victor through those well-remembered streets.

My most striking first impression was not visual but aural: the muted echoes of a battered city. The 1938 Berlin had assaulted one's ears with lively and strident crescendos, harsh, atonal, high-decibel; a medley of blaring car horns, squeaking brakes, snorting buses, clanging trams, shouting newspaper sellers. But now—like slow eerie drumbeats of a danse macabre—each sound rose and remained alone, the *clipclop* of often wooden-soled footsteps, the rattle of a handcart or an occasional tram, the chugging of a wood-fueled bus, the gear clash of an Allied army lorry. This absence of the constant roar of city life was more unsettling than the sight of bombed and shelled buildings, of jagged outlines of broken masonry framing bits of blue sky. I had been prepared for that, but not for a city hushed to a whisper. Yet Berlin was not a lifeless moonscape. It lived—albeit in something of a zombied trance—mirrored in the dazed looks of many of the people I passed, more often noticeable in men than women. But then the men were mostly old or elderly, bowed and bitter-faced; the few youngish ones who were about—emaciated shadows of the soldiers who had almost conquered an entire continent—looked pathetic and downtrodden in the tattered remnants of their Wehrmacht uniforms. The women were of all ages and, with so many men killed and hundreds of thousands in prisoner-of-war camps, they, not as formerly the Prussian male, dominated the scene.

Looking at the Germans around me my feelings were beyond hate or pity. I had been uncertain what my attitude toward them would or should be, but after my encounter with the railway children of Hamm I knew.

Our train, which had departed from Ostend in the evening, stopped at a tiny German country station, miles from anywhere, at about ten the following morning. On its single platform stood an RTO captain with three sergeants. Raising a loudspeaker to his mouth the officer ordered us to detrain to collect our haversack rations.

Passing one of his sergeants I said, "Odd place you've picked, haven't you, right at the back of nowhere?"

"That's why, Bomb," he replied. "You don't want to get your grub at a main station with crowds of half-starved Germans watching and begging kids swarming all over you like buzz-flies. Not pleasant, I can tell you. They'll be there all right when you get to Hamm, but you'll be up on your train and at a siding."

Hamm! Every child in Britain knew the name of that rail junction and marshaling yard, which the RAF had pounded more often and more fiercely than almost any other target in Germany. Jock and I were curious to see what was left of it. When the train pulled up at a siding some two hundred yards from the station we pushed the window down and looked out. The only signs of the recent war were a few burned-out trucks and some patches on the station building. Otherwise everything looked amazingly normal.

"So that's what they called 'saturation bombing,'" Jock said. "Forget it." He was about to close the window when we heard a small voice right beneath us whisper, "Hello, Tommy!"

We looked down. A seven- or eight-year-old girl, her hands outstretched and pleadingly cupped, was standing underneath it. Half of the Cadbury's Fruit and Nut bar we had been eating was still left and Jock threw it down to her. That did it. We had only seen a few Germans on the station platforms, no children anywhere, but suddenly hordes of them came running across the tracks. Seconds later they had lined up all along our train. "Tommy! Eh, Tommy komm! Please Tommy vat you got? Chockie, sandvich, sveets? Please, Tommy, hunger Tommy," they shouted.

The train windows rattled down, heads stuck out, and then manna from Britain: hard-boiled eggs, sweets, sandwiches, chocolate bars, apples, oranges, a few cans of sardines even, rained down on that jumping, laughing, crying, whirling troop of little dervishes. There was weeping, cursing, and fighting as the older children pushed the smaller ones aside. The soldiers were laughing. They enjoyed the spectacle. Like people amusing themselves throwing nuts at monkeys in a zoo. I was not going to join in. I went back into our compartment, took my haversack rations, walked to the coach door, opened it, and jumped down. Four children standing nearby turned to run away when they saw me come toward them.

"Hier bleiben!" I shouted, ordering them to stop. They did. A German-speaking Tommy was such a rarity it made them curious. The oldest, a blonde pig-tailed ten-year-old, shivering in the cold, came closer.

"Du sprichst Deutsch, Tommy?" she asked.

"Yes, I do."

"Hast Du was für mich?"

"Yes," I said, "for you and the other three, fair shares."

As I looked at that German girl I saw in a sudden vision the fear-dilated eyes in the tiny, shrunken faces of children of the Warsaw ghetto being herded together for the slaughter by German soldiers. A nightmarish image. It still haunted me years later, looking at my son and daughters when they were little. Could the father of that girl I was talking to have been one of those men in German uniform? *"Hast Du was für mich?"* What would he have had for the ghetto children but a smack with his rifle butt! And yet what had all this to do with her? What I was doing felt right and so it was right. I could not condemn all Germans, I could not hate all Germans, as the Nazis had condemned and hated all Jews. No, I neither hated Germans nor—with the exception of the children—did I pity them.

But then the Germans did not need my pity. They had, as I soon discovered, so much of it—far too much—for themselves.

Those were my thoughts as I arrived at the corner of Wilmersdorferstrasse and Kurfürstendamm. The architrave of its rather grandiose portico, an upright sentinel guarding a mound of debris, was all that was left of the house where my parents and I had lived. *Trümmerfrauen*, rubble-women, rusty hammers in their frost-reddened fists, hair tightly scarf-bound against the dust, were knocking crusts of mortar off still usable bricks and stacking them. Their contribution to the rebuilding of Berlin is remembered to this day, and the following lines written by one of them reflect something of the atmosphere of the Berlin of 1946:

> Our city's easy ladies
> Paint their lips a sexy red
> Think: to hell with all that debris
> Those who work there must be mad
>
> Had we followed their example
> Had we bed-hopped like those twits
> Berlin—evidence is ample—
> To this day would be in bits.

Having watched them for a while I turned around, intending to walk back to Kaiserdamm. But after a few steps I stopped. The house I had just passed looked familiar. Of course Aunt Manya, mother's cousin by marriage, and her daughter Rösl had lived here. We had spent quite a few evenings with them in the autumn of 1938. They had not emigrated, that I knew. And what had happened to them I could guess. Still ... Rösl was only thirty-five then. It would have been a miracle but she might have survived. I went in and began to climb the stairs to the fifth floor where Manya and Rösl's apartment had been.

2

"Heil Hitler, Herr Captain!"

Standing outside the door to the Bartmanns' apartment I could see myself again on the little balcony at the rear of their sitting room admiring Albert Speer's spectacular Dome of Light over the Sport Palast. Under this gigantic silvery halo, thrown on to Berlin's night sky by the beams of dozens of searchlights, Adolf Hitler was explaining to the world that the Czech Sudeten region was positively his last territorial demand. No lie ever spoken was exposed to more light; no lie ever spoken was swallowed more readily. This luminous pageant was beautiful and sinister, a reminder of the scene in the film of H. G. Well's *The Shape of Things to Come*, which I had seen in Vienna, where the enemy planes break through London's searchlight barrier and the bombs begin to fall.

It was the evening of September 26, 1938. In the living room behind me, the remnants of our cold supper still on the table, my parents, Manya, and Rösl were listening to Hitler on the radio. Father, mother, and Rösl sat quite still, concentrating on his words. Manya shifted nervously on her chair. A frail-looking diabetic in her mid-sixties, she was a bit of a moaner and not very bright, but Rösl, her daughter, was a delight. She had visited us in Vienna five years earlier. She had been thirty then, an elderly lady for me at thirteen, but her sparkling intelligence, quick Berlin wit, how she treated me as young man rather than boy, and—last but not least—her strong resemblance to my mother made me like her immediately. Though Mother and she were second cousins only, they looked like sisters. Both had the same oval faces, the same myopic dark-brown eyes, almost identical, slightly too fleshy noses, the same thick black hair, or "horsehair" as my mother referred to hers. Thirty-five-year-old Rösl's was graying while Mother's—she was fifty-one—was jet black. A miracle of nature? Father and I politely pretended it was. When he, the banker husband, checked Mother's household accounts each month, he always queried some items of expenditure—for the sake of good order and marital discipline, I suppose—but what she spent at her hairdresser's he never mentioned. Again like my mother, Rösl also spoke fluent French and English, and this, together with her intelligence and efficiency, had helped her to a much-envied job as assistant manager of the Air France office in Berlin, where the fact that she was Jewish did not matter. She believed that her position with the national airline of a great power gave her semidiplomatic status and, therefore, immunity from Nazi persecution; neither she nor her mother considered emigration seriously until it was too late.

Four visiting cards were pinned over the bell on the doorjamb. I read "Hinrichsen," "Dahlke," "Rebhuhn," "Kunzel." Should I ring and ask whether any of them knew something about Manya or Rösl? Still thinking about it I noticed a small oblong space on the upper-left door panel where the nameplate M. UND R. BARTMANN had kept it free of Berlin's grime. Why ask? That little rectangle, a shade lighter than the rest of the door, was their epitaph. The only one they would ever have.

I turned and as I walked downstairs I wondered if there still was a similar empty space on the door of our Vienna flat. Or had the new owners, covering it with their brass plate, denied my parents even so abject a memorial? On the staircase of that house in Wilmersdorferstrasse the thought slipped into my mind that my parents must not remain a mere two digits in the statistics of mass murder. Vague as it was, it stayed with me—God knows where—while I built my life until, one Sunday afternoon in the late Swinging Sixties, I sat down and typed the first words of *Last Waltz in Vienna*. I know that that book, in the hearts and minds of those who read it, lifted Ernst and Stella, my parents, off the conveyor taking the ashes of the industrially slaughtered from the fire ovens into the pit of anonymity. And, perhaps, by portraying their life and their death, it also did a little to restore to the nameless millions, who died with and like them, some of the humanity lost in the corpse count.

Walking back to Kaiserdamm barracks I asked myself yet once again: who were the guilty ones? Hinrichsen, Dahlke, Rebhuhn, Kunzel? Ought they to have seen the evil inherent in National Socialism before it was too late? Hitler had had his admirers everywhere. In every country there were those who had believed that he, better than anyone else, knew how to solve the problems of the times. My friend Jock, for instance. Or Joanna Cantrell, the very English, very upper-class daughter of a Regular Army brigadier. The apparent power of a dictatorship to get things done fascinates many—especially the impatient young.

Joanna—we met at the interpreters' course in Prince's Gardens and became friends for life—spent 1936, the year of the Olympic Games, in Germany to perfect her knowledge of the language. The Third Reich greatly impressed the eighteen-year-old. The cities and the countryside, Hitler Youths and Hitler Maidens, civilians and military, everything and everybody were so clean, so wholesome, so orderly. She saw a nation full of self-confidence and with an admirably clear sense of direction. When Joanna returned to England she found her own country supine, indolent, foundering. Convinced that the Germans had the answer to decline, unemployment, hopelessness, she joined the Anglo-German Friendship Society sponsored by Herr von Ribbentrop, the British Right's darling Ambassador to the Court of St. James's. It was not until 1938 that press photographs of Jews forced by grinning stormtroopers and civilians to scrub the gutters of Vienna proved to Joanna that the Nazis' sense of direction and hers were not the same at all. She resigned from the Ribbentrop circus. Nevertheless when the war started she was in serious trouble with the authorities. She managed to clear herself and eventually became one of Ian Fleming's assistants in Naval Intelligence. Yet before she was posted to Germany as a Control Commission officer-grade interpreter, she had to give an undertaking not to contact any of her prewar German friends.

The story Jock told me was not all that different. After he had joined us on the Ostend to Bünde train and we had started to chat he slipped in a few sentences of astonishingly perfect German. He had told us that he was an interpreter, but I had not expected an Edinburgh "laddie" to speak German almost like a native.

"How come you speak it so well?" I asked him.

"My mother's German-born," he replied, "but most of it I learned from my grandparents and friends in Münster. I spent my holidays there every year. I just picked it up. I liked Germany. To tell the truth, after Hitler took over I thought he performed miracles. Many of my Münster friends joined the Hitler Youth. They looked damn smart in their uniforms, and when they invited me to join their summer camp I was dead keen to go. Grandad didn't like it. He's a staunch Catholic and he hated the Nazis. We had quite a row when he tried to talk me out of it. I was sixteen, so naturally the more he said against it the more I insisted on going. We had a real ding-dong, I can tell you. But in the end he shouted, 'Ach, go to the devil!' and you might say I did.

"I loved it, at first that is. Plenty of sport, good food, great scenery, nice chaps. I had my doubts about our *Rottenführer*. I'd known him for years and thought him a nice lad, but in camp he suddenly behaved as if he were Hitler himself. You couldn't just talk to him. You had to stand to attention and report. And how the boys sucked up to him! *'Jawoll, Rottenführer!'* this, *'Jawoll, Rottenführer!'* that. Ridiculous, but I shrugged it off. In the evenings we sat round the campfire, roasted potatoes, and sang Hitler Youth songs. It was exciting and very romantic, there was a feeling of belonging—of, yes, comradeship, for want of a better word.

"But eventually what we were singing began to bother me. All about war, fighting, marching, victory, German valor, German greatness. I thought it a load of nonsense, but I kept my mouth shut, until, that is, they sang about German belonging to them today and tomorrow the whole world: *'Heute gehört uns Deutschland, morgen die ganze Welt!'* You know it, don't you?"

I nodded.

"When they repeated that chorus for the third time I got bloody angry. Suddenly I heard a voice yelling: 'You can keep your damn Germany, but you bastards can't have Scotland!' which, to my surprise, I recognized as my own.

"What an uproar! Can you imagine? 'Get on the next

train to your Scotland,' the *Rottenführer* shouted, 'or you'll be in real trouble. And you'd better not turn up around here ever again!' End of my Nazi period. End of my holidays in Germany. I wonder if that chap is still around? I'd like to know what he thinks now."

Thoughts and memories at the end of a long, a very long, mentally and physically exhausting first day in Berlin; one raising many questions and providing no ready answers.

The barrack room was empty when I got back. I went to the mess for an early supper and then to bed. Heaven knows how long I would have slept had I not been awakened by an earsplitting crash. I sat up and so did Jock in the bed next to mine. We rubbed our eyes, looked around, and then, much puzzled, at each other. Apart from us and a corporal picking up his dropped mess tin with an apologetic smile there was nobody in our room or the adjoining one. Of the fourteen beds in the two dormitories only three, Jock's, mine, and that corporal's, had been slept in.

"Sorry about that racket, but time you got up anyway," he said. "By the way, my name's Tolliver. What's yours?"

Having told him I asked, "How come there are only the three of us here?"

"Oh, the others are busy. Very busy," he replied.

"You're not telling me they're on duty already?" Jock said, looking at his watch. "It's half-past seven."

"Sure they are," Tolliver grinned. "They've been at it all night, you might say. Permanent night duty, sort of."

"You're pulling our legs," I said.

"Only a little. Enlightening the innocent about the facts of life is one of Uncle Tolliver's specialties. Ask me anything you like. After three months in this town I know the ropes. Anyway, people only sleep here if sleep's what they want. Few do. Every night is *Fräulein* night. That's why Berlin's licentious soldiery has that tired look. You may have noticed."

"How does one get a sleeping-out pass?" asked the hopeful Jock.

"Who needs one! Mind you, there's been a bit of fuss about chaps falling asleep at their desks. The other day all NCOs were given a lecture by the camp commander, a half-colonel I'd never seen before. 'I don't give a tinker's cuss who you pull through at night,' he said, 'but from now on anyone not at his desk at nine sharp will be on a charge.' Nobody will take any notice, of course. It's a good life. If you like that sort of thing. It so happens I don't. I'm choosy about where I sleep."

Tolliver was absolutely right. When we arrived at the Interpreters' Pool some minutes before nine there was no one there in spite of the commander's threat. Garrett's sergeant drifted in twenty minutes late.

"What are you doing here, Clare?" he exclaimed. "You're supposed to report to Captain Delaney at Lancaster House."

"How should I know?"

"Didn't I tell you?"

"Not a word."

The sergeant shrugged his shoulders. "Must have forgotten, mustn't I? Get on the next bus. You'll just make it. He's in room . . ." he checked his scribble pad, "506."

Lancaster House, the headquarters of the British Control Commission for Germany, a concave-shaped gray concrete edifice on the south side of Fehrbelliner Platz, was a typical example of Albert Speer–style Nazi architecture. With searchlights Hitler's master builder was as imaginative as are some passages in his memoirs, but his buildings were as he was during his years of power: megalomaniac, soulless, insensitive.

Having found room 506 I knocked, walked in, saluted, and reported.

Delaney, dark-haired with a permanent five-o'clock shadow, bushy black moustache, and delicately pale alabaster skin, looked at me disapprovingly with light-blue eyes.

"High time you got here. What's kept you?" he snapped.

I was about to explain, but he immediately shut me up with a brusque "Never mind now. We're late. Follow me."

We raced down the stairs to the inner courtyard where Delaney's jeep was waiting. Jumping into the seat next to the driver he motioned me toward the back.

Turning to me, the driver said: "I'm new, Bomb. Where are we going?"

"Drive off and follow my signals," Delaney ordered, and instead of telling the driver where to go he silently pointed his swagger stick in the direction he wanted. But when Delaney suddenly circled his cane in front of the driver's nose, he slammed on the brakes and stopped the jeep. "Why the fucking hell don't you tell me where you want to go instead of fumbling about with that thing . . . sir!" he shouted.

"I'll have you on a charge if you use foul language," the captain shouted back, but from then on, until we arrived at our destination, the headquarters of the British Sector's German Fire Brigade, Delaney gave clear verbal instructions.

I followed him upstairs to a big room on the top floor, where the chief fire office, the *Brandingenieur*, and his four *Brandmeister* for the districts Wilmersdorf, Charlottenburg, Tiergarten, and Spandau, which comprised the British Sector, were awaiting Delaney. They were in uniform and saluted, a greeting cursorily acknowledged by the captain.

"I want your report about the Poppek case," Delaney barked at the chief, "and let me tell you I consider your action gross insubordination . . ."

The chief wanted to speak.

"No, you hear what I have to say," Delaney cut him off. "You had no right to get rid of Poppek without my permission. I'm in command and I'll have no high-handed behavior from any German. That's it. Translate, Bombardier!"

When I had, the chief looked absolutely stunned.

"But you know why I dismissed Poppek," he said. "What else do you expect me to do with a man who raises his arm in the Nazi salute and shouts, 'Heil Hitler, Herr Captain!' when you come to inspect his station? You tell me."

I translated this for Delaney, thinking, What's that twerp complaining about? I quickly found out.

"I'd rather have a smart Nazi than a slovenly run fire station," Delaney replied. "Anyway, what have firefighting and politics to do with each other? Poppek ran a tight ship. His station was the most efficient in the whole sector. When he said 'Jump!' his men jumped. Best fire drill I've seen. I want that man back. Besides, that 'Heil Hitler' was probably just a reflex action. Translate."

I did not believe I had heard right.

"You don't really want me to translate this, sir?" I said.

"Of course I do. Are you telling me what I can and what I can't say? I mean every word. So get on with it."

"Is that an order, sir?"

"What else? Get going."

"I'll carry out your order, but under protest, sir."

"For the last time, translate exactly what I said."

"Captain," the chief replied, "eight months after the end of the Third Reich this was no reflex action. It was a provocation. That man is a Nazi. He will not be reinstated while I'm fire chief."

This I translated with pleasure.

"We'll see about that, won't we!" Delaney threatened, his pale cheeks flushing with anger.

"Before either of us does anything he may later regret, Captain Delaney," the chief said, "let me tell you that being a lifelong anti-fascist has not made me the least bit slovenly. And as for firefighting and politics, where do you get the idea that they have nothing to do with each other? You know that I was one of the most senior officers in the Berlin fire service before 1933 and that I lost my job because I was a social democrat. And I spent two years in Oranienburg concentration camp. No politics, indeed! You choose, Captain. It's either Poppek or me. I won't have a Nazi in my command."

I was about to translate, but the chief said: "Not yet, please, I have more to say. I do respect your position as representative of the British authorities, Captain Delaney," he went on, "but not your views on Poppek. If you want him back, then you must first dismiss me. And if you do, the district officers here will resign. Now please tell the captain."

As he listened to my translation, Delaney knew that he was checkmated. His bluster had failed. He may not have been blessed with much imagination, but even he realized the scandal that would result if he dismissed the chief for the sake of Heil-Hitlering Poppek. The press would report the story, Soviet Sector newspapers would make a gargantuan meal of it, British reporters in Berlin would pick it up, and a *Daily Express* headline, BRITISH OFFICER LOVES SMART NAZI SALUTE, would do him no good at all. He came off his high horse with the speed of a fireman slipping down a fire-station pole.

"Tell the Herr Brandingenieur I had not expected him to feel so strongly about this," he said. "He's really mak-

ing a mountain out of a bit of a molehill. Nobody's talking about dismissals or resignations. I merely pointed
out that he acted too hastily. Had he talked to me first
I'm sure we would have found an acceptable solution. In
view of our previous good relations, which I hope will
continue, I will take no further action."

The chief, after I had translated Delaney's words,
agreed. At this point he was quite ready to help Delaney
save face. A more or less perfunctory discussion of other
matters followed before we left. Although, as we drove
back to Lancaster House in silence, I was still fuming
about that three-pipped nincompoop, Delaney had actually confirmed what I had known all along. Interpreting
was not my cup of tea. I had plenty to say, but not as
somebody else's mouthpiece.

Tolliver was in the mess when I got there for lunch. I
sat down next to him.

"Did you ever meet a Royal Engineer captain called
Delaney?" I asked.

"If you mean the fire-brigade nutter with the swagger
cane, then the answer is, unfortunately, yes. I've interpreted for him. Why, what's he been doing to you?"

I told him.

"Delaney is a fool," Tolliver said, "but he isn't a Nazi.
He's tactless, fancies himself a great military discipli-
narian, like so many of the schoolmasters—that's what
he is in civvy street—who walk about here disguised as
temporary gentlemen. But he's also desperately keen to
do a job well about which he knows next to nothing. He
was probably in charge of fire drill at some Royal Engineers depot at home and that's what got him this job.
Like many officers throughout the British Zone, who
suddenly find themselves in charge of transportation,
public health, rationing, gas works, and electricity plants,
whatever, he's out of his depth. They all need German

experts to help them. And the best expert is of course the chap who did the job under the Nazis; hence, more likely than not, he was a party member. One after the other they get kicked out and there's your lieutenant, captain, or major left holding the baby. He doesn't give a damn about Nazi or non-Nazi, he wants to keep his expert. That's the dilemma. Admittedly, few would be so stupid as to say what Delaney did, but he was obviously impressed by Poppek's know-how. And I bet you Poppek speaks at least some English while the others don't and Delaney has no German at all."

I did nothing about Delaney, but my next job, with three perfectly charming British T-Force scientists, gentlemen it was a pleasure to be with, only strengthened my resolve to get out of interpreting.

T-Force's task was to hunt for German patents useful to British industry. It was very hush-hush. Although perfectly legal under the terms of Germany's unconditional surrender, which gave the victors absolute power over the territory, the people, and all the material and non-material assets of the German Reich, Whitehall did not feel all that comfortable about what, after all, was not the "sale" but the "snatch" of this—or any—century. Nor did they care for their allies to know too much about what they were after. The Allies, of course, all had their own teams out in the field. However, the Americans and the Russians preferred the inventors to the inventions while the austerity-ridden British preferred patents to men. Blueprints do not have to be housed and fed.

My T-Force doctors took me to the Askanier Works where unhappy-looking German technicians demonstrated a curious gadget. Two slowly turning spools transported a wire through little wheels and this reproduced bits of music and speech. I did not have a clue I was looking at the tape recorder's grandaddy, nor did I understand what my doctors and the Germans were so busily discussing. Oh yes, two of the T-Force team spoke excellent German. And they knew all the technical terms I did not know in either language. I was utterly useless. They did not seem to mind but I did. I had to get out of that game.

How? Simple. What Garrett valued at least as much as his whisky was a quiet life. I would ruin it for him, so thoroughly that he would never want to clap eyes on me again. No revolt, no insubordination, no offenses against King's Regulations, nothing risky, nothing bad. What I had in mind was a little psychological warfare.

3

"Snoek: Dutch for 'Pike' "

My Artillery training as a command post officer's assistant did not include lessons in strategy or tactics, but six years of war had proved the point that a pincer movement was wiser than a frontal assault. Hence the thrust of my psychological warfare was not aimed directly at Garrett. With evil cunning I encircled him with the lady interpreters in the pool. Spinsters of uncertain age, most of them, they were coyly and hopefully demure toward the colonel (and other mature officers), but bitchily conscious of their captain's status toward us NCOs. Our advantage over them was that, though they knew their German, we, whose mother tongue it was, knew it better. Like it or not, they often needed our help with its finer or more colloquial aspects. Asked for assistance I either pretended to be helpful and then confused them, or I claimed I was too busy when I was obviously twiddling my thumbs. It was easy to pull their unshapely legs or make sarcastic remarks about their simpering at the colonel, in short to be bitchier and nastier to the poor things than they had ever been to me.

It was mean and it worked. Garrett's peaceful life went up the spout. Every day one or the other female ran to him to moan about me. I got a dressing down but, as I did what little work I had conscientiously and well, he had nothing he could come to grips with. Then the Tiergarten British Military Government detachment solved his problem. Their resident interpreter, a Sergeant Singer, was going on extended leave and they needed a replacement. I, naturally, was Garrett's choice.

Having moved from Kaiserdamm barracks to the Tiergarten NCOs' mess, my first job was to find out what Military Government detachments actually did.

Each district, or *Bezirk*, of Berlin's four sectors was headed, but not necessarily controlled, by a *Bürgermeister*. He, his deputy, and his councillors were appointed, not yet elected. And in early 1946 many of them were still the men the Soviets had installed when the whole city was under their control. Their overall strategy, clearcut and shrewd, had been ably executed by the German communist leader Walter Ulbricht and his ten German-born functionaries, who were brought back from their Moscow exile by special plane on April 30, 1945, two days before General Weidling, Berlin's last Wehrmacht commander, surrendered. To find and put into positions of influence Germans who could be trusted to carry out Soviet policies was the Ulbricht eleven's priority task.

Moscow-trained Wolfgang Leonhard, the youngest member of Ulbricht's team, defected in 1948. In his book *Child of the Revolution* he vividly describes Ulbricht instructing his collaborators:

> What we've got to get right is the political composition of the Bezirks Administrations. We can't have communists as mayors; the Wedding and Fried-

richshain [Berlin's most proletarian districts] may be exceptions. In the working-class areas mayors as a rule should be Social Democrats and in middle-class precincts—Zehlendorf, Wilmersdorf, Charlottenburg, etc—we need men of bourgeois background, former members of the Zentrum, the Democratic or the German People's Party. Best, those who have a doctorate, an anti-fascist past and are prepared to co-operate with us. . . .

And now to our comrades. The first deputy mayor, the head of personnel and administration and the man who's in charge of education must be our chaps. And you've also got to find one comrade who's totally trustworthy. He's the one who takes over the police . . . it's got to look democratic, but all that really matters must be in our hands.

Then, in a scene not without touches of comedy, Ulbricht deals with the selection of a suitable candidate for the job of *Oberbürgermeister,* or governing mayor of all Berlin:

"Let's talk about the *Oberbürgermeister.* You've met Dr. Werner—how about him?"

Maron, Gyptner, and Winzer did not appear enthusiastic.

"I don't know, Walter, Dr. Werner doesn't seem to be quite the right man. And he is too old," one of them said.

Another remarked: "I've heard he's not all there in the head from time to time."

"What's that matter?" Ulbricht replied. "We've got our deputy."

And so, on May 17, 1945, Dr. Werner, a pliant, but not senile, civil engineer of no great distinction became *Oberbürgermeister* of Berlin while his deputy, the returned Moscow exile Karl Maron, held the real power.

The Ulbricht team got to Berlin eight weeks before the

Western Allies. It was time enough for the fast-working
Ulbricht and the Soviet Military Administration (SMA)
to establish their infrastructure for an eventual communist takeover of the city. The Western Military Government—once it had settled in—was not deaf to the
rustling of the totalitarian woodworms burrowing away
under Ulbricht's democratic veneer, but there was not
much they could do about it; not in the beginning, anyway. Communists were anti-fascists and, therefore, by
definition on the side of the angels. In their own countries communist parties were legal, the Soviet Union was
seen as a land of heroes and "Uncle Joe" Stalin as a rather
benevolent elderly despot. That was the situation. Its
consequence was Ordinance No. 1, promulgated on July
11, 1945, after the first meeting of the four sector commanders. It laid down that all orders and regulations issued by the Soviet commandant from the moment Berlin
was under "Allied" (Soviet) control were to remain valid
until further notice. With this freezing of the status quo,
Americans, British, and French shot themselves in the
foot.

No wonder they initially limped well behind the Soviets in their impact on the political life of Berlin. Then,
on August 17, 1945, the commander of the British Military Government detachment for Charlottenburg thawed
the status quo with his announcement that block and
street wardens were not to interfere in the private lives
of the people in his district. With this he drew attention
to a Soviet measure not even the con artistry of an Ulbricht could make look democratic: the continuance by
the Russians of the Nazis' house, block, and street war-
den system. Some of the newly red wardens were the
very same men who had done the very same job for the
Gestapo; one good reason, but by no means the only one,
why Berliners looked at their Russian "liberators" with
a strong sense of déjà vu. Four days later the U.S. Mili-

tary Government ordered the wardens in its sector to cease their activities. The British Military Government, always more hesitant about upsetting the Soviets, followed the U.S. example in early October, but by then Berliners had taken note that the Russians were not having their own way with everything any more.

Military Government detachments had to ensure that those wardens did not creep back in different disguise, that district officials worked not against but for democracy, to supervise the local administration, the courts, and the police; enforce, where necessary, the implementation of Allied Kommandatura decisions, and provide the link between local government and British Military Government HQ. Their officers and NCOs were Britain's men at Berlin's grass roots. Hard work in the beginning, it had become routine by late January 1946 when I went to Tiergarten. Life there was pleasant and relaxed, as was Major Banfield, the commanding officer. So nice and easygoing was he, and such a dolt was I, that my posting nearly ended with the Last Post being sounded over my early grave.

You see, I was besotted by the thought of owning a handgun. Everybody seemed to have one. Tolliver had a big Luger that I occasionally borrowed; feeling that heavy weapon in my greatcoat pocket gave me a *Herrenvolk* sense of power and superiority. When I asked the detachment sergeant major if he knew how I could get a pistol, he said, "That's no problem. Just go to Banfield and ask him for one. He's got dozens of guns handed in by the Jerries."

"Sure," Banfield said, when I asked him the following morning. "Pick one you like," and he gave me the keys to his bookcase. I selected a 9mm Belgian Browning automatic. Banfield gave me a box of ammunition, and I left, overjoyed with the new toy.

Sitting in my room that evening I had a great time playing with it. Having removed the empty magazine I polished and repolished its barrel with an oily rag until the metal sparkled under the lamplight. Then, succumbing to the lure of the weapon, I felt an urge to pull the trigger and hear the click of the firing pin. As if playing Russian roulette, I raised the unloaded gun to my right temple and gently squeezed the trigger. But before exerting the final pressure—in the best move of my entire life—I raised the barrel a couple of inches above my head.

No click—a thunderous explosion echoed through my room. Paralyzed by shock, as the room filled with cordite stench, I was none too sure I was not sailing skyward toward my ultimate promotion till an overwhelming need to visit the next-door bathroom convinced me I was still mortal. What I discovered there was no less horrifying. The bullet of the live round that had been hidden in the chamber of the gun had gone right through the wall, exiting at a level where it would have smashed the head of anyone using the bathroom. Getting that close to suicide and manslaughter concentrates one's common sense wonderfully. I resolved never to touch a firearm again; as far as they were concerned, I had shot into maturity.

The others in the mess must have heard the gun but no one took the slightest notice. They were cementing Anglo-German relations at the "grass roots" with their girlfriends. The Tiergarten mess, a large requisitioned German apartment, was liberty hall indeed. International friendships were being celebrated in high style all over the place. One never went into any bedroom, including one's own, without knocking first. A cosy home away from home it was; cosier, actually. Four German women cooked, cleaned, and butlered, the food was excellent, and the atmosphere was so homely that, unlike at Kaiserdamm, nobody ever slept out in spite of the major's order that all German visitors had to leave before midnight. It was strictly obeyed, too. Nobody wanted to risk being posted away from that ideal home.

During the day I either accompanied Major Banfield on his tours of inspection or sat in the office translating German documents. I was kept enjoyably and unexcitingly busy and left, when Sergeant Singer—who, unfortunately, had not fallen under a bus—returned, with keen regret.

When I woke up on my first morning back at Kaiserdamm, Tolliver was the only other person there.

"Where's Jock?" I asked him.

"Give you three guesses," he answered.

"Not night duty?" I said.

"Right first time," was the reply. "Jock's in love. Head over heels, as they say. With one of the waitresses in the mess. Straw-blonde, well curved, blue-eyed, young, the perfect German maiden. You better forget about him. Until, that is, he returns to sanity. And from what I've seen that won't be any too soon. Maybe a visit to the opera would be some consolation? Verdi's *Otello*. I've got two tickets."

That cheered me. On the day I had to report back to the Interpreters' Pool I needed something to look forward to. Once there I was trying to work out a new scheme for getting out of it again when Garrett saw me. "Oh you're back. Good," he said. That sounded ominous. "I want to talk to you. Come into the office."

What now? I wondered. Seeing the ladies smirk as I passed their desks I expected nothing good. But not so. Garrett's first words reassured me.

"I've gotten you transferred, Bombardier," he said, "permanently. You're being detached to HQ Military Government. Gave you a recommendation. You'll like the job. You'd best go there right away for your interview. Ask for Mr. . . . hang on . . . chap's got a funny name, I wrote it down." Having found the piece of paper he spelled it out. "S-n-o-e-k. He pronounces it 'Snook,' I believe. Sounds Dutch. If your face fits he'll be your new boss."

We had a Dutch-English dictionary in the office. I looked up *Snoek*. It was Dutch for "pike," the sharp-toothed fish, the dictionary said.

British Military Government HQ was a big yellow building on the former Adolf Hitler Platz, renamed Reichskanzlerplatz after the war. In its haste to drop the Führer's name the Berlin magistrate, restoring the previous one, had overlooked the fact that Hitler as last chancellor of the German Reich was being collectively honored and commemorated by that name as well. The mistake was eventually corrected when that square was designated Theodor Heuss Platz after the Federal Republic's first president.

Mr. Snoek's office was on the ground floor. He was a Dutchman; an elderly first lieutenant in the Princess Irene Regiment, formed by Dutchmen who escaped from the Netherlands and came to Britain during the war. Thin-lipped, sharp-nosed, small-eyed, he did bear some resemblance to his rapacious fishy namesake. He was friendly, chummy almost, and very frank.

"The way to get on with me," he said, "is not to bother me. Only come to me with problems you really don't know how to handle. I'm—what do you chaps call it? Yes—demob happy, that's it. In three months I go home and get my business going again. That's what matters to me. Right?"

I was not sure that was a question but responded, "Right, sir," to be on the safe side.

"Good," said Snoek. "Now, come with me and I'll introduce you to your colleagues."

I followed him down a few steps into a big room with

wooden benches along its walls and down the center. They were crowded with Germans, and more were standing.

Pointing to a big double door at the far end, Snoek said: "There, that's where we let the damn Moffens in in the morning . . ."

"Moffens?" I asked.

"That's what we Dutch call those bastards," Snoek chuckled, "not an endearment exactly. More like the French 'Boche' or your 'Hun,' and still too good for them. Now remember, the MPs open that door at eight-thirty and no more than two hundred are allowed in. That's the lot for the day. Never more. So they start queuing early and are half frozen by the time they come in. They deserve worse. My heart doesn't bleed for them and I hope yours won't either. And if there's any fuss you step on them. Hard! It's the only thing Moffens understand. As Churchill put it, they're either at your feet or at your throat. They're on their knees now and that's where they'll bloody well stay . . .

"See that big glass window in the wall over there?" he went on. "That is where you work, in the office behind it. I had it put in so you can see what's going on out here. Watch them. All the time. They often fight among themselves. A great nation! In victory supermen—in defeat they hate each other. Moffens! By the way, the MPs are just two doors away. There's a bell on your desk that rings in their guardroom. If there's trouble, the sight of the Redcaps is enough, it frightens them stiff."

Some of the Germans stood up and others just stared as Snoek walked past them. He took no notice. He opened the door to the office behind the window. Two corporals, each busy with a German standing in front of their trestle table, looked up.

Pointing his thumb at the open door Snoek snarled, *"Raus!"* at the two Germans. One of them tried to say something. "Are you deaf?" Snoek shouted at him in German. "I said get out. Now!" His thin lips curling back over his teeth, his eyes full of cold contempt, Snoek lived up to his name.

As soon as they had gone, the Dutch lieutenant became friendly again.

"Clare, meet Corporals Cooper and Belling," he said. "Belling's going, in three days. He's done his bit. You're replacing him. He'll show you the ropes. That's all." With that he left.

"He's all right really, you know," Belling said, "unless you're German. With him you only get into trouble if he catches you being nice to the customers. He's obsessed with being beastly to the Germans. With one exception, though—his German lady friend. Confirms the rule, I'd say; maybe fucking her is his way of getting even with his Moffens. Anyway, the one thing you've got to be good at in this job is saying no. That's the word you'll use more often than any other."

Belling and Cooper started to explain the job. No German could enter HQ Military Government unless they authorized his or her admission. They decided who was to be allowed upstairs to put his case to the appropriate department. Former members of the Nazi party or its organizations were usually refused, as were people whose requests would never be granted. Anyone trying to circumvent the proper German authorities by going straight to the British was inevitably thrown out. With people from the Soviet Zone, or Sector, who wanted to settle in the British Sector one had to be circumspect in case their move—scientists, pre-1933 politicians, expert technicians—could be in our interest. This also applied to persons wanting permits to travel to the British Zone.

"You get a lot of moaning about ration cards from those who claim they should be in a higher category,"

Cooper said. "That's got nothing to do with us. Off with them to the Germans. Now then, people who want British licenses to publish books, newspapers, magazines, start a theater, open a cinema, act, dance, perform, whatever, are dealt with by the Berlin Information Control Unit in Klaus Groth Strasse on the far side of Reichskanzlerplatz."

Most of it, Belling and Cooper assured me, was pretty straightforward, not half as complicated as it sounded. And if in doubt one phoned the relevant department either in the Military Government or at Control Commission HQ.

"Never," they added, "ask Snoek, unless there's absolutely no other way. It's not because he might blow up. It's just that he knows less about the job than we do. Mind you, sometimes it's easier for an officer to get through to the right people. That's when you go to him."

"And always listen carefully," said Belling, "to people from the Soviet Zone. Especially if they say they're in trouble with the Russkies. Pretend you send them to whatever department they want, but what you really do is send them up to Intelligence."

"Informers are a headache," they went on. "You get them by the dozen. Denouncing each other seems a favorite German sport. In the good old Gestapo days they denounced Jews or Commies, now it's Nazis or black marketeers. Most of the time there's nothing to it but envy, jealousy, greed, revenge, or trying to suck up to us and get some favors in return. But how can you know? Some could be genuine and come to us because they don't trust the German police. You've just got to play it by ear. You'll learn as you go along. And now we'd better get on with it or the natives out there will become restless. Just listen."

After two days in the job I would almost have wel-

comed a Poppek shouting "Heil Hitler" at me. Judging
by the endless procession of "anti-fascists" that passed
through our office he must have been the last Nazi alive
in Germany. Everybody had always been against Hitler,
had always believed in democracy, and Churchill clearly
had more admirers in Germany than in Britain. Yet when
questioned precisely about their activities during the
previous twelve years most applicants had problems with
their "short-term" memories. Long-term memory, however, functioned well. We did not ask, but were readily
told, which democratic party they had supported before
1933—mostly, it appeared, the Social Democrats: "The
German equivalent," as we were tactfully enlightened,
"of your Labor government." Whose vote, one wondered,
sometimes aloud, had made the Nazis the biggest party
in the Reichstag? Who actually had supported Hitler?
"Oh, the Germans," a mysterious foreign tribe with
which our visitors apparently had nothing in common.
Why else did they inevitably speak of "the Germans,"
never of "we Germans"? Amazing, too, how overpopu-
lated with attractive Jewish girls pre-1933 Germany must
have been, so many of our interviewees volunteered information about the Jewish girlfriends or fiancées they
had had, but unfortunately—"Well, you know what it
was like"—could not marry. Where had all those Jewish
lovelies come from? When Hitler became chancellor less
than one percent of Germany's total population had been
Jewish.

Skeptical one had to be, cynical one became. And yet,
looking into so many sunken, hunger-dulled eyes in so
many deeply furrowed, emaciated faces, saying no was
not always easy. Collectively they had brought their
misery upon themselves, but it was not a collective but
an individual who stood at the other side of my trestle
table. I often felt uneasy. Not from pity. Had I ever felt
that, the inability of the majority to understand that they

had only themselves to blame, their endless wailing about the injustice of their fate, their incessant self-pity would have killed it instantly. Not pity, but self-doubt disturbed me. Had I made the right decision when I turned somebody away? Should I have been more sympathetic? We had our rules, but if we wanted to we could help. If I referred somebody to the German authorities, I could just tell him to go, or I could pick up my phone, ring the appropriate German official, and ask him to do his best for the person I was sending him. Such a recommendation from HQ Military Government could work wonders. It was up to us to decide who was and who was not given the chance to present his case to those upstairs who had the final say.

One day, facing such a cadaverous man, I began to wonder what he might have looked like when Germany was on top. Remembering that every German had to carry an Identity card, which—unlike those we had in Britain—showed the holder's photograph, I suddenly said: "Give me your identity card."

"Yes, sir, of course."

And with that Pavlovian German reflex to obey immediately any order given by uniformed authority he handed it to me. I opened it and looked at his true face: double-chinned, hard-eyed, self-important, and in his left buttonhole—he had just told me how his local Nazi boss had persecuted him—there was the round swastika badge of the party member.

From then on, having first listened patiently to the usual "I was agin it" yarn, Cooper and I always demanded Identity cards. With the help of those "before" portraits, making one's decision about the "and after" presence was easier.

This is not—to say the least—a flattering portrait of Germans in the calamity of defeat, and, unavoidably, it is painted with the broad brushstrokes of generalization.

Of course not all the people who passed through that glorified porter's lodge of ours were like that. Some were out of the ordinary, and those I remember clearly after four decades. For instance, the young Waffen-SS soldier who had retained a conscience and the general's widow who had not lost her pride.

4

In the
Underground

One look at him as he came in was enough to tell me
he was not our usual kind of customer. He was eighteen
or nineteen. Young people rarely came to HQ Military
Government. His haggard looks were nothing special, but
the pain and sadness in his eyes were. In a colorless,
monotonous voice he asked: "Are you a British soldier?"

"Yes, of course," I replied to that curious question.

"Arrest me, please."

I looked at Cooper and Cooper looked at me. What sort
of a joker had we got there?

Understanding our skeptical glances, the youth said:
"I'm not mad. I mean what I say. Look." He threw off
his gray army overcoat, stripped off his shirt, raised his
arm, and pointed to a number tattooed into his armpit.
"There it is," he said, "my SS number. Will you arrest
me now?"

Cooper put his hand on my arm as if to calm and re-
strain me.

"Were you black or gray SS?" he asked.

All former members of the SS were in the Automatic Arrest category but it made some difference whether one had been in the black SS—Gestapo, the Deathhead Units of concentration and extermination camp guards named after their skull-and-crossbones badge—or in the gray, the Waffen-SS, the combat elite of the Third Reich. In general the former (unless recruited by the intelligence services of one or the other of the Allied powers) were treated more harshly, the latter more like prisoners of war. But sorting SS goats from SS sheep was complicated and confusing. On the one hand, men were switched between black and gray SS from 1939 onward, and on the other, major war crimes—the murder of the inhabitants of Oradour-sur-Glane, the execution of sixty-four British and Canadian prisoners of war during the fighting in Normandy, to name but two—were committed by Waffen-SS regiments.

"I was Waffen-SS," the young man replied, "a conscript. I didn't volunteer. In August '44 when I was called up Waffen-SS officers at the recruitment center took their pick. I'm nearly six foot. They went for big chaps. You weren't asked, you were told."

"So where have you been since the end of the war?" I asked.

"In hiding," he replied. Anticipating my next question he said, "I won't tell you where. The people who took me in were no Nazis, I'll tell you that. I won't give them away."

"Why d'you give yourself up now?"

"I want to feel clean again. I did nothing bad, I swear, but I know that terrible things were done. I didn't see any myself, but the older men talked. They bragged and laughed about what they had done in Poland and Russia. I laughed with them. I don't know why. Could be I was afraid, could be there's something in me that would have made me just like they were. I thought about it, a lot, but I don't know the answer. It frightens me, makes me feel dirty, smeared, ashamed. I hoped it would pass. It didn't. It's getting worse. Perhaps if I'm punished . . . I don't know. But I had to do something. Here I am. Will you arrest me now?"

I rang the bell for the military police. Two Redcaps came and took the boy away. I never forgot how he stood there, slim, tall, light-brown hair falling onto his forehead, those old eyes in his young face, the first German I had met about whose honesty I had no doubts.

The widow of the general was not racked by any guilt feelings. She was completely self-assured and disciplined; shabby but immaculate, she was the kind of person who would emerge even from a coal mine as spotless as she had entered it. The straightness of her posture made her seem taller and the calmness of her face more handsome than she actually was. Speaking with that upper-class German accent known as *gewaschene Schnauze*—well-washed snout—she said: "I want to join my daughter in Bad Pyrmont near Hanover. Could you please tell me where I have to go for a travel permit?"

"Would you first tell me who you are?" I said, resenting the somewhat superior air with which she had stated her purpose.

"My name is von Stülpnagel, Helene von Stülpnagel."

It rang a distant bell. I had heard it before, but was not sure of the context. I looked at her questionnaire. She had left blank the line where she should have replied to the question, "If married, widowed, or divorced state husband's or former husband's name and profession." Except for a cream blouse she was dressed in black. She wore a black tailor-made suit, a much-worn black coat unbuttoned over it, a wide-brimmed black felt hat, and black gloves. Widow's weeds.

"You did not complete your questionnaire properly,"

I reproved her. "You did not give your husband's name or profession."

"He is dead. I am a widow."

"Read the question again and then answer it," I said, handing her the form.

"Do I have to go outside and do it there?"

"No, or you'd be at the end of the queue."

"His name was Carl-Heinrich von Stülpnagel."

"Profession?"

"He was a regular army officer."

Now I knew. "The General von Stülpnagel who led the revolt against Hitler in France and was executed?"

"Yes." She was no chatterbox.

"Why didn't you mention it on your form?"

"Why should I? My husband is dead. I'm a German like any other German. I want no favors, nor would he have wanted any. He fought and he died for Germany, not for anyone or anything else. I have no home here anymore, so I want to join my daughter. I don't see what this has to do with who my husband was."

I signed her pass and sent her up to the Travel Permit section. I never saw her again, but that key sentence of hers, "He fought and he died for Germany, not for anyone or anything else," stuck in my mind.

Yes, Carl-Heinrich von Stülpnagel, German army commander in France and the most determined of the July 1944 officers, died a horrible death. While others fatally hesitated he acted, ordering the arrest of all Gestapo and SS officers in Paris. Once he knew that the plot had failed he shot himself, but the bullet did not kill; it only blinded him. He was nursed back to health, tried, and subsequently hanged with piano wire from a meat hook at Plötzensee prison on August 30, 1944.

There was no questioning his martyrdom. Yet his life and death, as did the lives and deaths of the other army conspirators, posed one of the most perplexing conun-

drums within the German enigma. Why did von Stülpnagel, a leader of the opposition against Hitler within
the army since 1939, and why did those other officers,
fight so hard for Hitler for so long and with all their
military ingenuity? Some, Rommel or Kluge, for instance, who were no anti-Nazis, vaguely supported the
conspiracy because they knew that the war was lost.
They wanted to save what could still be saved. But others, Olbricht, Stauffenberg, Beck, Tresckow, von Witzle-
ben, Stülpnagel, were long-standing antagonists of Hitler
and National Socialism. Why then did they serve and
abet the Gestapo state, as they all did, for so many years?

They fought for Hitler's Germany because they were
trapped and stamped, like Konrad Lorenz's ducks, by an
upbringing and by traditions that made them protagonists as well as victims of a uniquely German manifesta-
tion of patriotism. Fathered by the Napoleonic wars,
furthered by the long struggle for German unity, fostered
by the Kaiser-Reich, astutely exploited by Hitler, it was
a muddled, sentimental, romantic hotchpotch of Wag-
nerian "Valhallali-Vallhallaloh" around the shibboleth of
the Fatherland as a holy grail above and beyond politics,
above and beyond good and bad. A nationalist virus that
destroyed man's immune system against evil—his conscience. Senior German commanders in Poland, Lithua-
nia, Latvia, and Russia knew what was going on behind
their lines. They either collaborated or looked the other
way. Von Stülpnagel was no exception. On July 30, 1941,
when commanding an army corps in Russia, he signed
an order singling out Jewish members of the Komsomol,
the Communist Youth Organization, as principal insti-
gators of sabotage and partisan activity. It was, and
Stülpnagel knew it, a general death warrant for the instant execution of young Jews.

The leitmotiv of the generals who rose against Hitler
was not abhorrence of his crimes, but the recognition—

long delayed—of his profound contempt for them, all Germans and Germany, crystallized by Elias Canetti in these three sentences from his essay "Arch of Triumph":

> Once the Germans stop winning they are no longer his [Hitler's] people; and without further ado he takes away their right to live. They have proven themselves to be weaker, he can do without them, he wishes their annihilation which they deserve. The fact that so many still believe in him . . . makes no impression on him.

The truth of this, in other words Hitler's high treason against the German people, became evident to the leaders of the military resistance through their personal contacts with their supreme commander and through information from sympathizers in the Führer HQ. They knew now that the war was not for Germany's but for Hitler's sake. Yet, as Canetti points out, many Germans, in spite of all reverses, still believed in Hitler and his invincibility—the very reason why it was crucial for Germany and Europe's future that the assassination attempt should be bungled, that the putsch officers should prove yet once again the accuracy of Lenin's joke that German revolutionaries queue for platform tickets before occupying a railway station. Germany's hubris demanded that the July plot should fail and the war go on to the bitter end. Germany had not only to be defeated, but to prevent the birth of a new stab-in-the-back legend every German had to see, feel, and suffer defeat.

That brief encounter with Helene von Stülpnagel, which seeded my interest in the history and psychology of the men and events of July 20, 1944, took place on the morning of the day Tolliver and I went to the opera, more precisely the Städtische (municipal) Opera in what used to be (and is now again) Das Theater des Westens in Kantstrasse in the British Sector. Berlin's other opera, the State Opera, having been bombed out of its home in Unter den Linden, had moved into the Admiralspalast, a former variety theater, in the Soviet Sector. But once we had taken our seats and looked around—the performance was for Allied personnel only—one could not but conclude that both opera houses were firmly Russian-held. There was a handful of British officers, two British NCOs—Tolliver and I—a sprinkling of Americans, and—let us say—a pride of Frenchmen, but Soviet officers and their ladies were present in their hundreds. Wives, not German mistresses by the way. The Russians imported officers' wives—never those of Other Ranks—long before British or American "dependents," the official designation for wives and children, were allowed to join their husbands in Germany.

For me, like most people during the war a keen admirer of the heroic Red Army, this first close encounter with its officers was disillusioning. The Red Army Choir's rousing "Song of the Steppe" had created my image of tall, lean, valiant warriors, but look where I would I saw squat, broad-hipped, double-chinned men, their spare tires bulging under tight tunics. And their women? Were those the lynx-eyed markswomen with the many notches, one for each slain enemy, carved into their rifle butts? Could any of those overripe, heavy-bosomed, wide-bottomed mommas in "liberated" German finery ever have been a fiery partisan girl?

During the interval, when Tolliver and I promenaded through the corridors, I did spot my Soviet officer ideal. He was tall and lean, his face romantically handsome, his elegantly cut olive-brown uniform was of the finest cloth, his black riding boots were highly polished, and on his broad silver epaulettes this prince, nay, grand duke of a man, who would have stood out in any crowd anywhere, wore the three gold stars of a full colonel. Respectfully, as he passed in lonely splendor, all the other Russians and their wives made way.

"Look at him," I nudged Tolliver. "What a man! Did you see how they all move aside for him. What natural authority!"

"Natural, my foot," he grinned. "It's his smell, you know."

"His smell? What smell?"

"What's the color of the braid around his epaulettes?"

"Light blue," I said.

"Well, my boy, that's the color of the MVD, formerly Cheka, OGPU, NKVD, which by any other name smells just as foul."

Tolliver, educated at a good English public school, could be a bit patronizing and superior. I did not really mind being "my boy-ed" and liked him, but his reserve and his self-absorption prevented a real friendship. Good-looking, undoubtedly attractive to women, he showed no interest in them or in men either. He was happily in love with himself. He was well off, too. His father, one of the wise German Jews who got out early, had been in the film business and now owned a number of cinemas in London. Tolliver had also served in the Pioneer Corps. After the opera, when we were walking back to the barracks, we exchanged reminiscences about our time as "enemy-alien" laborers in that miserable outfit.

Maybe it was the tale of the foreign-born Moor in the Venetian army that got us on to that subject. When I mentioned that I had been in 77 Company Tolliver said: "Then you must know a Berlin school chum of mine. He was a corporal in 77. His name used to be Frohwein. It's Frewen now. Have you any idea what happened to him?"

I did; he was in Düsseldorf. We had been in Bünde at the same time and Frewen's naturally florid complexion

went purple when Jock and I told him that we were going to Berlin, where his fiancée lived. They had not seen
each other for seven years. Frewen was interviewed by
that practical joker, the Lübbecke captain, a day before
us. He asked for a posting to Berlin. The reply was that
there were no vacancies for interpreters there. Düsseldorf was screaming for more and that was where he was
going. Would I do him the favor, Frewen asked me, of
looking up his girl and her mother and help them if there
was anything they needed? I promised I would and then
forgot about it until Tolliver mentioned him.

Ella Fersen, which was her name, lived in Neu-
Westend quite close to Reichskanzlerplatz. So the following evening I went straight there after we had closed
shop at HQ Military Government. A small, gray-haired
woman with a deeply lined face cautiously opened the
door. When I told her who I was I got a torrential welcome.

"Here you are at last!" she exclaimed, making me immediately feel guilty. "We've been waiting for you, you
know. Paul wrote ages ago that you would visit us. Why
didn't you come sooner?"

I wanted to explain, but with her I did not have a
chance.

"Anyway, you're here now," she went on, "the first
person since 1938, when they got engaged, who can tell
Ella what Paul's like now. Such a long time! Particularly
for people so young. What a good boy he is. So faithful.
Isn't he wonderful?"

It was a purely rhetorical question. Although I was
quite prepared to confirm that Frewen, whom I hardly
knew and thought a bit of a bore, was indeed very wonderful, she did not give me the opportunity.

"There must have been so many temptations," she
continued, "but he never, never forgot my Ella. Childhood sweethearts they were, you know."

I made the sort of face that said I didn't, but wasn't it wonderful too.

"Yes, the Frohweins lived in this house. The children played together. He was always so sweet with Ella. He's four years older but he was always so patient with her. Extraordinary for a boy, don't you think?" She stopped, but not to hear my views. "Ella," she shouted, "Mr. Clare, Paul's friend, is here.

"Oh my goodness," she said, "here I am keeping you standing at the door! Come in, come in. Forgive me, I'm so confused. So many things have happened to us. All terrible. My husband's dead. Shot. No, not by the Nazis. The Russians killed him. They were drunk. Didn't Paul tell you? It was his bike. They wanted it. He didn't want to give it to them. They just shot him. Such a good man, he was. He stood by me all those years. I'm Jewish, he wasn't. He could have divorced me. So many got rid of Jewish wives. The Nazis pressed him. He lost his job. He was the headmaster of the local grammar school. They threw him out. He became a commercial traveler. Hated it. All because of me and because he was a decent man. And then when we thought the nightmare was over, he was shot."

She burst into tears, called for Ella the second time, got no reply again, realized we were still standing in the corridor. Wiping her eyes she led me into the sitting room.

She asked me to sit down and excuse her for a few minutes while she made some coffee and found out what Ella was doing. It was a sad and moving story, but I did not envy Frewen his future mother-in-law or, after Ella had joined us, his wife-to-be. She was small, chubby, and the shake of her pudgy hand was flabby; her rather expressionless face was neither plain nor pretty, but her hair, worn long and naturally wavy, was beautiful. Frewen himself was neither oil painting nor ball of fire, and they seemed well suited. Ella helped herself to coffee and rather more of the American cookies her mother's sister sent from New York than was good for her. She asked a few questions about Frewen more out of politeness than interest, it seemed to me. Then, chewing cookies, she lapsed into silence, leaving the conversation to her anyway unstoppable mother.

As the older Fersen went on and on, repeating herself over and over, and the mother-ridden young woman just sat and ate, I felt sympathetic and uncomfortable. To bring this awkward visit to an end I asked if there was anything I could do for them.

"How kind," the mother replied. "Indeed there is, oh yes, there is. Ella, you see, is an actress. And, even if I say so, a good one. She studied with Hermine Körner . . ."

What surprised me was not that this colorless young woman should fancy herself on the stage, but that such a famous actress and drama teacher should have accepted her as a student. But perhaps Ella, robbed by that overpowering mother of any personality of her own, showed genuine talent when that of a fictitious stage character filled her inner void.

". . . and she's been offered a part," Frau Fersen rambled on, "at a theater in the Soviet Sector. She wants to take it but I won't have it. My daughter won't work for the Russians. There are plenty of theaters in the Western sectors and more are opening. But my Ella—isn't it ridiculous?—before she can perform needs a certificate stating she was not in the Nazi party. As if anybody with a Jewish mother could have been."

"Surely this cannot be a problem," I said.

"You'd think so, wouldn't you, but it is, in spite of the fact that I'm recognized as a 'Victim of Fascism.' She's got to get it from the Kammer der Kunstschaffenden, the Artists' Chamber, that's the magistrate's department dealing with actors. It's in Schlüterstrasse, a side street of the Kurfürstendamm, number 45."

"So why doesn't she go, then?" I asked. I, too, in spite of the presence of the grown-up daughter, talked to the mother. Ignoring Ella was catching.

"She would, but I won't let her," she replied. "Ella may have to stand on line all day. She isn't up to it, she hasn't the strength."

Well-fleshed Ella said nothing.

"There's a British office in Schlüterstrasse. The British supervise the Germans, I'm told. They wouldn't see Ella, but if she were with you, well, if you wouldn't mind taking her there, you being a British soldier they couldn't not see you, could they? You they'd listen to. If you explained the special circumstances, maybe the British would give her this certificate. If it's not too much bother for you, of course. But you understand, don't you?"

I did. And I didn't like it at all. Chances were I would be told, and in no uncertain terms either, to go away and mind my own business.

Frau Fersen noticed my hesitation. "I know it's asking a lot," she wheedled, "but you'll do it, won't you? For Ella's and your friend Paul's sake, won't you?"

I did not know how to get out of it, and so I suggested that Ella and I should meet at four o'clock next afternoon at the Reichskanzlerplatz underground station.

When I got there she was already waiting. I thought she might be a bit livelier without her mother, but no, she only spoke when she was spoken to. If I asked she replied. Not that this mattered; the Berlin underground was no place for a chat. Once we had squeezed into the coach we were pressed tight, not like sardines (by comparison they are comfortable in their tins) but more like Mafia victims wrapped in concrete overcoats. Not exactly pleasant either, but odorless at least, which our imprisonment was not. The sweaty stench of unwashed bodies was overpowering. But then even habitually clean Germans could hardly smell like violets without soap, which had disappeared from the shops long ago. *Ersatzseife* came in reddish, sandy, crumbly bars, had a diabolic carbolic smell, and though strictly rationed was rarely obtainable.

All this was bad enough, but the furious battles between passengers attempting to get off the train and those trying to board it were infinitely worse. The very second the automatic doors slid open at a station the crowd waiting on the platform surged forward, a stampeding herd of bulls pushing everybody back into the coach. This scrimmage between boarders and leavers led to a chaotic, vicious, self-defeating seesaw. It was sheer mob hysteria, no one caring a damn for anybody else, everybody hating everybody else. A little patience, a little common sense, discipline, and fellow feeling, qualities Berliners had amply displayed under bombs and shells, but apparently lost in the moral degradation of defeat, could so easily have avoided this ugly spectacle.

Our train approached Kurfürstendamm. "Hold tight to my left arm," I whispered to Ella jammed against me. Then, so that people would see my greatcoat sleeve with its two white stripes, I raised my right arm in a perfect Nazi salute and began to push in the direction of the exit doors. At first I politely asked in German whether we could please pass. Nobody took the slightest notice. Then I shouted at them in spicy English. That made them shrink back, leaving just enough space for us to eel through.

The train stopped. The door slid open. A human battering ram of boarders hurled into me. I kicked and I yelled, I hit out right and hit out left. This stopped the mob and I could reach the platform, but the second I did they crashed forward like a storm-whipped wave carrying Ella back into the coach with them.

Ella awoke and screamed. I went berserk. My sudden feeling of hate was so intense it was near murderous. I lashed out, dragged people back by their coat collars, stamped on their feet, pulled at their hair, raged like a maniac. Later, when I had calmed down, I sensed that the behavior of that underground crowd had triggered feelings beyond and beneath the rational, and I thanked God for my Tiergarten resolution never ever again to carry a gun; had I had that Browning on me heaven knows what I would have been capable of. I got Ella out. The train left. I looked around. From behind its windows people with anger-distorted faces were shaking their fists at me.

I had forgotten my misgivings about taking Ella to Schlüterstrasse in all this turmoil but as we approached it they came back. Silently I cursed Frewen, Tolliver, Ella, her mother, not least myself for getting me involved in something that really was none of my business. That afternoon, I was sure of it, was bound to continue as unpleasant as it had begun.

5

"... The Victor Potent in His Rage"

—MILTON

Schlüterstrasse 45 is now the Hotel Bogota, a name somewhat farfetched for a Berlin hostelry, yet one not unconnected with the city's history. For by calling it after the capital of Colombia the late Heinz Rewald, a Berlin Jew who bought and converted the house in the 1950s, acknowledged his gratitude to the South American republic that had given him refuge from Nazi Germany. And thus, with that ironic twist typical of Berlin humor, the onetime home of Dr. Goebbels's principal instrument for squeezing Nazism into German culture and Jews out of it, the Reichskulturkammer, became a Jewish-owned tourist hotel.

At the inauguration of this Reichs-Chamber of Culture on November 15, 1933, Goebbels declared: "No one, however high or low, has the right to use his personal freedom at the expense of our concept of national freedom, and that applies also to all creative artists." Translated into plain language this meant you either conformed or you were refused membership in the main chamber and its subsidiaries for theater, film, literature, music, the press, the visual arts. But without it you could not work in your profession, no matter whether you were a great composer or the oompah-pah'er in a Bavarian brass band; literary lion or scribbler of pulp literature; painter of world renown or dauber of kitsch souvenirs; box-office manager or box-office star. If you were neither social democrat, communist, Jew, or "Jew-infested degenerate," you could still be refused membership if your face did not fit. On the other hand if something in your background was not Nazi-kosher—a Jewish granny, say—then a Nazi of substance, possibly even Goebbels himself, might, once you had been through the door of his bedchamber, open that to the Culture-Chamber for you.

Hans Hinkel, a senior official in Goebbels's Propaganda Ministry and a *Gruppenführer* (lieutenant general) in the SS, was the chamber's director. His qualification for being one of the arbiters of German culture was, among other things, his authorship of a book titled *Europe's Jewish Quarters*. His office, now presumably one of Hotel Bogota's better double rooms, was on the fourth floor of Schlüterstrasse 45. Two floors above it was the Reichskulturkammer archive with its close to 250,000 files containing the personal histories of its members during the Nazi era. This treasure trove of information Herr Hinkel, namesake of Chaplin's *Great Dictator* and no less inept, left behind him at the end of the war, when by a lucky fluke it fell into the hands of the British. The Soviets had overlooked it when they were in sole control of the city, but now they would have happily given Molotov's—if not Stalin's—eyeteeth for those files. A hint that a Hinkel file full of letters proclaiming utter devotion to the Führer could possibly be lost might have tipped the balance in their favor with quite a few prominent and popular German artists who did not want to work for the Russians in spite of the *Payok* food parcels and other privileges they offered.

In 1946 the Reichskulturkammer archive was held (nominally on behalf of the four Allied powers) by the Intelligence Section of British Information Services Control, which also supervised the magistrate's department issuing those "free from Nazi-infection" certificates Ella needed.

At Schlüterstrasse 45 a German porter showed us to the elevator. We got out on the fourth floor, turned left and went through an open double door into a large waiting room. At its far end we found a narrow corridor that led to our destination—the last door on its right marked MAJOR W. WALLICH, RA, INTELLIGENCE SECTION ISC; STAFF SERGEANT J. HURST, SECRETARIAT.

I knocked, opened the door, and found myself looking at a very rotund staff sergeant gleefully hopping up and down on his chair while singing, "Victory, victory, victory!"

"Congratulations," I said, "what did you win?"

He looked around, got up, and closed the door to the adjoining office. "Oh," he replied, still smiling, "I won my bet. The major said that Chamberlain when he came back from Munich landed at Croydon. I bet him a quid it was Hendon. I was right. It's not often you win a bet or an argument with him. Anyway, what can I do you for?"

I felt much happier. This jolly chap would not throw me out when he heard what I wanted. I told him the Ella story.

"Where's the girl?" he asked.

"She's waiting outside."

"Hm—it's all most irregular," Staff Sergeant Hurst said. "We'll have to see, won't we, what the old man thinks. He won't bite you, not today that's for sure. He's just gotten the good news. He's going to be broadcasting controller for the British Sector, what he's always wanted. So you could be lucky. Hang on."

He went into the major's office. When he came out he said, "He'll see you both. Bring your Ella in."

Dwarfed by his large, hand-carved, overornate desk, formerly that of SS Gruppenführrer Hinkel, Major Wallich looked tiny. His face was fine-boned and aristocratic, his small nose curiously shaped, its tip tilting so sharply downward it almost touched his upper lip.

He listened to Ella's story and looked at her documents.

"I'm sorry," he said, "but I cannot give you the certificate you want. Only the Germans can do that. But I'll tell you what I can do. I'll sign a letter saying that as far as this office is concerned you can act anywhere in the British Sector or the British Zone. That should do."

Ella was as overjoyed as Ella could be and when she held the signed letter in her hand she actually embraced me and her lips touched my cheek—by her standards a volcanic emotional eruption.

Signing Ella's letter was Walter Wallich's last official act in ISC Intelligence. Digging up other people's past, interrogating, doing police work, was never the right job for this very private and sensitive Cambridge scholar. Even worse for a man of his absolute integrity—he told me this years later—was the inner doubt whether his decisions were truly impartial, or, without his being conscious of it, influenced by the memory of his father's tragic death. The elder Wallich, distinguished Berlin Jewish banker, highly decorated World War I officer and staunch German patriot, threw himself off one of the Rhine bridges at Cologne after the Reichskristallnacht of 1938. His sons, Walter at Cambridge and Henry (a future governor of the U.S. Federal Reserve Board) in

America, were abroad, and safe, but for him, one of those many German Jews who—like von Stülpnagel and his caste—had succumbed to the "Fatherland" syndrome, death in the waters of the most mythology-flooded of all German rivers seemed the only alternative to a life away from his beloved country.

When we left Schlüterstrasse the rush hour was over on the underground. I got out at Kaiserdamm station, knowing that Ella would reach home safely. I walked to our mess for supper, and there was Jock. He looked thinner and a bit tired, but his eyes were sparkling, if over deepened rings underneath. Being a discreet soul, I did not ask the personal questions to which I was dying to have his answers. Instead we talked about the Interpreters' Pool, where Jock still was, and my job at HQ Military Government, until Jock ended it, saying: "She's wonderful. I'm delirious. What else d'you want to know?"

"Everything."

"Well then, she's an angel. I've never been so happy in my life. I've never experienced anything like it. And when it comes to 'subject normal' there's never a no, no matter how often I want it. It's heaven, absolute heaven."

"You two have to keep your strength up," I said. "You live together so what d'you do about food?"

"Ay, the first is true," Jock grinned, "and the second isn't much of a problem. I eat here when Uta's on duty. Then she also gets a meal. Otherwise we, and that includes her mum, buy stuff on the black market, or I get something from the Winston Club . . ."

This, the British Other Ranks' club on the Kurfürstendamm, supplied the British soldiery in Berlin (and a fairly substantial proportion of its younger female population) with the most effective aphrodisiac of the time: food.

Any newcomer on his first visit to the Winston, seeing with what amazing speed mounds of spam and cheese rolls, buns and cakes disappeared from the soldiers' plates, had to believe the British Army starved its men. A keen observer, however, would soon notice that the soldiers were filling not their stomachs but the haver-sacks they kept hidden under the tables. Loading them to the brim cost practically nothing: about twelve Reichsmarks, the black-market rate for two cigarettes. Four Gold Flakes' or Players' worth of Winston Club "shopping" could feed a *Fräulein*, and her family, for a couple of days. Finding the black market was no prob-lem. It came to you. Everywhere and anywhere, in the streets, in cafés, on the underground, on the tram, in-deed right outside the entrance to the Winston Club, Germans stopped you, asking if you had cigarettes to sell.

"So you see," Jock said, "with our NAAFI ration of two hundred fags a week for a few bob we manage fine. Why ever did we two idiots not want to come to Berlin! It's paradise."

"And where exactly is this Garden of Eden of yours?" I asked.

"Not far from here, in Schillerstrasse. It's a small flat, one room and a kitchenette. Belongs to her mum. What more do we need? It's perfect. Except for the bloody toilet. That's in the house across the backyard. Not much fun these cold nights. Things could freeze up."

"What about the mum?" I asked. "How's she taking it?"

"Fine. No problem. As I said, it's her place. We live with her."

"What, three of you in one room!" I exclaimed.

"Ay," he said.

"But Jock . . . !"

"Och, that's okay. Mum doesn't mind. She just turns over and goes to sleep."

I thought Jock's novel form of ménage-à-trois a bit extreme—even for Berlin, which, with its air containing more particles of eroticism per cubic centimeter than any other city's, never was a place for celibates. Indeed Berlin's most popular song, almost its anthem, Paul Lincke's "Berliner Luft," is a celebration of the invigorating air from the plains of Brandenburg to which so many occupiers have succumbed. Should they have strained for greater valor when discretion so clearly was not the better part of it?

That man does not love by air alone was no problem in Berlin, where the desires of thousands of lonely soldiers were stilled by the many more thousands of lonely women whose husbands or boyfriends were either dead or dimming memories in prisoner-of-war cages dotting the globe from Iowa to Siberia. The nonfraternization order—a sop to British and American public opinion—banning any but strictly formal contacts between victors and vanquished was so universally disobeyed it had to be dropped. Nature is informal and the victor potent not only "in his rage." All nonfraternization did was to give two now forgotten words to the English language: *frat* for the Tommy's or GI's German girlfriend and *fratting* for their relationship. Usually starting as soulless barter—sex for cigarettes, chocolates, nylons, food, and other treasures from NAAFI or PX—it often developed into something deeper. The young, healthy, and well-fed boys from Leeds or Cincinnati were attractive, and the aura of victory gave them added glamour, particularly for German women brought up to believe that winning was the highest military virtue. And to the boys from Leeds or Cincinnati, Northumberland or Wyoming, it was a revelation how German women then looked up to their men, made them the focus of their existence, cosseted

them, deferred to them, embraced them often and with
an eagerness and warmth for which Anglo-Saxon femi-
ninity was not exactly famous. Exposed to such emotional incandescence many a dishonorable intention
melted into love, leading to heartbreak or—more rarely—
marriage.

My "frat"—in this respect at least I was no different
from the genuine Tommy—was Anita. Or rather that
was what she, christened plain Anna, called herself, tag-
ging on the "ita" to make her name—and herself—more
exciting, more bewitching, more Copacabana. Tolliver—
nothing if not outspoken about anybody but himself—
having met Anita, pronounced her a pill. That was a bit
harsh. Anita was never unpleasant and a bore only when
she, yet again, reminisced about the Berlin Press Ball.
Had Tolliver, with his usual sarcastic grin, said instead,
"That's not a woman, my boy, but Germany's silent
majority you're sleeping with," he would have been close
to the truth, though Anita actually was anything but silent. Which was all to the good, for from her chatter I
learned more in a couple of days about what the German
in the street, man or woman, was really thinking than I
had in all my weeks at HQ Military Government.

Anita, another plus, was five years older than I and,
as she told me right away—she was honest in everything—an "experienced" woman. When Hitler became
chancellor she had been eighteen, a young thing utterly
uninterested in politics. She wanted to enjoy life, go to
the cinema, dance, have lots of boyfriends and pretty
dresses. For her, freedom, justice, tolerance were abstrac-
tions just as meaningless as National Socialist ideology,
but she liked the idea of a strong Germany, was glad that
the chaos of the Weimar years was over, and admired
Hitler for ending unemployment and creating prosperity.
Yes, she had given her *ja* to the Führer, although like the
majority she had been neither Nazi nor anti-Nazi, and

yet again, when that majority—far from being silent—cheered Germany's miracle man, her voice had swelled the glory choir. But all that was politics and did not matter to Anita half as much as the annual Press Ball, which, from 1933 to 1939, became the highlight of her life. Her chance to attend it came because, like everything else, this most elegant and distinguished event of the Berlin social season was taken over by the Nazis and turned into a swanky, ostentatious spectacle. Where formerly hundreds of white chrysanthemums had sufficed to decorate the Exhibition Halls at the Funkturm, Berlin's Radio Tower, there now had to be thousands. More florists were engaged and Anita was one of them. When the job was done she caused some mild amusement because she refused money and asked for a complimentary ticket instead. She got it.

A dreamy look coming into her gray-green eyes was my warning that Anita was off to her Press Ball wonderland once again; little flower girl in white ball gown on cloud nine of her seventh heaven, floating along through halls thronged with the stars of stage and screen, famous writers and composers, Hohenzollern and lesser princelings, women fair and women fat sprinkled with sparkling jewels, *Direktoren, Professoren, Doktoren* in white-tied elegance, officers of the Wehrmacht in gala uniforms, gold-embroidered diplomats chatting up party grandees trailed by handsome adjutants: Anita among the haut (and demi-) monde of the Third Reich, Cinderella waltzing beyond the chimes of midnight into the early hours of the morning. The very time, I reminded her one evening when she had told me that tale just once too often, when elsewhere in the "Night and Fog" of Berlin and Germany the Gestapo was busy hauling its victims out of their beds.

Anita collapsed into tears.

"I know that," she sobbed, "and I knew it then. Everybody did. But what on earth was I to do? Sit at home in sackcloth and ashes? I was young. Good things were happening, too. Plenty. And what about all those foreign statesmen? They knew so much more than we did. And the Gestapo was nothing to them. Yet they crawled after Hitler all the way from Berlin to Berchtesgaden! Guilt, guilt, guilt! Where? Why? Yes, in 1942 I did see Jews being taken away. For resettlement in the East. That's what one was told. And one believed it. Perhaps because one wanted to believe it, I don't know. You tell me what one could have done in times like those. Tell me!"

I did, but what I said did not sound wholly convincing to me, because I had not forgotten the afternoon in late October 1938 when I, strolling along Kurfürstendamm, saw a hundred or so handcuffed Polish Jews under SS and police escort being marched to prison. From there they were to be deported to their native country, which had already announced it would not let them in. What could I have done? Protest? And have myself beaten to pulp? What did I do? I looked away, thanking God I was an Austrian and not a Polish Jew.

What ought Anita, what ought any German to have done in 1942 when they witnessed the "removal" of German Jews? Was it typically German that they, too, but for one minor public protest that actually did take place in Berlin, looked away? To citizens of a free society it was an incomprehensible and guilty silence, but not to those who have experienced totalitarian rule. Here— from *Galina*, her autobiography—is Galina Vishnevskaya's (Russian opera star and wife of the great cellist Mstislav Rostropovich) description of the wartime deportation of an Estonian family that had been living in Russia since before the Revolution:

An Estonian family by the name of Gerts lived in the apartment across from us. . . . They were hauled off with all their belongings to Mother Siberia. I clearly remember old Fenya, her feet swollen, barely able to move, leaning on her grown children. . . . She was wailing at the top of her voice, as over the dead. All of the neighbors gathered on the stairway to watch. Russians enjoy seeing other people suffering. For some reason they feel sorry for themselves at such moments. . . . No, I don't recall that anyone was outraged; such scenes had become commonplace. On the contrary many even tried to find a justification for this monstrous lawlessness [and said]: "What can you do in times like these?"

To talk about the present with Anita instead of about "times like those" was, naturally, less problematic. Her, and Berlin's, favorites just then were us, *die Tommies*. The image of the English gentleman, his fairness, his devotion to the spirit of cricket, was so firmly implanted in the German mind that it survived Hitler, Goebbels, even reality, with ease. The Americans, *die Amis*, came next. They were not quite in our league because they were tougher, particularly their military police, which earned them the epithet "Russkies in well-pressed pants." The French at that stage were not taken very seriously, hangers-on to the coattails of the real victors. But basically all three were seen less as occupiers than as the Berliners' liberators from terrible "Ivan," the hated and despised Russian soldier.

Although I knew that everything Anita told me about the behavior of Soviet troops during the final weeks of the fighting and the early ones of the occupation was true, I nevertheless resented her saying it. The Germans had brought it upon themselves. What right had they to complain! Who had invaded whom first, I asked her, the Germans Russia or the Russians Germany? Would she answer that! I would have none of her "Yes, buts" as in "Yes, Hitler attacked Russia, but German *Landsers* [pet-name for the ordinary soldier] were never rapists." So who committed so many crimes worse than rape? "The SS!" was the instant reply. What were they, extraterres-trials or Germans? And Hitler and Germany, what were they, opposites or one? She gagged at that, found it dif-ficult to swallow, but conceded the argument in the end. Yet with her, as with so many Germans of her and the previous generation, it was a reluctant and superficial acceptance. What their brains acknowledged did not then really penetrate either their consciousness or their con-sciences.

Anita witnessed the arrival of the Red Army in the small village some twenty miles east of Berlin where an aunt of hers lived and where she had fled from the bombing. At first the behavior of the Soviet troops had been exemplary. Everybody heaved a deep sigh of relief and everybody, villagers and refugees, started to mock the Nazis' scare propaganda about Russian bestiality. The horrifying shouts, "Frau komm!" began on the sec-ond day. Old women were raped and girls not yet pu-bescent, wives in front of their husbands, mothers before the eyes of their children; by one man if you were lucky, by half a platoon if you were not. Drunk or sober, Ivan was unpredictable. Sometimes, if a woman resisted, he would shrug his shoulders and go away, but a bullet in the head or a bayonet in the belly was just as likely. Most women submitted, perhaps consoling themselves with the bitter joke: "Better an Ivan on your tum, than an Ami bomb on your head." Anita was lucky, because it happened to her only once. After, by the standards of the time, lengthy Russian foreplay. *"Frau komm,"* the Ivan said. Pointing to the relevant part of her anatomy Anita said, "I sick." "I rubber," he replied.

Why the men of the cruelly disciplined Red Army were allowed their savage rampage is still unexplained. One word from Stalin would have stopped it, as it did some weeks later when the order had been given and Red Army officers shot on the spot any man caught in the act. Was it Russian mentality to accept that the victorious soldier is, and must be allowed to be, "potent in his rage"? Was that why Stalin did not foresee either the world reaction to his troops' conduct or its eventual consequences for his plans for Germany?

In the late 1950s, when the Berlin newspaper publisher and veteran Social Democrat Arno Scholz visited Moscow, he was asked by a senior Soviet functionary, "When will you Germans at last stop talking and thinking of those less than pleasant events that occurred when our soldiers marched into your country?"

"Let me answer you," Scholz replied, "with the first verse of a nursery song known to every child in Germany. It goes like this:

> Cockchafer, cockchafer fly afar
> My Daddy is away at war
> My Mummy is in Pommern town
> But Pomerania was burnt down.

And that, my friend, commemorates something that happened during the Thirty Years' War three hundred years ago."

Scholz was right. *Frau komm!* was the most effective anti-Soviet and anti-communist slogan ever coined. The Russian officers who set up the Soviet Military Administration for Germany had no illusions. They knew what damage had been done. To help them achieve their aim, one Germany—communist if possible, neutralized if not—they used, as always, the carrot and the stick. The "carroteers," the men with the task of changing the Berliners' image of the Soviet Union, were the Soviet culture officers, the best-educated and probably most intelligent of all the Russians who arrived in Berlin in 1945.

6

"Very Pretty, Herr Oberst"

Yet it was not a *Kultura* carrot, but an iridescent flower, Berlin's cultural revival, that sprouted out of the dung heap of pillage and rape thrown up by the Soviet *soldateska*. Much against Colonel Sergey Tulpanov's will, his agitprop seed crossbred with Western cosmopolitan ideas and then—nurtured by Berlin's native artistic potential (diminished but not destroyed by National Socialism and war)—it foliated and blossomed, until it wilted under the twin pressures of currency reform and blockade in late 1948.

Materially it was the worst of times, spiritually and intellectually it was the best of times. In the words of Berlin art critic Hans Borgelt[*] this short span that he called the "Golden Hunger Years" "offered nothing less than the most exciting cultural life this city had brought forth since its proverbially 'Golden Twenties' . . . both

[*] Hans Borgelt, *Das war der Frühling in Berlin* (Berlin: Schneekluth, 1980).

periods having in common a greed for new experiences, heated discussions, critical freedom, wealth and quality of productions, internationality of programs, and also the fact that our own creative powers were not much in evidence in either of them . . . after twelve years of near total isolation there was an enormous need to catch up."

Almost as soon as the last shot of the Battle of Berlin had been fired, the Russians ordered theaters and cinemas to reopen: if still usable, in their own premises; if not, in public buildings, schools, town halls, or drill halls, any place that could be speedily adapted. Such haste had two reasons: first, under the Soviet system culture and politics are reverse and obverse of the same propaganda coin; therefore one man, Tulpanov, head of the Political Department of the Soviet Military Administration, was responsible for both; second, there was the urgent need to prove that the country of Pushkin, Tolstoy, Dostoyevsky, Chekhov, and Gorky was cultured and civilized and the excesses of her soldiery "mere accidents of war" best forgotten.

Tulpanov, a bear of a man with traces of Asiatic ancestry in his features and a Yul Brynner–style shaven skull, had the threatening presence of a Mongol warrior, an impression this consummate actor on the political stage cleverly cultivated and exploited. Apart from his bulk he was also in other respects not unlike Hermann Göring, one of whose many offices, that of chief of the Prussian State Theaters, the Soviet culture supremo had—so to speak—inherited. Both men charmed with false joviality, both were most convincing when telling their biggest lies, both shammed disarming frankness when most devious, and at their affable best both were at their most dangerous. But to slyness and brutality, the main weapons in Göring's armory, the fluent German-speaking Russian added a keen intelligence honed at the universities of Leningrad and Heidelberg. A communist party functionary for many years, Tulpanov was well versed in political wile and guile. And, again not unlike Göring, he knew how to achieve some popularity by being blunt about the quirks of the system he served when it suited him. A good example is the following story told by Boleslav Barlog,* postwar Berlin's most successful theater director.

Barlog, a man of strong views and almost childlike honesty, told Soviet culture officers exactly what he thought whenever they asked his opinion about a Russian play or film. Although he lived and worked in the American Sector, it was still a gutsy and näive thing to do. After yet one more heated argument between Barlog and a Soviet officer, Frau Barlog put her foot down. "From now on," she insisted, "you just say it was all very pretty and not another word."

The first ever Russian color film, *The Stone Flower*, was launched on Berlin with a great propaganda fanfare. Supposedly far superior to Hollywood Technicolor, it was heralded as yet another unique Soviet achievement. The Barlogs were of course invited to the festive première. The film was dreadful and the color awful. But before Barlog could slip away, there stood Tulpanov.

"Well, Herr Barlog," Tulpanov inquired, "and how did you like our *Stone Flower?*"

Frau Barlog secretly kicked her husband's shin, and he docilely replied: "Oh, very pretty, very pretty, Herr Oberst."

"Indeed, Herr Barlog?" the colonel said. "That surprises us. We Russians found it damn boring. Why don't you tell us the truth? We've quite enough arse-crawlers who find everything we do wonderful."

Only a Tulpanov (or, formerly, a Göring) would make such a remark. But then reputedly he had his own direct

* Boleslav Barlog, *Theater Lebenslänglich* (Munich: Drömer, 1981).

telephone line to the Kremlin and appeared to wield more power than the Soviet marshals, first Zhukov, then Sokolovski, who were his nominal bosses.

His principal assistant in cultural affairs was the diminutive and dynamic Major, later Lieutenant Colonel, Dymshitz, who, like many other officers of his department, belonged to the more liberal and open-minded Leningrad "Culture Mafia," duly replaced later on by stricter party-line men from Moscow. Dymshitz, in civilian life a professor in the arts faculty of Leningrad University, spoke excellent German, and his knowledge of Germany's history, her literature, and her theater was profound. Virtually all Russian culture officers were carefully selected specialists. The British, Americans, and French were much more haphazard with their appointments. Only U.S. Theater Chief Benno Frank, in pre-Hitler days a well-known Jewish-German actor/director, was in their league. But his background, left-inclined views, and appallingly German-accented English—a few elocution lessons from Henry Kissinger would have done Benno a world of good—limited what influence he had on his WASP superiors.

Still, as a Western culture officer Frank was the exception, and Pat Lynch, the British Theater and Music Officer, the rule. Lynch was a charming Irishman from Cork, but no match for the Dymshitzes of Berlin, where Pat arrived in early 1946, a couple of weeks or so after me. He never left it again and became a true Berliner—the first ever, though, to speak authentic Berlinese with an Irish brogue.

To chew over old times Pat and I met at the Kempinski Hotel in Berlin in June 1981, a few months before he died.

"Tell me," I asked him, "what were the criteria by which they picked you as British Theater and Music Officer?"

"Hit or miss!" he replied. "You ought to know yourself. How else did anyone ever get a job with the CCG?"

"Come on, Pat," I said, "that's not true. I mean you had your qualifications. I was told you were an opera singer."

"Opera singer—me arse!" he laughed out loud. "I sang in the chorus of the Ilford Amateur Operatic Society. Sure, that's nothing. No, I was a schoolmaster at a local and not very distinguished boys' prep school. They only took me, you know, because there was a war on and a shortage of teachers. I had a B.A. but no teaching experience at all. Still, it went all right for a while. It was English I taught. Well, you know yourself the way young lads love to take off their teachers and after a while some parents were complaining that their little darlings had started to talk like little Cork men. By that time the war was over, teachers, real ones, were coming back and I thought I'd better look at the job ads in all the newspapers. In the *Daily Telegraph* there was one from the CCG offering temporary civil service jobs in Germany. That interested me now because I knew some German, you see. Not much, and I taught meself, but I had enough to get along with. I've always liked Wagner and wanted to read his libretti in the original, you know. So I bought some Linguaphone records and taught meself.

"Anyway, I wrote in and a couple of weeks later I was at Prince's Gardens, which you know yourself, being interviewed by a panel of three: a red-haired lady, a major, and an elderly civilian. Now I had no idea what the job they wanted me for was. They wanted to know was I interested in music. So I told them I love it and all about our Ilford amateur group, went on a bit about Wagner, I really know his work like, and after we'd chatted on for about ten minutes they asked if I'd like to be British Theater and Music Officer in Berlin. Well, that

took the wind out of me. Would I like to do it? Jeez, would!

"They made some commotion about how urgently I was needed, saying they'd speed up the documentation. Well, to cut a long story: one week later I was in Berlin; the man they'd been waiting for, eh? You must be joking! Nobody, but nobody, had bothered to tell Lamont—the half-colonel running Berlin Information Control—about me. Sure, typical, first thing he knew he had a new Theater and Music chappie was when I walked into his office and introduced meself. Your man was livid. Not only did he know nothing about me, but he'd promised the job to some friend of his. He would have loved to send me back home on the next train. He couldn't do that, but what he could do and did was to give me a hard time. Luckily he was promoted away a couple of months later and with George Bell, his successor and a former schoolmaster like me, I got on well. And that's how it was."

It was not surprising that the Russians seemed way ahead of their allies during the first year of the occupation. They had a lot going for them: Tulpanov's power and single-mindedness, his understanding of the link between culture and politics, his officers' superior qualifications, the fact that they were unhampered by nonfraternization nonsense in their dealings with Germans, their ability to gild the agitprop carrot with their *Payok* parcels, their familiarity with German customs, a point of considerable importance. Even something as apparently trivial as a handshake mattered. Not knowing that Anglo-Saxons do not pump hands at every possible and impossible occasion, many a German artist felt deeply hurt when, on meeting a British officer, his outstretched arm groped the air for a responding clasp that

never came. This, of course, was interpreted as
rogance of the new master race and unfavorably
pared with the surface amiability of Dymshitz and
colleagues.

But then, neither being nice to Germans nor cultural
affairs ranked high on the Western powers' original list
of priorities. They considered it more urgent to bring
bread than circuses to the population; if the Russians
wanted to provide dancing bears, so be it. It appeared a
sensible attitude only for a while, because British, American, and French officers meeting Germany's intellectual
elite, then still concentrated in Berlin, recognized fairly
quickly that the mind needed sustenance just as much
as the body. The result was that glorious competition for
the spirit of Berlin germinating the "Golden Hunger
Years," which the East, in spite of the excellence of its
representatives, never had a real chance of winning. Certainly those "less than pleasant events that occurred
when our soldiers marched into your country"—to recall
the marvelously understated words of Arno Scholz's
Moscow interlocutor—played their part in this, but they
alone were not conclusive. The decisive factor was that
the West allowed artistic and spiritual freedom. Admittedly this was within the unavoidable constraints
of an occupation regime, but these were mild compared
to the pressures and manipulations of totalitarianism,
which—however much the men from Leningrad tried
to temper them—became stronger with the passage of
time.

For twelve years German artists had lived under a totalitarian system of their own, which many had hated
and despised, though many had also compromised with
it. In any case they had no desire for a repeat, and what
Borgelt termed "the greed for new experiences after
twelve years of near-isolation" was directed toward the
free West, not toward the regimented East. In conse-

quence, as more and more theaters opened in the Western sectors, as more publishers of books and newspapers were licensed, and as film studios began to prepare new productions, much German talent, which until then—directly or indirectly—had worked for the Russians, moved away from their sphere of influence.

Dymshitz tried to counter this trend with increased activity and more perks. He opened an artists' club and restaurant in the Soviet Sector. Called Die Möwe (The Seagull), membership was open to any of Berlin's *Kulturschaffenden*, "culture makers" (a word from the Nazi vocabulary still used in the defunct German Democratic Republic), no matter where they worked or resided. It was a successful failure. People supped at the Möwe all right, but with a very long spoon when politics were dished up. And Dymshitz also discovered that there's many a slip betwixt indoctrination and intoxication. By and large Die Möwe did less for him than for his colleague Major Mosyakov, who ran the place and developed a thriving black-market business selling food, drink, and cigarettes through the back door, until, having been informed on by a colleague, Major Ausländer, he was shipped to the Archipelago for eighteen years.

For my involvement with Allied cultural policies in postwar Germany and with her *Kulturschaffenden* I have to thank Tolliver, one of my three good fairies. Oppenheimer, the first of them, gave me the push; Tolliver, the second, the steer; and the third, about whom more later, the introduction determining the future course of my life.

It started like this: one morning Tolliver left Kaiserdamm a corporal and in the evening when I saw him again he was a sergeant. I congratulated him—not without envy—and asked: "How come?"

"I've had a new job these last two weeks," he said.

"You secretive bastard!" I reproached him. "You might have said something."

"Well, I was on a two-week trial. So why talk about it? It could have gone wrong. Anyway, as you see," he pointed to his stripes, "it didn't. But, honest, I was about to tell you anyway. You see, we've got a vacancy and when I mentioned your name to the major he said that he knows you and if you're interested you can come for an interview."

"Who's the major?"

"His name's Sely. He says you were at the same interpreters' course."

"So he's managed to get his 'major's crown'. Yes, we were together at Prince's Gardens. He's bright, but arrogant, stuck-up. Not my cup of tea. Anyway, what's he doing?"

"He's head of Information Services Control Intelligence Section."

"What, that outfit in Schlüterstrasse?"

"Yes. How come you know?"

I told Tolliver about my visit there with Ella.

"That's it," he said. "Hurst's been demobbed and I've taken his place. But not as the major's secretary. That's a German girl now. The work and the section are expanding and we've got a new slot for a second sergeant. Well, d'you want it?"

That was tempting, in spite of Sely being the boss. I thought him pompous and patronizing. And he put my back up even with such a friendly and harmless remark as his "Careful, dear boy, don't break anything" when he overtook me on the icy steps of Charlottenburg station.

But the first time I saw him he did impress me. One afternoon during our excruciatingly boring interpreters' course, when I was fighting postprandial somnolence, the door opened and a most distinguished-looking officer

came in. Very big, well over six feet, of powerful phy-
sique, graying temples framing a suntanned face with
sharply chiseled features, he was strikingly handsome.
As I was sitting and he so tall I could not see what his
two-rank insignia were, but from his appearance I assumed that he was a lieutenant colonel on a tour of inspection. I jumped up and stood to attention. The other
NCOs followed my example and our middle-aged lady
lecturers stopped open-mouthed in mid-sentence. With a
colonelish nonchalant wave of the swagger cane in his
gloved hand the officer graciously indicated "Carry on."
But standing I had seen that he was a mere first lieutenant with the laurel-wreathed crossed spade, pickax, and
rifle badge of the Pioneer Corps on his cap. I, one of those
"enemy aliens" who, until the summer of 1943 when I
transferred to the Royal Artillery, were only permitted
to serve in that "navvy" unit, hated it so much that I
refused a Pioneer Corps commission when offered one
by a War Office Selection Board. That spade and pickax
cap badge was a big chip on my shoulder, and I was too
much of a snob myself to want to be seen ever again,
even as an officer, with that "gravedigger's" emblem on
my uniform. I was not all that impressed with the new
arrival anymore.

But the impact he, Kaye Wolve Frederick Sely, born
Kurt Wolfgang Friedrich Seltz in Munich, had on our lady
lecturers was so devastating it was comical. In their eyes
the eagerness of women long unmanned, they fluttered
round him, pressed him to take tea with them, twitter-
ingly approved every word that came from his lips, and
from the next morning on it was he who was running
the course. It became alive under his guidance and far
more relevant to work we would be expected to do in
Germany. He made us act the roles of Military Government judges, counsels for defense or prosecution, as German defendants or as court interpreters. He set up mock

conferences between British and German officials in which we played all the parts. Suddenly the course was fun and worthwhile. He was friendly, but talked down to us NCO's in the manner of one who sits socially on a higher perch. Neither Freddy Gross nor Peter Schnabel, both from Vienna and the first "alien" officers we had in 77 Company of the Pioneer Corps, had ever behaved like this. They expected, and got, the respect due to the King's Commission, but neither on nor off duty did they ever show any caste consciousness. And neither Gross nor Schnabel would ever have made that remark to Joanna Cantrell that Sely made to her when we were all together in Bünde waiting for our postings.

I had invited Joanna to come to the army cinema with me. We liked each other and I had a bit of a crush on her. I stood in the street outside the officers' mess, but it took a long time before she came. She, the brigadier's daughter used to military punctuality, had never been late before. When she appeared she was not at all like the young woman I knew. Her face flushed, her dark eyes flashing with anger, she would, had a broomstick been handy, have grabbed it and flown off there and then to the nearby Brocken, the Harz mountain where according to German legend the witches hold their sabbath. I could just see her stamping, dancing, howling with the coven around the effigy of the person who had so enraged her—the newly promoted Captain Sely.

"That bloody man," she fumed. "How dare he lecture me about what company I keep! He asked me what I was doing tonight and I told him that I was going to the pictures with you. You know what? He had the infernal cheek to tell me that officers don't mix with Other Ranks. Who the hell does he think he is! Telling me what I can and what I can't do. That he's married to the widow of a navy paymaster captain must have gone to his head. Sleeping with the English upper crust doesn't make him upper-crust English. Trying to be more British than the British, that's what he's doing. Phew! Don't you ever be like that, George."

Sound advice, which I occasionally forgot.

That incident had turned me against Sely. His thinking me not good enough to go out with Joanna had been hurtful at the time, but was it important? What Tolliver had told me about the work in Schlüterstrasse sounded fascinating. My job at HQ Military Government had become routine, and there was nothing the least bit constructive about it. And to make sergeant at last was no mean attraction either. I asked Tolliver to fix an interview with Sely.

A few minutes before 5:00 P.M. on the day, I was walking along the narrow corridor to what used to be Wallich's and was now Sely's office. I was about to approach the door to his secretariat when the sound of loud laughter, a woman's, stopped me dead.

"Ach, Herr Major! Nein, nicht doch, Herr Major, also bitte, bitte, Herr Major," she giggled.

A basso profundo male voice, Sely's, declaimed:

> His body is perfectly spherical
> He weareth a runcible hat.

Then he said: "If you want your new hat, Fräulein Rose, try and get it."

Something heavy bumped against the door. It flew open.

I was looking at the massive, though by no means spherical, back of the great Sely himself, the broad-brimmed red lady's hat sitting on his head making a somewhat unusual and flamboyant topping to the service dress with Sam Browne he was wearing. Jumping up and down in front of him, her arms outstretched trying to retrieve her hat, was a well-proportioned young woman. Spotting me she stopped in mid-jump.

"Oh, mein Gott!" she exclaimed.

Sely turned round. I saluted. "You're wrong, Rose," he said to his secretary, "it's Bombardier Clare."

7

Matters of Intelligence

Sely, minus red hat, sat down behind the Hinkel desk and pointed me to the armchair in front of it. With a bit of a flourish he produced a prettily chased silver snuff-box from his breast pocket and opened it. Having seen actors in Restoration comedy, but never anyone in real life, take snuff, I watched with much interest how he gripped a pinch between thumb and forefinger, lifted it to his nose, sniffed right, sniffed left, and then, by wiggling each nostril with his thumb, encouraged the brown powder on its voyage up his nasal passages. His nose—focal point of these proceedings—proudly prominent and elegantly aquiline, had a slight tilt to the right. Not only this eagly beak but his looks altogether reminded me of paintings of sharp-faced inquisitors of the Holy Roman Catholic Church, which, combined with his size—how he towered over that huge desk, which had so dwarfed Wallich!—made him seem perfect casting for the role of ISC Intelligence chief.

He offered me the open snuffbox.

Saying, "Thank you, sir, but I'd rather stick to cigarettes, if you don't mind," I declined, but I appreciated his gesture.

"Snuff's better for you, you know," he said, "but if you must, smoke by all means."

I took out my Gold Flakes and lit up.

"Tolliver tells me you think of joining us. Good. You and I know each other and so we know what to expect."

He might! I was not so sure anymore.

"Tolliver also mentioned," he went on, "that you've been here before, have some idea of what we do. You met Walter Wallich, didn't you? What did you come to see him about?"

I told him the story.

Pressing the tip of his nose down as far as it would go against his upper lip and imitating Wallich's voice, Sely said: "I'm Walter from Potsdam and straight as a rod, I'm serious and noble and not like you lot, if I sold just one fag my soul would rot, I'm Walter from Potsdam and black-market not."

Speaking normally again, he said: "Not my work, by the way, but that of the resident wit of Walter's mess. Not very good, but certainly true. Walter's one of those rare birds who've high principles and actually live up to them. For this job, though, he was the wrong man. In a way he misunderstood it. He thought it was only concerned with leaving no stone unturned to find the worms underneath. It's part of it, but not what we're really about. Now, Clare, you already know a bit about what we do here. How would you explain it in your own words?"

"Well, sir, you denazify people in cultural affairs: actors, writers, musicians. Isn't that it?"

"Hm, not quite, but before I explain it I'll tell you a joke. And don't stop me if you've heard it. There's this man," Sely began, "standing at the corner of Schlüter-strasse/Kurfürstendamm watching a chap sweep the road and being pretty clumsy about it. He looks on for a while and then asks: 'For how long have you been a road-sweeper, mate?' The other stops, looks up, and says, 'If you must know, since yesterday.' 'So what were you do-ing before?' 'I was a bank clerk. But I was also a party member and this is my punishment.' 'Ha-bloody-ha,' his questioner laughs, 'don't I know all about it? I too lost my job because I was in the party.' 'What did you do then?' 'I was the local roadsweeper here.' "

I had not heard that one before.

"I told you this story, which is all over Berlin," Sely went on, "because it lampoons mindless, indiscriminate, and useless denazification. What's it matter whether roadsweeper, butcher, baker, candlestick maker was or was not in the party. We waste time, energy, and money catching those little fish in our net. But the big sharks bide their time and swim around it. I'm not talking about people who've committed crimes, of course, but about the ordinary common or garden party member. Leave him alone and let him get on with it.

"What we really ought to do is proscribe jobs and func-tions, not people. Anyone who actively supported the Nazis ought to be barred, at least for ten years, from politics, the judiciary, education, the police, the higher reaches of finance or industry, the arts, literature, jour-nalism. You see, many pillars of the Third Reich, clever and powerful men, never joined the party. Instead of squeezing nine million former Nazis through the dena-zification sieve we'd only have to deal with candidates for what—two hundred thousand jobs at most. You're a field gunner. So you know you don't just pepper the countryside with your shells, but you aim at specific tar-gets. Well, that's exactly what we do here in this office. We're targeted at a small number of highly influential professions. Our job—I don't think Walter quite saw this—is not to throw people out, but to see that the right ones get in. How does all this grab you? Want to work with me?"

"Very much so, sir," I replied. "What would my job be?"

"Your job?" Sely smiled. "Your jobs, you mean, plural. Now, let's see. You'll do interrogations. On your own, or together with Tolliver, sometimes with me too. Have you got shorthand?"

"No, sir, but a good memory and I write quickly."

"Right, that'll have to do then. You'll take the minutes at the meetings of our Four-Power Committee. It's a subcommittee of the Allied Kommandatura Cultural Affairs Committee. It consists of Captain Gouliga for the Soviets, Michel Bouquet for the French, Ralph Brown for the Yanks, and I, who advise them on denazification. We always meet at this office. It's centrally located, we hold the Hinkel files and we supervise the Spruchkammer. That's the German denazification panel for cultural affairs.

"Ah, that reminds me. You'll also look after the German staff. We've thirty-two of them at present. Our own lot is ten and then there are the twenty-two who work for the Spruchkammer. Strictly speaking they are employed by the Berlin magistrate, but de facto they're ours. They get the ration cards plus the one meal per day for those working for the British. That, of course, gives us the influence we need. They've got to be here because we hold the Reichskulturkammer archive. They've access to the files, but only through this office. That's crucial. We have control. And yes, Spruchkammer verdicts are legally valid only once the Allies have approved them. Now, the chairman of the panel, Alex Vogel, needs some watching. He's a lifelong communist. Give you three guesses whose interests come first with him. Wolfgang Schmidt, the Spruchkammer's secretary, is the kingpin. His office prepares each case for the tribunal and at the hearings he acts as public prosecutor. He's not a communist, more a leftish social democrat, but he's also an old and close chum of Vogel. They jointly led one of the few genuine anti-Nazi resistance cells in Berlin.

"One more thing: every file must be returned to the archive at the end of the day. I'm not worried about Herr Hinkel coming back to burn them. That bastard is in safe hands in an internment camp. But we've also got in this building the 'Kulturbund für die demokratische Erneuerung Deutschlands.' They're on the second floor. Johannes R. Becher is the head of this so-called cultural association for Germany's democratic renewal, a communist front. Heard of him?"

I shook my head.

"In the twenties he was a promising young progressive poet. Now, after many years in Moscow, he's a Stalinist hack. I'm trying to get him and his Kulturbund out of here, but our betters in Lancaster House and HQ Military Government are dithering as usual. Well, what's new about that? Now, here are two documents for you to study. They're our bibles."

Saying this Sely handed me "Control Council Directive No. 24," subheaded "Concerning the Removal from Office and Positions of Responsibility of Nazis and Persons Hostile to Allied Purposes," dated January 14, 1946, and "Allied Kommandatura Order No. 10" titled "The Elimination of National Socialism and Militarism from Public and Economic Life," issued March 10, 1946.

"But have you got anything to do with militarism, sir?" I asked.

"Oh, yes, I'll show you." Sely opened his desk drawer, took out a cigar box and pushed it over to me.

"Well, look at it and tell me what you think," he said.

It was a well-known brand. I had often seen those
boxes at tobacconists in Vienna. On its lid it had a picture of a lone sentry in early-nineteenth-century uniform
and the caption underneath, taken from a German nursery rhyme, read "Lippe-Detmold eine wunderschöne
Stadt, darin ein Soldat" ("Lippe-Detmold is a lovely town
with a soldier in it").

"What's wrong with that, sir?" I asked, greatly puzzled.

"Can't you see it's fervent militarist propaganda?"

"No. It's an old trademark."

"Ah, that's what you and I think, but not the major
who runs the Censorship Branch in Bünde. He sent it to
me as an example of that German militarism that's got
to be stamped out. He thinks we ought to ban it. I replied
saying I thought it a case of a smoke without a fire. He'll
never forgive me, of course. We get all sorts. Now, about
your transfer . . ."

"How long will that take, sir?"

"A couple of days should do it. We've got high priority.
And yes, there's another job you'll have to get your teeth
into right away. First thing you've got to do. You get the
Furtwängler file from the archive and update it with all
the recent newspaper cuttings on him and his case. Anything you can find. Everything else can wait. Get in
touch with press section and Pat Lynch, the Theater and
Music Officer in Klaus Groth Strasse. You've got about
four weeks. Show what you can do."

I could not resist saying, "You're sure, sir, that's all
you want me to do?"

"Not quite, Bombardier," he replied, "there's something else. Two 'sirs' per day, one in the morning and
one in the evening, will do me."

Automatically—and much to his amusement—I said,
"Very good, sir."

What had happened to him? I wondered. Could my previous Sely image have been that wrong? Yet here he was fooling around with his secretary's new hat like a schoolboy, imitating Wallich, relaxed and friendly, and during the whole interview he had treated me not as a subordinate but more like a colleague. He was different. What had changed him?

Whatever the answer, I now had no doubts about working for him—"with him" he had actually said—and I looked forward eagerly to my transfer from the Military Government "glasshouse" to ISC Intelligence, expecting the contrast between the common herd queuing at Reichskanzlerplatz and the artists, some world-renowned, I would meet at Schlüterstrasse to be no less than antipodean.

It was not only naïveté, though that played its part, that gave me this impression but also the Austro-German cultural climate in which I had grown up. Artists were not considered ordinary mortals, and the grandest of them, the divinely gifted, *die Gottbegnadeten*, were adored as Olympians. The English-speaking public does not endow even its greatest thespians—from before Garrick to after Olivier—with comparably super-human status. For the Anglo-Saxon the theater—from before Shakespeare to after Stoppard—is a place of entertainment rather than enlightenment, but the German cherishes it as a *Bildungsstätte*, Friedrich Schiller's "moral institute," for cultural and spiritual edification and—not to be forgotten—intellectual snobbery. One had one's annual subscription to the theater and the concert hall not necessarily because one loved the play or the sound of music, but because one wanted to be seen at the play and sound off about music. In Germany social climbing was easier and quicker up the culture than the money ladder.

Well aware of this, the Nazis used the arts for their purposes. Although most of the leaders were philistines they nevertheless fully supported what they called "German" art, perfuming the party's musty lower-middle-class odor with culture to make it smell sweeter in the upturned noses of the conservative upper class. Nazi Germany flattered, cosseted, and rewarded its artists (provided they were "Aryan," served it, and did not talk either too much or too loudly out of turn) as never before. Hitler liked to surround himself with the popular and famous at social functions and to the Olympians he was generous not only with titles and decorations but also with donations varying from cash sums to country estates. Another bonus, after Goebbels had denounced critical freedom as a typically Jewish perversion, was that from then on reviews had to be either friendly or bland. Many performers were also exempt from war service until September 1944, when the propaganda minister ordered the closure of theaters, opera houses, and other places of entertainment, with the exception of cinemas. But even then only the less prominent had to report to the labor exchanges, while the fate of the *Gottbegnadeten* was decided by Hitler himself. In a way he, too, was a child of Austro-German cultural traditions.

Neither war nor its aftermath changed that German attitude. This was reflected in a report we received in October 1946 from our Hamburg Information Control Unit, then commanded—this by the way—by Lieutenant Colonel Freddy Gross, five years earlier our first alien second lieutenant in 77 Company of the Pioneer Corps. It stated: "In respect of denazification there is a German belief that all persons connected with the arts should be regarded as a different kind of human being. They are considered to live in a different world and should, therefore, be treated in a different way."

A point of view we did not share in Schlüterstrasse. In theory, that is. In practice we, and that included "Torquemada" Sely, did not respond in quite the same way to an unknown bit player as we did to, say, a film star or the bearer of a famous name. Unlike German artists we were merely human.

8

When Music Was
Not the Food
of Love

Of all the famous names in German art there was none
more illustrious, none more controversial, than that of
that most august of all Olympians: Wilhelm Furtwängler. That much I knew. What I did not know when I
began to update his file was how it would lead me—via
the highways and byways of the German psyche—into
the complexities of the artist's moral and political responsibility under a totalitarian regime.

The curtain raiser to the Furtwängler drama, and it
was nothing less than that, was his first postwar visit to
Berlin in response to a Tulpanov-backed press campaign
for his rehabilitation and return. It culminated in the
"Berlin calls Wilhelm Furtwängler" open letter published in the Soviet Sector's *Berliner Zeitung* on February 16, 1946. Leading off with a reference to the maestro's
recent sixtieth birthday it said:

You are about to begin a new chapter in your life, which, of this we are certain, will continue to be dedicated to your art. German music is endeavoring to play its part in overcoming the greatest crisis in our history by concentrating without compromise on its true national values—this German music cannot do without your creative collaboration. The artist expects new and forward-looking impulses to come from you. We all need you as interpreter of the classical and modern, German and foreign, creations of musical genius to enable us to experience them in that masterful perfection that today, more than ever before, holds the most profound appeal to one's conscience. For what is such mastery if not the strictest and purest service in the great task we all are called on to undertake? All of us who want to build the new democratic Germany in the spirit of humanity need the high symbol of artistic perfection, which for us Germans, after the barbaric relapse of National Socialism, is the clarion call to self-knowledge. That is why we, why Germany, needs the artist Wilhelm Furtwängler. Your birthplace appeals to you to return to it. The home of your true fame and worldwide success so indissolubly linked to the Berlin Philharmonic Orchestra appeals to you to come back. We are confident that you feel a strong inner need to work again in the city that you, continuing the great tradition of a Bülow and a Nikisch, filled with the living present.

This piece of somewhat high-falutin' prose was signed by Dr. Werner, the Soviet-appointed governing mayor, by Johannes R. Becher of the Deutsche Kulturbund, and by many other prominent personalities including Sergiu Celibidache, the Romanian conductor, who substituted as the Berlin Philharmonic's musical director in Furtwängler's absence. He was no Soviet puppet, nor were many of the other signatories.

Furtwängler's positive response to the *Berliner Zeitung* appeal and the Russians' offer to fly him to Berlin came from Vienna. In February 1945, alarmed by warnings, from Albert Speer and the lady doctor who was Himmler's wife's personal physician, that the Gestapo intended to arrest him, Furtwängler had fled from Berlin via Austria to Switzerland, where his family was living. Until then the careful Swiss—prudently balancing between Germany and the Allies—had treated him as a respected guest, but after Germany's defeat many Swiss, often those who had been most pro-Nazi before, were rabidly anti-German. Noisy demonstrations against Furtwängler were used by the Swiss authorities, anxious lest the presence of so prominent a German offend the victors, as a welcome excuse to request his departure. Leaving his family in Switzerland, he moved to half-occupied, half-liberated Austria in the autumn of 1945.

On March 10, 1946, Furtwängler landed in Berlin—and a hornets' nest of intrigue. Tulpanov had his triumph. He was giving back to the German capital its most glorious living cultural monument.

"No way," as they say, did the U.S. authorities share the Russian colonel's enthusiasm for the conductor's return. On the contrary, many Americans considered Furtwängler a former Nazi stooge, and his arrival aboard a Soviet aircraft at a Soviet airfield proved to them that he was now about to become a Russian one. Their suspicions were further fueled by the cordial reception prepared for the maestro. As his plane touched down, he was welcomed by representatives of the Soviet Administration, accompanied by a German delegation led by the inescapable Becher. One of the Russian officers, a Captain Barski, immediately attached himself to Furtwängler as his "minder" and drove him to his "grace and favor" apartment in the pheasantry of Frederick the Great's Sans Souci palace at Potsdam. The official seals having been removed from its entrance, Furtwängler found his old home in the exact condition in which he had left it a little over a year earlier. Everything was clean, tidy, and in perfect order; even his concert grand, which the Russians had had to recover from some Red Army soldiers who had "borrowed" it, was back in its appointed place.

Never a subtle politician, Furtwängler, attempting to pacify the Americans at his press conference, only made matters worse by naïvely declaring that he was in Berlin in a purely private capacity—as if flying private German individuals through the air with the greatest of ease were a Soviet habit.

The official American response was a curt and icy statement from General Robert A. McClure, chief of the U.S. Information Division, in which he pointed out that any former Prussian state councillor—a title Furtwängler had accepted in 1933, but stopped using after the November 1938 pogrom—was automatically banned from public life by Control Council Directive No. 24 until cleared by the appropriate denazification commission. And to ensure that Furtwängler had no illusions about working with his beloved Berlin Philharmonic before the Schlüterstrasse Spruchkammer had dealt with his case, McClure stressed that the orchestra had its official seat in the U.S. Sector and performed under a U.S. license.

Furtwängler was stunned. On the day before his departure a Viennese tribunal had denazified him. He had not fully comprehended that Austria was once again a separate and independent state and that the writ of her courts, therefore, did not extend to Germany. Fortunately so, because the country that gave the world Hitler, Seyss-Inquart, and Kaltenbrunner, to name only the three stars of its native horde of Nazi leaders, was too busy burying her own past to dig properly into that of her prominent and useful residents. Austria's priority was not justice but restoring her image as a dear little land of wine, women, and waltz.

The Soviets, who showered protest notes on the Western powers like confetti whenever they suspected them of having overlooked one i-dot in a four-power agreement, did not give two kopeks for Control Council Directive No. 24. Or McClure. They offered Furtwängler the directorship of "their" State Opera. He thanked them but politely declined. One dictatorship had been enough. Besides, saying yes to the Soviets was tantamount to saying good-bye to the Berlin Philharmonic, the virtuoso orchestra he had created. Before returning to Vienna he grasped the Spruchkammer nettle and applied for denazification.

The American insistence, supported by the British and the French, on the letter of the law was absolutely correct, although everybody including McClure knew that the *Staatsrat,* the state councillor title, was a mere honorific. Awarded by Göring in his capacity as minister-president of Prussia, it gave no political power, entailed occasional representational duties, conferred some privileges, unimportant except for one—Göring's personal patronage, which obliged his arch rival and arch enemy Goebbels to treat *Staatsräte* with circumspection. Everybody, again including McClure, knew that Furtwängler had never been a Nazi. But, and that was the question, had he willingly allowed the Hitler regime to use his genius and world fame for its own purposes?

Undoubtedly the Nazis understood and exploited music's universal appeal for their national and international propaganda. At home and abroad they used the harmonies of Germany's classical composers to drown the thump of truncheon and jackboot. Before the war the performances of the Berlin and Vienna philharmonics, the Leipzig Gewandhaus, and other good German orchestras in foreign capitals were meant to demonstrate that National Socialism was in tune with the highest aspirations of German culture. During the war, playing in countries allied to Germany, in neutral and even in occupied ones, under the batons of Furtwängler, Karl Böhm, Clemens Krauss, the young and fast-rising von Karajan, these same orchestras conveyed the message that the nation that had produced Bach, Beethoven, Mozart, Haydn, Schubert, Wagner, Brahms, Richard Strauss, could not be fighting in any other cause but that of Occidental civilization. The only German conductor who, with the exception of one concert in Denmark, avoided visiting the occupied countries, saying privately that he had no wish to follow the Wehrmacht's tanks with his music, was Furtwängler.

But in the virtually unanimous view of American intellectuals, of Arturo Toscanini, Thomas Mann, and many other prominent refugees from fascism and Nazism, Furtwängler had, by staying in Germany, not only served but actively supported the Third Reich, an opinion that was shared by many U.S. occupation officials in Germany.

The Furtwängler controversy, or rather controversies, did not begin in 1945 or 1946, but had its origins in 1933, when his adversaries were not liberal opinion leaders but their very antagonists: the Nazi bosses. Naturally Goebbels was suspicious about the man who wrote in an essay published in 1928: "German music must be conceived as European music. That is what it always was and that is what it must remain. Attempts to bring nationalism into music, which are being made everywhere, must lead to its decline."

The propaganda minister's misgivings about Furtwängler were amply confirmed on April 11, 1933, when he read the maestro's open letter in the *Vossische Zeitung.* Clearly addressed to Goebbels it drew his attention to:

Recent events within German musical life, which in
my view are not an essential concomitant to the res-
titution of our national dignity, for which all of us
are so grateful ... as an artist the only divide in art
I recognize is that between good and bad. But the
distinction that is now being made with theory-based
relentless severity is between Jew and non-Jew, even
if the political attitude of the person concerned gives
no reason for complaint ... great artists are rare and
no country can do without them without damaging
its cultural life ... therefore, in plain words, men
like Klemperer, Bruno Walter, Max Reinhardt, etc.,
must also in future be allowed to serve their art in
Germany.

It was early Nazi days but, although the new regime
had not yet fully revealed its true character, to write
those words after the Reichstag fire and the brutalities
that followed it required some courage. More than a year
later, when Furtwängler took up his pen yet again to
challenge Goebbels, by protesting against his decision to
ban Paul Hindemith's opera *Mathis der Maler,* no one of
any intelligence could still be ignorant of how the Nazis
dealt with their opponents. In the Nazi view, expressed
with typical venom by our Schlüterstrasse predeces-
sor Hans Hinkel, Hindemith was a composer "enthusiastically celebrated by the disciples of Jew-infected
Music-Bolshevism, deeply rooted in the spiritual and
weltanschaulichen attitudes of the Weimar Republic, so
abhorrent to National Socialism."

The *Deutsche Allgemeine Zeitung* published Furtwängler's daring defense of Hindemith with near equal
bravery on November 25, 1934, but only after its editor
had made sure that the author was fully aware of the
possible consequences for himself.

"Certain circles," Furtwängler wrote,

have fired their opening shots in a campaign against Paul Hindemith. They claim that he is unacceptable to the new Germany. Why? What are their accusations? First, foremost, and purely political: that he has Jewish connections and played the viola in the Amar Quartet, which has had Jewish members for many years. Furthermore that he, even after the National Socialist revolution, made some gramophone recordings together with Jewish refugees. The facts are that we are talking about a group of string instrumentalists who joined together long before the present government came to power, nor are they "émigrés." One of them, Goldberg, was an outstanding leader of the Berlin Philharmonic until a few months ago when he decided to become a soloist, and the other, the Austrian citizen Feuermann, universally recognized as one of Europe's best cellists, was a much respected teacher at the State Academy of Music in Berlin for many years . . .

Furtwängler did not restrict his defense of and help for Jews to words, however brave, in place of deeds. He protected Jewish musicians and assisted them with their emigration. Nor did he cease his efforts on their behalf after the Reichskristallnacht pogrom of 1938, when helping Jews became more dangerous than ever before. In December 1946 F. L. Kerran, a British diplomat and onetime adviser to King Zog of Albania, published a letter in *The Times* of London (one document I obviously did not have when I prepared my file) that bears witness to this:

"While visiting at the beginning of 1939 in Vienna the well-known Jewish singing teacher Dr. Walla Hess," Mr. Kerran wrote,

I heard a pupil of Mme. Hess, a young but very poor Jewish youth, whose magnificent voice greatly im-

pressed me. This youth was "on the run" and expected any moment to be arrested by the Gestapo. I
immediately got in touch with Furtwängler in Berlin
and he promised to help any way he could. Within
48 hours he flew to Vienna from Berlin, saw and
heard the boy at a secret rendezvous. He gave me a
letter as to the quality of the boy's voice and musical
ability and did the same for Mme. Hess. With these
letters and the support of Sir Adrian Boult the Home
Office granted permission for both of them to come
to this country.

Goebbels was not lying, merely exaggerating hugely,
when he complained, "There's not a single filthy Jew left
in Germany on whose behalf Herr Furtwängler has not
intervened."

But although Furtwängler had never for one moment
been attracted by Nazi ideas and ideals, which at one
time or another appealed even to some of the civilians
and soldiers who later led the July 20, 1944 resistance
movement, he, unlike, for instance, Dietrich and Klaus
Bonhöffer or Hans von Dohnanyi, was not made of the
stuff of which martyrs are made.

After the publication of the defense of Hindemith,
Goebbels hit back hard with a major speech. In it he
denounced Furtwängler for disloyalty to National Socialism, "not only the political and social but also the
cultural conscience of the nation, and the new German
state." Furtwängler resigned his directorship of the State
Opera, an office specially revived for him in 1933, his vice-
chairmanship of the Reichsmusikkammer, and on December 5, 1934, he withdrew from public life into what
later came to be called "inner emigration," a sort of re-
fusenik term invented postwar by some German writers
who were trying to defend themselves against Thomas
Mann's accusation, also aimed at Furtwängler, that it

would have been their duty as artists to quit Germany in protest against Nazism.

In this Mann was a little holier-than-thou, because initially his own departure from Germany had not been an act of defiance against Hitler. On February 11, 1933, eleven days after the Nazi leader became chancellor, Mann set out on a long-planned lecture tour to Amsterdam, Brussels, and Paris. A two-week holiday in Ascona was to follow. There he received a message from his daughter Erika, who was in Munich, warning him not to come back; the Nazis were out to get him. Mann, instead of returning to Munich as he had intended, decided to stay in Switzerland and await developments. Yet in spite of repeated requests from friends and members of his family to speak out against the German regime, he, in order to protect his and his publisher's financial interests in Germany, remained silent for another three years and only donned the mantle of spiritual leader of the German emigration after the Nazis' final sequestration of his German assets. This was an ambivalence not unlike Furtwängler's, except that the conductor, having spoken out openly, then remained in Germany quiet and compromised, while Mann, once his self-imposed silence had ended, became the most authoritative and effective German voice opposing the Third Reich from abroad.

Furtwängler's "inner emigration" was short-lived. He and Goebbels met in February 1935 and the result of their talk was that the conductor, thinking he was thereby freeing himself of any personal responsibility for its future course, agreed to the publication of a statement in which he acknowledged Hitler to be the sole arbiter of German art. The world in general and the Nazis in particular saw it as the maestro's surrender—a view that Hitler's presence and that of the other principal Nazi leaders in the hall of the Berlin Philharmonic on April

25, 1935, the date of Furtwängler's return to the rostrum, apparently confirmed.

The concert, given in support of Winter Aid, the Nazi's favorite charity, began with Beethoven's *Egmont* Overture. This was followed by his *Pastorale* and Fifth symphonies. When the last chord of its coda had died away, there was stunned silence. Then the audience went wild. A sheer endless standing ovation, growing in intensity till it seemed more a demonstration than just applause, celebrated the maestro's reappearance. Seventeen times Furtwängler was called back to the podium and not once, to everybody's amazement, did he raise his arm in the Nazi salute, obligatory at any function Hitler personally attended. To avoid it, Furtwängler kept his baton in his right hand. "Heil Hitlering" with the little white stick stabbing the air would have looked ridiculous.

All the photographs, except one, taken on this occasion show the conductor thanking the audience by bowing somewhat stiffly from the waist. But the one used by most newspapers in Germany and abroad was the odd one out, portraying Hitler shaking the conductor's now batonless hand. Around the world that handshake photo was seen as further evidence that Furtwängler had betrayed his ideals.

One of the most painful reactions was the "Letter to German Intellectuals" that Furtwängler's friend, the violinist Bronislav Huberman, published in the *Manchester Guardian* in the following year. Beginning with a mention of his earlier correspondence with the conductor, to whom he referred as "one of Germany's most representative spiritual leaders," Huberman said.

> Dr. Furtwängler has spoken out openly on his own behalf and on that of "all true Germans" against the shameful persecution of people for "race-

contamination." I do not doubt for one moment that his indignation is genuine and I am convinced that many Germans, possibly even the majority, share his view. But what have those "true Germans" actually done to turn this shame away from their own consciences, from Germany, from all of humanity? . . . Where in Germany are the Zolas, the Clemenceaus, Painlevés, Piquarts, in this monster Dreyfus Trial against the whole of a defenseless minority? . . . Before the whole world I accuse you German intellectuals, you non-Nazis, as the truly guilty of all Nazi crimes.

Yet Furtwängler's early public protests had been the nearest anyone in Germany ever came to emulating Zola, Clemenceau, Painlevé, and Piquart. In any case Huberman's comparison between Furtwängler's later silence and the steadfast bravery of the four Frenchmen's fight for justice was unrealistic: the cockerel of the Third Republic and the predatory eagle of the Third Reich were hardly birds of the same feather.

However, if contrasted with the dialectic acerbity of an anti-Furtwängler pamphlet produced by the German communist composer Hanns Eisler, Huberman's remarks were almost mild. Eisler, who spent the war years in the United States and afterward moved to the German Democratic Republic, accused Furtwängler of aiding and abetting "murder, arson, robbery, theft, fraud, torture of the defenseless, and above all silencing the truth. . . . Staatsrat Dr. Wilhelm Furtwängler has proved in word and deed that he uses his art and abuses the great works of Germany's classic composers to prettify Hitler's bloodstained hangmen regime."

So why, instead of compromising, did Furtwängler not emigrate? Material considerations obviously had nothing to do with his decision to stay. The language of his art was universal and, though he was one of Germany's highest earners, he would not have incurred any financial losses—more likely the opposite would have happened—had he moved to Britain or the United States. One reason was his highly, perhaps overdeveloped sense of mission: the conviction that his continuing presence and music making gave solace to all "true" Germans who felt as he did. This view was shared by many, including the Jewess Dr. Bertha Geismar, his former personal assistant. Having emigrated to England, where she became Sir Thomas Beecham's secretary, she wrote in her memoirs: "Furtwängler did more to preserve a decent mentality in Germany by staying in the country than others who left."

Thinking about this argument in 1946 one saw the flaws in it. For as long as Hitler added success to success, for as long as the cheering majority worshiped the ground he trod on, solacing the decent mentality of a silenced minority with beautiful music meant tilting at inexorably grinding windmills. But the ideology perverting and destroying Germany's nobler traditions did its initial work by gradual erosion rather than sudden onslaught. Hence Furtwängler could harbor the illusion of saving some of their essentials by his art and example; such faith in his country's humanist achievements—of which music was perhaps the greatest—also purblinding him to much, if not to all, of what was happening. In this, however, he was far from unique. Even after the regime had fully revealed its bestial face, men politically more aware than he and of much firmer convictions resisted acknowledging the truth.

One of the most moving testimonials to how strong a hold the idea of that other and better Germany had over men's minds comes from a Jew born in Austrian Poland, the author Manès Sperber, onetime communist comrade and lifelong friend of Arthur Koestler. Here, in an excerpt from his autobiography,* Sperber describes how he reacted when he heard the first rumors about Auschwitz in his Paris exile:

> It took some time before we could really believe the rumors about this lunacy, because we assumed that even Hitler, in spite of his fanaticism, would still retain that realistic sense of purpose he had so often demonstrated during his rise to power. But there was also another reason for our disinclination to accept such horror as possible: the deep and indestructible bond between us and German and Austrian culture. One knew Hitler was capable of any crime, but how was one to think it possible that thousands of Germans and Austrians could be found who were willing to exterminate innocent and defenseless human beings! . . . What was it I defended myself against that so many months had to pass before I was prepared to trust those rumors of industrialized mass extermination? *I defended myself against the rupture with Germany.*

I, not Sperber, put that last sentence in italics. If he, the Jew in his Jewishness, so defended himself against the rupture with Germany that he could not for a time believe Auschwitz to be possible, can one condemn the German Furtwängler in his Germanness for not abandoning his native country years before Hitler embarked on his greatest crime? It must remain a moot point whether by staying he did preserve, and to what effect, that "decent mentality" of which Dr. Geismar spoke, but he certainly could do more to help the persecuted from inside than from outside, where he would have been a seven-days propaganda wonder. How much did Toscanini damage Mussolini? How much Mann, Hitler?

* Manès Sperber, *Bis man mir die Scherben auf die Augen legt* (Munich: Deutscher Taschenbuch Verlag, 1982).

The dictators were not defeated by the intellectual opposition abroad or by what there was of it at home; they were defeated by the nowadays pejoratively called "military-industrial complex" of their enemies.

Yet by staying in Germany Furtwängler did become the Third Reich's most impressive cultural advertisement and alibi. However reluctantly, he did accept Göring's Staatsrat, was—if only for a short time— vice-chairman of the Reichsmusikkammer, and on three occasions he did dignify Nazi functions with his music and presence. As festive finale to the Nuremberg rally of 1935, where Hitler proclaimed his infamous race laws, Furtwängler conducted the *Meistersinger* at the opera house, a performance he repeated, allegedly at Hitler's behest, at the jubilant post-Austrian Anschluss party rally of 1938. And in honor of Hitler's fifty-third birthday he conducted a special celebratory concert.

There were occasions when he, like many German non-Nazis, did trim. And, again like many German non-Nazis, he persuaded himself that bending his spine before Hitler would strengthen his backbone in confrontations with the Führer's minions. But there was also the fact that the maestro off the concert platform was more human than Olympian, vain, touchy, and insecure. Especially when it came to von Karajan. Knowing that Furtwängler recognized in this greatly (if not yet "divinely") gifted, ambitious young man, and not at all reluctant party member, the only conductor who might one day challenge his own supremacy, Göring and particularly Goebbels, when they wished to manipulate Furtwängler, only needed to mention von Karajan's name. Conducting *Ein Heldenleben* is one thing, leading one is quite another. To the Karajan threat Furtwängler responded as to nothing else, even the Führer's gifts.

After his divorce and second marriage in June 1943, when Furtwängler was in financial difficulties, Goebbels

sent him a message saying, "The Führer desires to do-
nate to his meritorious chief conductor a house built and
furnished to your specifications."

When I read the copy of Furtwängler's reply I had to
admire his probity. After many flowery expressions of
gratitude he wrote that he felt regretfully unable to accept such a generous present at a time when so many of
his fellow citizens had lost their houses and homes.

When I had finished my work and the file was ready to
go to Sely, I sat and looked at the closed folder for a long
time. The Spruchkammer would have to give its verdict,
but on what? That no one could live under a brutal dictatorship without becoming tainted? Compromising
with evil to prevent worse, a defense I was to hear many
times, is always futile, but to know this after the event
was as easy as, except in a very few cases, it is difficult
to recognize malignancy in its infancy.

Years later, when I came across Huberman's letter
again, it struck me how many of those who claimed pre-
science about Hitler also served Stalinist communism,
in cruelty the mirror image of Nazism. Why did Huberman, no communist like Eisler, not send a similar letter
to, say, Shostakovich? The year was 1936 and Hitler's career as a mass murderer was, so to speak, still in its kin-
dergarten stage, while Stalin's had already reached
maturity. Millions of kulaks, men, women, children, had
been shot, starved, or deported to Siberian labor camps.
The world knew about it. It knew about the thousands
of arrests that followed the murder of Kirov in 1934, it
knew about the decree "On Combating Crime Among
Minors" that authorized the death penalty for children
from the age of twelve, and the Moscow show trials had
already begun. Why did Huberman write to the German
but not the Russian? Did he too—inhaling the fumes of
the opium of the great and good of his time (and be-

yond)—hallucinate that Left is always right, no matter what?

This may be one-half of the explanation. The other, it comes out clearly in Huberman's words, was that Russia and Germany were not measured by the same yardstick. Rightly! That in that vast country on the fringe of Europe one autocrat had succeeded another seemed less significant to the Western mind than the decline into barbarism of Germany, a heartland of European culture and civilization for many centuries. The resulting shock was and is so profound that it has still not been overcome. What Germany truly lost during the years of her intoxication with Hitler and brute power was not the war, but herself.

But toward the end of March 1946 such thoughts did not occur to anyone in Berlin, German or Allied. Minds were concentrated on an event of more immediate urgency: the forthcoming ballot of all Berlin's Social Democrats on whether or not their party and the communists were to unite in one single "anti-fascist" political organization. Its outcome was to determine the future of Berlin and profoundly influence that of the whole of Germany.

9

Ballot and Ballet

Heaven knows how she did it—first thing in the morning too and after a rush-hour journey on the Berlin underground—but Eva Rose always arrived at Schlüterstrasse with cheerful smile and springy step. I, being an early bird by nature and having my own transport, a bike bought for two hundred cigarettes from our mess-shuttle tram driver, was usually at the office before her. While she made our NAAFI* coffee and toasted her one slice of dry bread on her little kerosene stove, we often had a chat. By the time Sely got in, around nine o'clock, the coffee was ready and Tolliver and I joined him for "morning prayers" to discuss the day's business. But on the last Wednesday of March, Eva Rose, looking thoughtful and preoccupied, trundled rather than danced into the office.

"Hey, what's bitten you?" I asked.

*British PX

"Ach, Mr. Clare, if only I knew what to do!"

"Why, what's the problem? Boyfriend trouble?"

"No, nothing silly like that. That ballot! I'm not sure what to vote for. Should I be for or against the Communist and Social Democrat merger?"

"But that's a ballot for party members only," I said.

"Well, I am," she replied. "I'm a Social Democrat. We all are in my family. Oh, if only my dad were still alive! He'd know what to do. Why of all people did a lifelong Social Democrat like him have to die in an air raid? He was also in the *Reichsbanner*, the socialist defense force, you know, and was a founding member of the secular school movement as well. I think of him often, but even more so now. What would he say?"

When we had this talk my work on the Furtwängler file had further softened the tones in my picture of Germany. Where once there had been only the blackest blacks, more and more shades of human gray had filtered in. Nevertheless the danger of a possible Nazi revival still seemed real to me and so anything with an "antifascist" label had my sympathy. Had such a united left-wing block existed in the early 1930s, I reasoned, Hitler would never have come to power. I advised Eva Rose to vote for the merger. She thanked me, but, instead of brightening up, her face retained its solemn expression. I felt a bit huffed. Obviously my lucid argument had not convinced her. But I said no more about it. Considering how wrong I was, this was just as well.

The flaw in my premise, and I suppose she saw it, was my ignorance of how before 1933 Stalin's Comintern had regarded the Social Democrats rather than the Nazis as the real enemy. In those decisive years its agent, that same Walter Ulbricht who now agitated for working-class unity, had even cooperated with the Hitlerites to achieve the one aim German extremists of Right and

Left had in common—the destruction of the Weimar democracy.

Perhaps my views were also influenced by my antipathy for Kurt Schumacher, the leader of the Social Democrats in the British Zone of occupation. One had to admire the courage of this one-armed World War I veteran, a sick and dour man after ten years in concentration camps, but I could not abide either his messianic righteousness or his criticism of the Allies. When he said, "While others [meaning France, Britain, and the Soviet Union] were signing alliances with the German government some of us were already rotting in concentration camps," he was far from wrong, but I thought the time for a prominent German to say this in public had not yet come.

Schumacher had not forgotten or forgiven the Communists for undermining the Weimar Republic and he saw Ulbricht's Soviet-sponsored anti-fascist bloc in Berlin for what it was: a potentially dangerous model for the whole of Germany. How simple-minded Harold Laski's "Let capitalist governments mistrust one another . . . but governments like the Russian and our own are the surest hope of peace . . . ," or the Labor Party's 1945 election slogan, "Left understands Left," must have appeared to Schumacher. He knew that what Ulbricht had in mind when proclaiming "unity" had nothing to do with either understanding or respecting the Social Democrats' point of view.

Schumacher's opposite number in Berlin, Otto Grotewohl, the chairman of the Social Democrat Party's central committee, vacillated for a while before becoming a fervent merger advocate. The party's functionaries in Berlin split into two camps, but the force of Schumacher's personality and arguments began to tip the balance in favor of the antimerger faction. In spite of this Ulbricht was still convinced that he would win. The master manipulator relied on the fact that out of 230 appointed city councillors 100 were Communists, many of them in sensitive positions, and that of the 81 Social Democrats not all were opposed to unification. But his Russian masters were less confident and were undecided whether to allow the ballot in their sector. Even after General Clay had stated that the U.S. Military Government would not recognize the validity of a merger unless a genuinely secret poll produced a clear majority for it, the Soviets prevaricated. Saying neither yes nor no they kept asking for more detailed information and asserted that the Social Democrat district organizations in their sector had not yet applied for permission to hold the ballot. Then, at the very last moment, the Saturday before polling day, they finally banned it in their part of Berlin.

On Sunday, March 31, 1946, only Social Democrats in the Western sectors were able to vote on the question: "Are you for or against an immediate union between the Social Democrat and the Communist parties?" Two Soviet Sector districts, Friedrichshain and Prenzlauer Berg, defied the Russians and opened polling stations, but soon Red Army soldiers, forceful missionaries of "People's Democracy," arrived, closed them down, and departed with the ballot boxes. It was this act that finally shattered what illusions I still had about our Soviet allies.

Of the 32,547 registered Social Democrats in the Western sectors 29,610 voted against, 2,937 for the immediate merger. The first free and secret election on German soil since 1932 had produced an overwhelming vote for liberty. What in fact was the second battle for Berlin—although the world at large inasmuch as it took notice at all, saw it as a minor local event—had ended in the Soviet Union's first serious setback in Germany since the end of the war. She had suffered a defeat in the very city where she had enjoyed her greatest triumph—her victory in the first epic battle for Berlin, the stuff of legends. And Soviet propagandists and hagiographers were no slouches in spinning them. For instance, the one about the Red Army having slain the Nazi dragon on its own, or its sequel that the Western Allies, in spite of the relevant agreements, were the Soviets' "grace and favor" tenants in Berlin. In other words, while they were in Berlin on sufferance, the Russians "owned" the whole of the German capital by right of conquest.

In truth the Russians' hold on Berlin resulted not only from their soldiers' valor, but also from what, except for Hitler's own follies, was the most blinkered decision of the war: General Eisenhower's order to his armies not to advance on Berlin. He gave it when his forward units—two days before the Soviets started their final offensive from further away—were less than fifty miles from the capital. Partly out of loyalty to the Soviet ally, partly because he considered Berlin militarily unimportant, the supreme commander did not change his mind, even in the light of Winston Churchill's prescient warning about "the special importance the capital of the Third Reich is bound to possess in the final catastrophe of National Socialism and *after. . . .* "

And indeed, if anything, Berlin's importance after that catastrophe was greater than before. If Eisenhower did not agree with Churchill about this, Stalin certainly did. He wanted the whole city, and the merger between Social Democrats and communists was but one crucial further step toward this aim and toward the greater one that Lenin had defined in the sentence: "He who has Berlin has Germany, and he who has Germany has Europe."

The votes of some thirty thousand Berlin Social Democrats in a ballot, which but for the Western Allies controlling three-quarters of the city would never have been held, foiled Stalin's plans and prevented a shotgun wed-

ding with the Communists analogous to that which did
take place in the Soviet Zone. Its unforeseen but eventually vital by-product was the change it wrought in the
relations between the Western powers and the Berliners.
Britain, France, and the United States were now no longer just occupiers. They had become Berlin's defenders
and protectors from totalitarian tyranny. This gave the
Western presence in the city a moral legitimacy in the
third battle for Berlin, that of the Soviet Blockade and
the Allied Airlift, which carried more weight not only
with Berliners and other Germans but also with the free
world than that derived from the unconditional surrender.

The day of my debacle as Eva Rose's political advisor
would have stayed in my memory in any case, but that
particular Wednesday was unforgettable also for another
reason: my first visit to the State Opera and the Soviet
Sector. In my almost three months in Berlin I had never
been to that part of it. Had access been as difficult then
as it would eventually become, I would probably have
been more curious about it, but there was no Berlin wall,
there were no checkpoints; one just walked or cycled in,
took the underground or—as I did—the elevated S-Bahn. I
got out at Friedrichstrasse station and as I had plenty
of time I ambled through the streets. They looked a bit
more desolate, perhaps, than those of the Western sectors, where some modest restoration efforts were becoming visible, but there was not much to it. The one
obvious difference was the many red flags and streamers
with their slogans and, of course, the ubiquitous Stalin
poster with his pronouncement that the Hitlers come
and go but the German people remain. I did see some
unarmed Red Army soldiers in their filthy boots and
dirty uniforms, but as a rule Other Ranks and NCOs

were confined to barracks, so they should not see even the little that was left of capitalist civilization.

The inside of the Admiralspalast, the former variety theater that was now the home of the State Opera, having been refurbished on Russian orders, looked quite splendid in its traditional opera-house red, white, and gold. To the marshals, generals, and colonels of the army of the great revolution tradition was tremendously important; when it came to opera and ballet none of them, from Supremo Stalin down, had any time for leftish modernistic frippery. This was the salvation of Tatiana Gsovsky, owner of Berlin's foremost ballet school. A White Russian émigrée, she saw herself on the next train to Siberia when the Red Army entered Berlin. The Russian officers who knocked at her door, however, carried neither chains nor leg-irons but *payoks* and flowers. "Ah, Madame," they laughed when they noticed her fear, "who bothers about that sort of nonsense nowadays? That's ancient history. No, we haven't come to talk about your past, but about your future. Please do us the honor and accept the position of Maîtresse de Ballet and Chief Choreographer of the State Opera."

Eighteen-year-old Ilona Kortmann, one of the principal dancers of the State Opera ballet and a Gsovsky pupil since the age of seven, had told me this story. She, her mother, and I first met in my HQ Military Government "glasshouse." Having pressed the bell on my table I waited for the next in the queue to come in. Two women entered and I just sat there, momentarily speechless, staring like an open-mouthed yokel at the younger of the two, a slim and willowy girl. Not in films, not on the stage, let alone in real life, had I ever seen beauty of such breathtaking perfection. From under her wide-brimmed hat glowing chestnut-red hair, framing a face of Botticellian grace and delicacy, cascaded down to her shoulders.

Intensely blue eyes looked straight at me with almost childlike innocence and a disconcertingly penetrating steadiness of glance. The girl's skin, pale, of translucent sheen and slightly freckled, covered prominent and aristocratically narrow Slavonic cheekbones, the shadowy hollows under them accentuating the fineness of her bone structure. Her lips, generous without being voluptuous under the small straight nose and too thickly smeared with lipstick of too bright a red, consolingly proved that this miraculous creature was human after all.

The mother—the likeness was obvious, she had the same red hair but cut short, and dark brown eyes—was very attractive, yet she could never, not even when she was much younger than the forty or so years I guessed her to be, have matched the daughter's beauty.

Trancelike and entranced I did what I had never done before. I got up, went over to the two women, and shook hands. They told me their problem. It was a familiar one, the same as Ella Fersen's. Ilona, who until then had only appeared at the State Opera, had been asked to give a solo performance at a British Sector theater and needed the relevant certificate. But that was not the only parallel. Ilona too, to use Nazi terminology, was a "half-caste," a *Mischling*, of the first degree. Neither she nor her mother volunteered that information. I found out, because noticing the foreign accent in the mother's German, well polished but nevertheless discernible, I, having recovered my composure, now looked at their questionnaires. Kortmann, the family name, was as German as one could get, but the mother's first name was Salka—that puzzled me.

Salka? My mother had had an aunt of that name. I could not stand the poor woman, because her German, amply laced with Jewish expressions, and spoken with the singsong intonation of Yiddish, offended my assimilationist ears, touching the racial insecurity buried deep in the head between them. Frau Kortmann's German had nothing of the Polish ghetto or *shtetl* about it, but it sounded a little hard. I saw that she had written "Protestant" where religion had to be stated on the form, but then discovered that her place of birth was Lemberg, the same town in Poland where my mother was born.

"Are you Jewish?" I asked her.

"Yes, I am," she replied, "though not by religion anymore. I converted when I married my husband. He's German, of course."

"Why didn't you tell me?"

"It didn't occur to me. Ilona is the reason for our visit. I came because legally she's still a minor. In any case the days when racial origins mattered are over, thank God."

I liked her. She let her daughter do the talking, very different from Frau Fersen, and though it must have been obvious to her how I had warmed to them she did not, when I told them about Schlüterstrasse, try to wheedle me into doing anything for them. She did, however, invite me to visit them and meet her husband and I accepted with pleasure.

In the 1920s Kurt Kortmann had been the chief conductor of the orchestra at the UFA-Palace am Zoo, that big and luxurious cinema my parents had talked so much about after their visit to Germany in 1929. But in the early 1930s new technology—the talkies—made him and his musicians redundant. Perversely this turned out to have been a stroke of good luck, because in the short interval between losing his job and the Nazi takeover he made a name for himself as a composer of film music, backroom and background work ideal for an Aryan with a Jewish wife. This, with the help of various ruses, good friends, good luck, and some careful economy with the truth, enabled Kortmann to continue to make a good living.

Visiting the Kortmanns became an almost weekly ritual. Instead of flowers I usually brought a haversack of goodies from the Winston Club, which was only a few steps from their large flat on Olivaer Platz. My hosts supplied coffee or wine and we sat there talking till late. After two or three visits I discovered to my own surprise that what attracted me was not Ilona but her parents. She made me feel uneasy. For one thing I felt a little shy in the presence of so much beauty, too ethereal for somebody as earthy as I took myself to be. But she was also highly strung, if not to say neurotic, and I found it difficult to cope with her tenseness and abrupt changes of mood. I was too young then to look for reasons, but the very strong and obvious love her parents had for each other may have been too exclusive. It did, however, create an atmosphere of warmth and closeness that made the Kortmann home a kind of sanctuary for me from the rougher world of khaki, mess halls, barracks, and also Anita's simplicities. But when Ilona asked me to come to the State Opera and see her dance I naturally accepted with a show of enthusiasm.

She had given me a complimentary ticket for a seat in the tenth row of the stalls. In front were Russian officers and their wives, next to me Americans with their girlfriends, instantly recognizable by the sheerness of their nylons and the thickness of their makeup, and behind us were the Germans of the Golden Hunger Years seeking escape from harsh reality in art and from the unspringlike cold in a well-heated theater.

Ravel's *Bolero*, described by the composer as "My masterpiece, but, unfortunately, it contains no music," was the first item on the program. Tatiana Gsovsky danced the principal part herself. She and her girls were in tightly clinging black dresses. Their faces, painted white like geishas', were expressionless, their bloodred lips unsmiling, and, with the exception of Ilona, who of course needed none, they all wore wigs of flaming red hair. This, combined with the sinuous swaying of their bodies to the monotonously sensuous rhythm of the *Bolero,* first conveyed sexual submissiveness; but then the dancers, whipped on by the ever rising crescendos of drums and cymbals, gyrated faster and faster in ever more wanton abandon until—with the final, climactic "rumba-ba-rum"—they collapsed on to the stage, the audience bursting into ecstatic applause.

Ravel's *Daphnis and Chloe,* with Ilona as Chloe, followed after the interval. She looked lovely and, as Kortmann had so proudly said of his daughter, was highly talented, but neither the story nor the music nor the dancing really spoke to me. I was bored; the thing seemed to go on interminably and I longed for it to end, although I knew that another chore, a visit to Ilona's dressing room, had yet to be endured. Fortunately for me—I loved the *Bolero* but did not know what to say about her solo part—the dressing room the girls shared was chock-a-block with visitors, mostly Russian officers, but also a few Germans. As everybody was trying to outshout everybody else, I, having spotted Ilona and squeezed myself near her, had no need to lie. It did not matter what I said. In that high-decibel din she could not possibly understand it anyway.

My duty done, I walked back to the S-Bahn station, half-regretting that I had left so quickly. Perhaps there might have been a chance to meet and have a few words with a Soviet officer. Quite a few of those in the dressing room had spoken German. What were they really like? Not that there would have been the slightest chance that any of them would say what he really thought, but not only words clothe or disclose a person. However, my first opportunity to observe a Soviet officer at close quarters came one week later.

10

Meeting the Committee

"Morning prayers" with Sely would last anywhere from two minutes to half an hour or even longer. It depended on what mood he was in and that again depended on how his own morning prayers had gone. As a practicing Catholic he attended early mass daily and if afterward—all gruff and overdosing on snuff—he had Tolliver and me in and out of his office in record time, we knew that the colloquy with his father-confessor had not been all with milk and honey. The reason the husband of the paymaster captain's relict knelt uneasily in the confessional was prettily obvious. On many an evening it came tripping along our office corridor to fetch the major, too elegant and attractive to be mistaken for a maiden aunt. But when our boss felt good he would sit us down, and then Tolliver and I were in for a treat: half an hour or so of jokes, mostly Jewish ones, brilliantly told by this son of an arch-Bavarian Catholic mother and a Jewish judge.

Sely paired a talent to amuse with an apparently inexhaustible repertoire.

After one such pleasant morning session on the day before the meeting of the Four-Power Denazification Subcommittee, the major told Tolliver to get on with his job and me to stay.

"Tomorrow you'll take the minutes for the first time" he said, "so I think I'd better give you a bit of background on the others. Now then, our froggie is Michel Bouquet. Charming and a first-rate linguist with perfect German, Russian, and English. Mind you, Michel doesn't say much in any language. Sometimes he gives one the feeling that the whole thing bores him. Maybe it does, maybe he's just being superior and French. He doesn't miss anything, though. On the other hand our Yank, Ralph Brown, is anything but reticent. In that he's very American, but otherwise he's no more so than you and I are British. Correction: that's not quite true. He's been naturalized, we're still waiting. Ralph is a Berliner who emigrated to the U.S. He was attached to Counterintelligence before transferring to the U.S. Information Division. He's a civilian, like Bouquet, but both of them rank as majors. Our Soviet member, Captain Alexander Gouliga, speaks fluent German and some, but not much, English, although I suspect it's better than he lets on. So watch what you say. I'll say this for him, though; for a Russian he's easy to get on with and pretty cooperative on the whole. I can see a question mark on your face. What is it?"

"I've been wondering why you want me to take the minutes. Rose tells me she used to do it and I don't think she's any too happy about the change."

"Tough luck, isn't it! I think Gouliga will be more relaxed and perhaps even more open without a German in the room. But of course you dictate the minutes to Rose from your scribbles afterward. She'll type them out.

By the way, don't be too detailed. None of that 'Mr. So-and-so said and Mr. So-and-so replied' nonsense. Just summarize the points and the results of our discussions. That's all we need for the record. Now, there's something else about tomorrow. The Gouligas have just had their first baby, a little boy. Michel, Ralph, and I clubbed together and bought a layette."

Sely got up, went over to the big wardrobe and book-case standing against the far wall. He opened it, took out a parcel, and gave it to me.

"You take it. I'll come with a bottle of champers tomorrow and when I call you, bring it all in, nicely presented on a tray. Rose will get it ready for you. She knows all about it. She bought the present. That's it, then, unless you have any more questions."

When I came out of his office and Fräulein Rose saw the parcel in my hand, she said, "We've also got something for the young father, look." Some artist on our German staff had painted a congratulations card showing on its cover a happily smiling baby in a high-necked Russian blouse lying on a map of Berlin. The message inside said in German and Russian, "A hearty welcome to a new Berliner from Schlüterstrasse's old Berliners."

When I marched into Sely's office with my tray next morning they were sitting on his other Hinkel heirlooms, the powder-blue settee and matching armchairs around the coffee table across the room from his desk.

"This is Sergeant Clare, gentlemen," Sely introduced me. "He's joined me recently. He'll take our minutes in the future. No objection, is there? Good. Before we get to our agenda there's one extra subject I've got to mention. It concerns the continuing increase in the population of the Soviet Union. My confidential sources at the Soviet HQ in Karlshorst tell me it's gone up again," he paused for effect and then added, "by one little Gouliga!

Our congratulations to you and your wife, my dear Captain, and here, with our very best wishes, is a small gift from us three."

Handing the parcel to Gouliga, Sely said to me, "Pop the cork, Sergeant, so we can wet the baby's bottom." I did, and poured the champagne.

During Sely's little speech Gouliga had blushed to the roots of his thick thatch of straw-blond hair but, having clinked glasses and emptied his in one go, a happy smile lit up his broad Slav face as he replied to the toast. "Well, Major Sely," he said, "for once, just for once, your information is correct and," he winked, "I can't say *nyet*. So instead, also on behalf of my wife, I'll say *Ochen spassiba* to you all. How kind! Thanks again. May I open it now?" He unwrapped the parcel and, one by one, produced little knitted booties, panties, and bonnets.

They were "ah-ing" and "oh-ing" like young mums at a tea party as they admired each tiny item until I, with my most innocent expression, asked Sely, "Excuse me, sir, d'you want this minuted?" They all laughed.

"You just do that, Sergeant," Sely said—my promotion had only just come through—"and by tomorrow you'll be back to bombardier."

"Good man, that new sergeant of yours, Kaye," Ralph Brown said. "It's high time we got on with it. If we don't start now we'll never get through in time for lunch."

"Food's all you ever think of, Ralph," Bouquet teased him, but he obviously had a point. Brown was a very big young man.

"Coming from a Frenchman I'm not sure whether that's a flattering or offensive remark," Brown replied, "but be that as it may, Kaye's ordered our table at the 'Embassy' for one-thirty so we'd better start."

It was actually up to him to get things moving. The chairmanship of all Allied Kommandatura committees rotated monthly among the four powers. It was the Americans' turn that month and so Brown was in the chair.

As I got to know him I had to revise my first impression of Ralph Brown as merely a jolly chap who burst into cackling laughter every now and then. Behind that corpulent jollity was a quick brain, a clear concept of what he wanted, and the shrewdness needed to get it. But I could never quite make up my mind whether the end was not always more important to him than the means.

"Right," he said. "Furtwängler's of course the first item on our agenda. Not that I think that there's much to be said about his case at this stage. He's applied for denazification and we'll just have to wait for the Spruchkammer decision."

"And how long will that take?" Gouliga enquired.

"You'd better ask Kaye," Brown replied. "He's got the Spruchkammer here."

"I've talked to Schmidt," Sely said. "He doesn't think they'll be able to deal with Furtwängler before the autumn or later. He tells me Alex Vogel, their chairman, thinks so too."

"That is unacceptable," Gouliga complained. "It's ridiculous to force the world's greatest conductor to queue up like everybody else. The whole fuss was totally unnecessary, anyway . . ."

I wondered what annoyed him more, the delay or Sely's hint that Vogel, the communist, was in no hurry either to clear Furtwängler.

"I'm sorry, Captain," Brown interrupted him, "but we can't agree with you there. A four-power principle, a Control Council Directive also bearing the signature of your Marshal Zhukov, is at stake here. But as for the delay, if you insist, we can ask Major Sely to tell Herr

Schmidt to speed things up. No doubt he'll have any number of excuses why it's impossible, but we can try."

Gouliga shrugged his shoulders.

"Incidentally, Captain," Sely said, "what applied to Staatsrat Furtwängler also applied to Staatsrat Gründgens. Yet there he is in your sector, undenazified, rehearsing for his first postwar première at your Deutsches Theater."

"Neither of those two were Nazis and you know it," Gouliga replied.

"You may well be right," Brown said, "but it's for the Spruchkammer to say so, not for us. Whatever each of us may personally think about those two men we're all bound by the directive."

"But I must protest," Gouliga said, "against Major Sely bringing up the Gründgens case. It's not on our agreed agenda. In any case, what happens in the Soviet Sector is a matter for the Soviet authorities and no one else. So I'm not willing to discuss it."

"Come, Captain," Brown replied, "you know that the directive applies to the whole of Berlin, indeed to the whole of Germany. Germany's greatest actor and her greatest conductor are in the same boat. I see no reason why this issue should not be raised in our committee."

"I refuse to talk about Gründgens, Mr. Brown," Gouliga said. "I have not been authorized to do so and there's nothing I can say. You know I go along with you wherever I can. I too know that directive, but I've got my instructions and you don't expect me to go against them. Now do you?"

That was very frank. Would he have been that open if a German had been present? I wondered.

"All right. Captain Gouliga, I'll make a suggestion," Sely said. "We'll record that the Gründgens case came up in our discussion, that in your view this committee should not deal with it, at least at this stage, that its other members disagree with your standpoint, and that we therefore require a ruling from the Cultural Affairs Committee or, should it so decide, from yet higher authority."

Before Gouliga could reply, Brown objected. "No, Kaye," he said, "that's not a good idea. If we throw this into the lap of our senior committee they'll merely come back to us wanting to know what we think we're for. We're supposed to give them solutions, not problems. My suggestion is that we record our disagreement and request Captain Gouliga to convey our view on the Gründgens case to his superiors and then come back to us. The Cultural Affairs Committee will know about the problem from our minutes. There's always time to go to them if the Soviet response is entirely negative."

Gouliga nodded. Sely thought for a moment. Then he said, "Yes maybe that's the better way. What do you think, Michel?"

"I like Ralph's suggestion," Bouquet affirmed. "Captain Gouliga must have an opportunity to talk to Major Dymshitz and perhaps Colonel Tulpanov before we go any further on this."

Sely turned to me. "Have you got this down exactly as Mr. Brown said it? It does need to be recorded verbatim. I'd better dictate it to you here and now, so everybody knows exactly what will appear in the minutes."

When this was done Brown said to Gouliga, "Personally, I don't think Gründgens should have any problems with his denazification. Anyway, nothing like the problems he had with your chaps, Captain."

Much to Gouliga's visible discomfiture, Brown had alluded to the tragicomical linguistic screwup that led to Gustaf Gründgens's arrest by the MVD after the war, and nine subsequent months in Russian internment camps. As Generalintendant, or director-general, of the Prussian State Theater, Gründgens held a title that in the Red Army was that of a quartermaster general. His Russian interrogators were convinced they had caught one of the Wehrmacht's top commanders, Hitler's Ludendorff so to speak, and Gründgens's explanations of Germany's theater hierarchy cut no ice with them. Some prominent German actors and directors intervening on his behalf eventually managed to convince senior Soviet officers, including Colonel General Bersarin, Berlin's first Soviet commandant, that a mistake had been made. But finding Gründgens took time. There was no central internment camp administration, records, if any, were chaotic, and three-quarters of a year passed before Gründgens staggered out from behind the barbed wire into the welcoming arms of Dymshitz and Tulpanov.

The atmosphere had become a little tense when Bouquet, whose sharply lined and wrinkled face made him look older than his forty or so years, tactfully changed the subject. "I see, Kaye, our next point is the case of Leopold Ludwig. A British Military Government court has sentenced him to one year in prison for falsifying his *Fragebogen*. I'm not criticizing it, but isn't that verdict a bit harsh?"

"Well," Sely said, "we've yet to see whether he'll actually serve the whole of it, but in my view he'd deserve to. If we'd let the chief conductor of the Städtische Oper in our sector get away with it, then all the smaller fry would have an excellent excuse for falsifying their questionnaires too. Ludwig denied on his *Fragebogen* that he had been a party member. But what did we find when we checked his file? He had been in the party, which he, an Austrian, had actually joined when it was illegal in his own country. When I showed him the evidence he just shrugged his shoulders. 'Oh, was I?' he said. 'I'd forgotten all about it.' No, Michel, I think it's a just sentence."

"Certainly the man's committed a serious offense against Military Government regulations," Bouquet went on, "so he has to be punished, but a whole year? Won't he come out more of a Nazi than he ever was? What harm can he do? He isn't going to play the 'Horst Wessel Lied,' is he? Three months would have been enough to make an example of him. I agree denazification is necessary but don't we all too often, as you English say, pour out the baby with the hot water?"

"Bathwater," Sely corrected him.

"Sorry. Anyway, you know what I mean. We can't ignore our directives, certainly not, but we could interpret them with a little more attention to the individual and his circumstances."

For Bouquet, who had been quietly puffing his Gauloises most of the time, that was quite a speech. What his words reflected was the general French skepticism about the whole denazification business. If one could have de-germanized the Germans the French would have been enthusiastically for it, but dividing them into goodies and baddies seemed a futile exercise to the one occupation power that sincerely hated all Germans. Though that in itself was nothing new, the intensity of the feeling was. German atrocities, such as Oradour, were of course part of it but the true cause lay deeper: in the unadmitted but ever-present awareness of how shamefully so many French had abased themselves before the Germans when they had been the occupiers.

Yet, strangely, in spite of this, the Germans resented the French least of the three Western powers, a strange phenomenon explained by an unnamed German to the historian Michael Balfour (director of British Information Services Control in Germany in 1946 and 1947) in

these words: "The British like us, but don't always notice that we're there; the Americans like us, but treat us
as badly behaved children; the French hate us on equal
terms."* This equality of hate—and guilt—was another
factor that made the French reluctant to rummage too
much in the recent past, particularly as not a few of the
officers and officials in the French Zone of Occupation
had been Pétainists or collaborators, or both. However,
the French, from motives more opportunistic than be-
nign, did, as Bouquet said, pay attention to individuals
and circumstances, in the sense that if an individual had
qualifications valuable to their interests and the circumstances were that he was willing to serve them, then
they nonchalantly whitewashed his brown stains. In
short: the French were just as cynical as the Russians
about denazification but, being weak, were more elegantly diplomatic about it.

"I quite agree with you, Michel," Brown said, "that
Ludwig will nowadays conduct the 'Marseillaise' or 'God
Save the King' with the same verve with which he played
the 'Horst Wessel Lied,' but I don't think that's the point.
A three-month sentence isn't all that dreadful and quite
a few people would take that risk and falsify their *Fragebogen*. But one year, that's different."

It was one o'clock, but there were still three points on
the agenda. Brown rushed through them and at precisely
ten past one, when Fräulein Rose came in to report that
Sely's driver, Herr Gleicher, and the staff car were waiting downstairs, they were ready to leave. Now that Gouliga was standing up I saw how slim and smart he looked
in his waisted olive-brown tunic with the wide silver
shoulderboards, on them the four little gold stars of a
Red Army captain, and his red-striped black trousers.
With a little curtsy Rose handed him the hand-painted

---

* Michael Balfour, *West Germany* (London: Ernest Benn, 1968).

card from the German staff. Gouliga looked at it, thanked her, and then, an impish grin on his face, he showed it to the others.

"Did you have a good look?" he asked when they had all seen it.

They said they had and thought it a nice gesture.

"Ah," he said, "but I bet you didn't notice that my little Russian is stretched out over the whole of Berlin, not just the Soviet Sector. Now did you?"

Rose was quickest off the mark. "As the inside message reads, Herr Hauptmann," she said, "your baby son is a Berliner and it's to all Berliners that the whole of Berlin belongs."

After that little scene they left for the Embassy Club, but Rose's words were by no means the final ones in connection with that morning's proceedings. Gouliga, as promised, reported his colleagues' views on the Gründgens case to his superiors and within days, on April 27 to be exact, a specially summoned Soviet Sector tribunal declared the former Staatsrat and Generalintendant untainted by Nazism. Following this blitz-denazification rolls of thunder reverberated through Schlüterstrasse as Wolfgang Schmidt, banging every door on his way, stomped into Sely's office like a raging bull, demanding that the Western powers protest to the Russians against this usurpation of his Spruchkammer's prerogative in cultural matters. When Sely asked whether Alex Vogel, his chairman, supported him, Schmidt replied that Vogel was ill, too ill even to answer his telephone. But when the Allies, all four of them, eventually came up with a well-nigh Solomonic solution, Vogel recovered overnight. The decision was to cut Gründgens, figuratively speaking, in two. One half of him, the actor, it was agreed, had been cleared in the Soviet Sector, but the other half, the director, would remain banned until

Gründgens had been denazified all over again by the Schlüterstrasse panel.

If only I could have found such a crafty stratagem to solve the problem of the too-irascible Wolfgang Schmidt. My fear, which Sely shared, was that his sharpness with former Nazis might lead to unfortunate consequences. A short while before I joined ISC Intelligence a woman had thrown herself from a fourth-floor window in Schlüterstrasse. The horrified Eva Rose had been an eyewitness of this suicide, a tragedy that had had nothing whatever to do with Schmidt, who had never even met that woman. Yet I was afraid that his intensity could cause a similar incident. My difficulty was that he was not one of our German employees but a magistrate functionary, yet if something went badly wrong at Schlüterstrasse it inevitably reflected on those who had the real power there, and that, of course, was our section.

11

Ziegfeld's
Follies

It may seem absurd but even now, over forty years later, I still have problems with Wolfgang Schmidt. When writing about him I want to be fair to that staunch anti-Nazi, who had risked his life more than once under the Third Reich; yet the rage in him, constantly on the boil, caused me a lot of trouble. True, he kept it under control most of the time, but every now and then it would spill over and I have not forgotten those outbursts: a release for him, but for me, who had to restore the balance, a burden I could have done without.

There also was his unfortunate appearance—an almost uncanny likeness to Joseph Goebbels. Ironic it was, but in looks our Nazi-hating Spruchkammer secretary could have been the late unlamented Nazi leader's younger brother. Both had the same slight, slim bodies with disproportionately large heads, the same slicked-back dark hair, the same deep dark eyes, the same thin lips with the same misanthropic downturn at their corners. And when Schmidt got excited, then—just as with Goebbels when he worked himself up to an oratorical climax—strands of that neatly combed hair would shake loose, fall on to an unusually wide forehead, and thereby draw attention yet once again to a curious anatomical imbalance.

Beyond physical characteristics the two men also had in common the capacity to hate with fanatical intensity. That icy glitter that came into Goebbels's eyes when he spat out the word *Jew* also glinted in Schmidt's when he faced a former Nazi. There was of course nothing wrong in treating Nazi activists with severity, but Schmidt sometimes went too far. When his rage got the better of him, he did not shrink from personal abuse, and his body language, as he sat coiled like a wildcat about to jump, could seem so menacing that the more timid were ready to confess to almost anything just to get away from him. At those moments I had to interfere to prevent the interrogation becoming too reminiscent of a Gestapo examination.

Sely, Tolliver, and I also spent a good deal of our time interrogating denazification candidates, applicants for British licenses as publishers or whatever, or those who looked for work in positions that came under our control. Our primary task, however, was slightly different from Schmidt's. He had to ascertain for his panel whether someone applying for denazification had been a dedicated Nazi, while we were mainly concerned with those suspected of falsifying their Military Government questionnaires. But what he did and what we did, naturally, often overlapped.

By a lucky fluke I have three such interrogation protocols among my papers—documents that not only illustrate that aspect of our work but also convey something of the flavor and mentality of the time.

* * *

Kurt Viek was a lawyer and writer. I interrogated him together with Schmidt in one of his gentler moods.

According to the record my first question was: "Why haven't you resumed your work as solicitor and public notary, Herr Viek? That's your profession, isn't it?"

"I haven't been readmitted to legal practice yet," he replied.

"Why ever not?" I asked. "On your questionnaire you state that you were not a member of the Nazi party, so you're not affected by denazification regulations."

"Well," he said, "I've no idea why, either. Unless it is that I was supposed at one time to become head of the National Socialist Lawyers' League for my party district. Anyway, the discussions with Frank, its chief and later governor of Poland, led nowhere. You see, I could not supply the so-called greater Aryan family tree proving that there were no Jews in my ancestry as far back as the late eighteenth century."

"And apart from being a lawyer you're also a writer?" I asked.

"I wouldn't say that, but I do have manifold literary interests," was his answer.

"Did you ever publish any of your writings?"

"Yes," he said, "but nothing sufficiently important to be mentioned on my *Fragebogen*."

At that point I must have decided to change tack and surprise him with a very direct personal question.

"Would you, Herr Viek, describe yourself as an honest man?" I asked.

He shrugged his shoulders but did not speak.

"All right," I said, "I have here a booklet you wrote. It's called *Where Wotan Found His Last Resting Place*. I've read it. It's pure Nazi propaganda. It should have been mentioned. It clearly says on the questionnaire: 'List the titles of all publications from 1923 onward to the present that were written in whole or in part, or compiled or edited, by you.' Well?"

Viek again remained silent.

I waited a minute or so before saying: "Well then, let's look at another aspect of your past. Did you ever apply for Nazi party membership?"

Viek obviously had problems with words like yes or no.

"I did defend some stormtroopers in the courts before 1933," he replied.

"Why stormtroopers in particular?"

"They just happened to come to me."

"Did Jews also just happen to come to you and ask you to defend them?"

"Yes, but not that often. I was in a boxing club, you see, and some of my fellow members were stormtroopers, others communists. That explains why quite a few of my clients were brownshirts and maybe some of them persuaded me to try to join the party."

"I'm not quite clear, Herr Viek, about what you're really telling me," I said. "Are you in fact saying that you did file an application for party membership—in January 1933, perhaps, when Hitler became chancellor?"

"I don't know the year or the month," he asserted, beginning to lose his temper. "What does it matter? It doesn't interest me."

"It should," I said, "because so many people who joined the party in 1933 were just opportunists, while most of those who joined it earlier were convinced Nazis and you, Herr Viek, became a member in 1928."

"That's the same nonsense I've already heard from the Americans."

"They're also well informed. So, let me ask you again, were you or were you not a member of the NSDAP?"

"I seem to remember," he replied, "that I did declare

my willingness to join the party at one time or another, but I don't know whether they actually accepted me."

"Were you never given your membership number?"

"I don't recall that I was."

"Would you then by any chance recall whether you ever filled in any *Fragebogen*s during the Nazi regime?" I asked him.

"Oh yes," he said, "on several occasions."

"How come you knew your party membership number then and gave it on those documents, when you can't remember it now?"

I waited, but no answer came.

"And how come," I went on, "you also knew then the exact date you joined the party?"

Silence.

Viek's Reichskulturkammer file was on my desk. I opened it to where his old *Fragebogen* was, turned it around so he could read it, and placed his Military Government questionnaire next to it.

"Look at those two documents," I said, pointing to the columns concerning party membership, "and then tell me why what you wrote in our *Fragebogen* so totally contradicts what you wrote in the Kulturkammer one."

"I suppose I'll have plenty of time to think of an answer," Viek replied. "Your courts will see to that."

Speaking for the first time Schmidt said, "Why don't you stand by what you believed, tell the truth, and admit that you were a Nazi?"

I let that sink in and then asked, "Herr Viek, do you admit that you falsified your Military Government *Fragebogen?*"

For once we got a straight answer. "Yes, I do," he said.

"Right, now we've got that settled, tell me when you joined the party."

He hesitated briefly and then, pointing to his Kulturkammer file, he said, "I wrote 1928 here; I can neither confirm nor deny it."

"Why did you falsify your *Fragebogen*?"

"To make things easy for myself," he replied. "Why, after all, was I told to fill one in when you had all the evidence anyway? Surely only so I would be tempted to falsify it. You set me a trap. Why else did you order me to come here?"

"You do not seem to realize that you have to obey the orders of the Military Government," Schmidt said, "or that anyone who has any contact with the occupation authorities has to complete his *Fragebogen* without being given any explanations. In any case, you're trying to stand things on their head. It's not we who're being interrogated; you are."

"And you were told to come here not because we were out to trap you but because you wanted Military Government permission to publish some of your writings," I added.

"I didn't know that," Viek said, "but I shall tell the truth from now on. And I withdraw my remark about you setting a trap for me. What's going to happen now?"

"You are resident in the U.S. sector," I told him, "so your case will be passed to the U.S. authorities. At some time in the near future, whenever it suits you, report to Mr. Westrum at Rothenburg Strasse 12. There's no great hurry."

"What, you're not arresting me right away?" Viek blurted out. "What if I run away? I was illegally in the British Zone only a couple of weeks ago."

"I know that, Herr Viek," I lied "but why should we arrest you? We don't go in for dramatics of that sort. We're not the Gestapo. You'll appear before a Military Government court in due course, that's for sure, but we have so many cases like yours there's quite a queue. It'll take a while till your turn comes. Where would we put you in the meantime if we arrested you? And remember, if you try to flee we'll find you no matter whether you're in the British, French, American, or, you'll be surprised to hear, even in the Soviet Zone." Which was another lie.

Viek at least never claimed an impeccable anti-Nazi record, but Franz Mohr, a journalist born in Cologne in 1914, did exactly that on his application for a license to publish a magazine. Having been given provisional clearance by our Düsseldorf Information Control Unit he was already on the editorial staff of a Cologne illustrated weekly.

When he came into my office I welcomed him, according to the interview protocol, with the words: "So you're the man who hates filling in our *Fragebogen*s. Anyway, that's what my Düsseldorf colleagues have told me. Why, if you've nothing to hide?"

"I've filled in about twenty since the end of the war," Mohr said. "Enough for one lifetime, wouldn't you agree, Mr. Clare?"

"I would, I suppose," I said, "but you overlooked some of the questions on the one I've got here. Tell you what, let's go through it together and do the thing properly now."

I started to read: "Father's name: Hermann Mohr; Profession: Architect; Mother: Maria Mohr née Derichs. Fine, but you did not fill in your parental home address . . ."

"Oversight, sorry," Mohr said. "Cologne, Stadtwaldgürtel 69."

"Right. Now you write here that you went to Paris to study at the Sorbonne. And you go on to say you didn't want to stay at German universities because you objected to their militarist and National Socialist outlook.

That's interesting. But you don't give any dates for your stay in France."

"Oh, that's true. I went there in 1937. I can prove it. I've managed to save all my French documents," Mohr said. Opening his briefcase, he took out his Sorbonne registration certificate and handed it to me.

"Thank you," I said. "Now let's read on. You say here that you had trouble with the Gestapo because of your friendship with Jews at the Sorbonne, some of them refugees from Germany."

"Yes, the Gestapo in Paris reported me to the Gestapo in Cologne because of it."

"I would have thought that the few Gestapo men in Paris in 1937, the year of the Paris World Fair, would have had more important things to do than watching a student."

"Perhaps it wasn't the Gestapo who reported me," he replied. "Apart from the Jews from Germany there were also other students from the Reich there, and most of them belonged to the National Socialist Students' League. One of them must have spied on me."

"Were you a member of that organization?"

"Oh, no, of course not."

"Ah, yes, you did say you went to France because you disliked how things were at German universities. Yet what about those other German students? If, as you say, most of them were Nazis why did they, like you the anti-Nazi, study at a French university?"

"I don't know," Mohr answered. "One didn't talk about those things. It was too dangerous."

"Yet you befriended Jews. Wasn't that just as dangerous?"

"Well, yes, and that was how I got into trouble. When I went back home in the summer of 1939 because of the enemy war threat, the Gestapo interrogated me for two hours, accusing me of having been chummy with the Jewish clique. They let me go after I told them a lot of lies—for instance, that I had Jewish contacts only because one could get a first-rate lunch at the Jewish students' canteen for a mere two francs."

"And that was not your motive?"

"Well, I was short of money, but no. I lied to the Gestapo but not to you."

"Fine. Now you say here that you were sent to a concentration camp, yet again you don't give the date."

"That was during the war. They arrested me on January 23, 1943," Mohr answered, "but I expressed myself badly on that *Fragebogen*. That's what comes from having to fill in so many."

He paused. Maybe he expected some reaction from me to his little joke.

When none came he went on, "I was supposed to be sent to a concentration camp, but wasn't actually because of my health. I had had meningitis with bone-marrow complications, could hardly see, and had to walk with a stick. It was very painful."

"You must have been very fortunate to fall into the hands of such humane Gestapo men," I commented. "I'm sorry but I find that story difficult to believe."

"Well, I also had a friend, a Nazi high-up. He helped me."

"Isn't that a bit surprising in your case? You have repeatedly stressed that, even though you were only eighteen and a half when Hitler came to power, you always were an anti-Nazi and never wanted to have anything to do with them. Yet such an important Nazi was a friend of yours? Tell me, Herr Mohr, do you know that we have documents where we can check the truth of what you're saying?"

"Yes, I've heard," he said.

"Do you perhaps want to amend or change anything you've written on your *Fragebogen* or told me?"

"No."

"All right. I'll now read out from your *Fragebogen* the questions concerning membership in the NSDAP and its organizations and how you answered them. Please listen. 'Were you a member of the National Socialist party?' Your reply: 'No.' 'Were you a member of the National Socialist Students' League?' Answer: 'No.' 'Were you a member of the Reichschamber for the press?' 'No.' 'Did you ever fill in a Reichskulturkammer *Fragebogen?*' 'No.' Those were your statements, Herr Mohr, and the young lady there who's writing down everything we're saying has also recorded your assurance that you lied to the Gestapo but not to me. Yet here", I said, taking his Kulturkammer folder out of my desk drawer, "is your file and here, over what is undoubtedly your signature, is the *Fragebogen* you just said you never filled in. According to it you joined the Nazi Party on May 1, 1933, immediately after your eighteenth birthday, when you became eligible for membership. At the first opportunity. And here, look, you, who so disliked the Third Reich's universities, give your membership number in the League of National Socialist Students. You have some explaining to do, haven't you?"

"Well, Mr. Clare," Mohr said, "that's a long story."

"It's my job to listen to long stories. Go ahead," I replied.

"As you've stressed," he began, "I was just over eighteen in 1933. So when the Nazis took over my parents thought it would be a good idea and help my future if I joined the party. So somehow this was done . . ."

"Somehow?" I interrupted. "What is that supposed to mean? You applied for membership, completed and signed the application form, and were accepted."

"Well, yes, I forgot about that. I know everybody you talk to will tell you the same. It's no excuse, but you see inwardly I always was an anti-Nazi. I can produce dozens of witnesses who can testify to that. I did everything I could against them. That they eventually arrested me and almost sent me to a concentration camp proves my true political convictions."

"And so you felt inwardly justified in falsifying all your twenty British Military Government *Fragebogen*?"

"Honestly, it's been a burden on my conscience. But knowing what I truly felt during the Third Reich I did not think the mistakes I made in my youth need haunt me forever. Especially as I resigned from the party in 1943."

"Oh, come off it, Herr Mohr!" I exclaimed. "Stop playing games with me. You did not resign; they threw you out because you had forged documents, the very same reason you're in trouble now. That's why you were arrested."

"I did it to help a Jew get out of Germany. Like you he's now a sergeant in the British Army. And I also faked papers so some soldier friends of mine could get special Berlin leave. But by now you probably won't believe anything I say."

"Sorry, but that's how it is," I said. "You've been stupid beyond belief. Had you told the truth you would have gone before a denazification panel that might well have decided in your favor. As it is you will be tried by a Military Government court and you'll never get a license."

"But to err is human, can't you understand that?"

"A man who had the courage, as you say, actively to oppose the Nazis must also have the courage to tell the full truth about himself."

"I feared for my job. I am a passionate journalist. It's my whole life. I love my work, so much so it destroyed my marriage. Surely you have the humanity to understand my motives."

"I'm not judging those or you, Herr Mohr," I replied, "or the truth of your anti-Nazi convictions. That's not my job. You can explain all that to the court. I'm only concerned with the fact that you lied on your *Fragebogen*. I now want you to write out a confession."

Mohr did and when he gave it to me he asked, "May I say one last word and please don't think I'm merely saying it to move you. This will be the death of me."

According to the protocol I lost my patience at this point.

"For heaven's sake, don't give me that tragic death or suicide bullshit," I snapped. "Take what's coming to you. You've nobody to blame but yourself."

Mohr and Viek were more or less routine cases. Tolliver or I dealt with those. Sely reserved for himself the more complex ones, those involving prominent personalities or people who also had dealings with the Soviets. Another category he liked to interview were nutty characters who amused him, like one Arnold Ziegfeld. Sely's interrogation of that author and publisher is not recorded as a dialogue, but as a summary.

Ziegfeld had published books, some written by himself, on religion, the humanities, political science, geography, the demography of Germany's border areas, constitutional history, economics, and also fiction.

"In spite of his political past," the summary says, "Z. considers himself a suitable candidate for a license as publisher. Stressing that he does not think of himself as a businessman first and foremost, but as someone devoted to science and literature, he asserts that he, having been born a U.S. national in Japan and growing up in a truly international atmosphere, had, therefore, always opposed German militarism and National Socialism. He describes himself as a cosmopolitan who worked all his life for better international understanding and the brotherhood of nations. He moved to Bremen as a youth and thus completed his education in a city famed for its liberal and democratic traditions, which had strongly influenced his own outlook. In 1910 he became a German citizen by naturalization.

"Major Sely draws Z.'s attention to the following facts:

"1. He had joined the Nazi party in 1921. His membership had lapsed, but he rejoined in 1937.

"2. He had been an SA stormtrooper from 1934–43.

"3. He had been an active political speaker on behalf of the SA and his local party organization.

"4. He had held office in the Foreign Section of the NSDAP, which controlled and coordinated all Nazi movements and cells abroad.

"5. From 1941–45 he had his son educated at a 'Napola,' boarding schools supervised by the SS and intended to produce the leadership elite for Nazi Germany's future.

"Z. admits that all this does not sound too good, but adds that one had to understand the circumstances and the times. He only became a party member in 1937 because he was in the SA, and he only was in the SA because all members of the Stahlhelm, the war veterans' political organization to which he had belonged, were automatically transferred to it in 1934. He had joined the Stahlhelm one year earlier because he had believed it to be the one political grouping able to resist National Socialism. Had he refused party membership only two possibilities would have been open to him: abandon publishing or emigrate. Had he gone abroad, how could he have worked against Nazism? He had no alternative in 1937 if he wanted to go on publishing books of religious and educational character. It was not true that he joined the party in 1921. Living in Munich he had applied for membership in its sports section, a sort of forerunner of the SA, but two months later he had withdrawn his application.

"Major Sely points out that Z. considered it appropriate to mention his 1921 party membership on his Reichs-kulturkammer questionnaire but not on his British *Fragebogen.* Z. replies that many young Germans sympathized with the early Nazis in Munich because they all suffered under the conditions of the Treaty of Versailles. It was so difficult then to know which road to take and he had felt himself a German nationalist. Other nationalist parties did not gain the trust of young people. The NSDAP did, because it combined the ideals of nationalism and socialism. Later, after Hitler's party had shown its true face, he had no longer favored it.

"About the books he had written he said:

"*England's Decision* (1939) had been positively reviewed in *The Times,* because he understood so well the English mentality. In it he described Britain as an imperial power and demonstrated that her policies were traditionally anti-European. Britain's Continental policy had always been the 'balance of power.' She had, therefore, always prevented Germany from becoming too strong. He had written it to show his readers the British concept of Germany and thus further their understanding of the overall European situation.

"*France, the Reich's Eternal Enemy* (1941) had been neither written nor published by him, but by a member of the Army High Command.

"*Germany, Europe's Conscience* (1941) expressed his view that Germany as the heart of Europe is responsible for the whole of it. The European question depends on whether Germany is a vacuum or not. Germany must take the lead in the creation of a federated Europe. Hitler tried to achieve this by force. That was wrong. His book advocating the idea of feudal states on the medieval pattern was really an anti-Nazi tract, a protest against Hitler's brute power policies.

"As for his son and the Napola: there really had been no other choice. Berlin's schools had been closed down, all other boarding schools were crowded, hence the Napola in Billstedt had been the most suitable one. The boy was a bit of a loner who needed to learn how to live in a community. Yes, the teachers had been Nazis but rather moderate ones. But he was sure even if Hitler had won the war his son would not have become a fanatical Nazi. He, the father, would have influenced him in a different political direction.

"Referring to his activities as a political speaker for the SA and the party and its Foreign Section, Z. says that all this had been nothing but camouflage. To stay in publishing he had to do it. Maybe one or the other of his speeches had intentionally exaggerated the Nazi point of view, but most of them had been on such harmless topics as geography. And, had he not worked for the party's Foreign Section, he would never have been given permission to visit England or to write about it. He was also a member of the Anglo-German Brotherhood.

"Major Sely informs Z. that he appears to have a somewhat confused image of himself. No 'internationalist' and opponent of the Third Reich would have sent his son to a Napola, nor did Berlin's schools close down in 1941, far from it. Only 100% Nazis had their children educated at Napolas. So what percentage Nazi would Z. say that he had been?

"Ziegfeld replies that he had been an anti-Nazi throughout the existence of the Third Reich and had, therefore, wrongly been classified as a fellow traveler and put into category IV.

"Ending the interview the major advises Z. to appeal for recategorization, warning him that should he be put into Group V there would still remain more than a modicum of doubt as to whether he would get a British license. However, why not try? He had enjoyed their talk. Perhaps if Z. reapplied after having been fully denazified, one would meet again. He was sure a new book on Britain from his pen would make fascinating reading."

I can just see Sely saying this tongue in cheek, his eyes as gentle as a doe's, the smile on his lips looking somewhat cramped with barely suppressed laughter. He was a good actor, but spoke no less than the truth when he said that he had enjoyed their talk. He must have—hugely.

Incidentally, the lucky fluke by which I got this and the other documents actually has a name. It is Eva Meyer, formerly Schlüterstrasse's Fräulein Rose. Having read my *Last Waltz in Vienna*, she wrote to me via my publisher. No other lady's reemergence from my past could have given me such joy, and it was she who helped me to obtain those papers. What struck and surprised me most when I read them was how fair we were toward those lying veteran Nazis. Now, one does not have to be born in Britain, or with a cricket bat in one's cradle, to know what fairness means, yet there is something unique in its British concept, which by mixing it with more than a smidgen of tolerance and a shot or two of apathy turns a noble ideal into a practicable human quality. We, I think, learned it during our years of service in the wartime British Army; my first teacher was Sergeant Lowe, my near illiterate section sergeant in the Alien Pioneer Corps' 77 Company. That story, even if it takes us away from Berlin for a few moments, is one that should be told.

12

Private Levin and Sergeant Lowe

Throughout its long, proud, and sometimes unorthodox history, the British Army never had a regiment as outlandish and extraordinary as the Alien Pioneer Corps. Nor can there be anything like it ever again. What was so singular about it was not that its soldiers spoke German better than English—after all, so did George III's Hessians—but that, with a few exceptions, they were all Jews, refugees from Germany and Austria with some Czechs and Hungarians thrown in. And by army standards many of them were elderly, the average age being nearer forty than twenty; men who had been in mid-career as doctors, scientists, teachers and lecturers, judges, lawyers, writers and journalists, bankers and businessmen, when, Hitler threatening their survival, they had fled their native countries. Hence when I joined the Alien Pioneer Corps, the only unit in which so-called enemy aliens were then allowed to serve, I, at twenty, was one of its "children."

That was in the summer of 1941. In the autumn of that
year, after initial training in Ilfracombe, I was posted to
77 Company at Long Marston near Stratford-upon-Avon,
where I met one of the kindest and best-read men I have
ever known. He, Hans Levin, had the bed next to mine
in our Nissen hut and this former German judge, a man
in his late forties, became my intellectual, and I what
may be laughingly called his "military," mentor. I could
not say how he felt about his task; mine was hopeless.

To begin with, Levin was unbelievably ugly. His high
forehead—with woolly graying black hair atop it—
descended to a pair of eyebrows so thick and bushy they
nearly covered his sad dark-brown eyes, mirrors—as he
put it—of five thousand and some years of Jewish history. His looks, I regret to say, actually reminded one of
a rather melancholy orangutan, just as much out of his
natural habitat in a zoo as Levin was in the army, an
impression much enhanced by his wide, blunt nose—its
nostrils flaring sideways rather than forward—and a
thick-lipped, much too large mouth. The lines that
framed it were so deeply cut into the flesh of his face
that his cheeks seemed to balloon out. This in turn made
the receding line of his chin look worse than it really
was. So unfairly had nature treated him, one could not
but suspect anti-Semitic tendencies in his very genes.

Yet this paragon of homeliness was married to a juno-
esquely beautiful and loving German blonde with not
even the slightest trace of Jewish blood in her veins. She
had resisted the Nazis' blandishments to divorce the ugly
Jew and live happily ever after in the "new" Germany
after her husband, like thousands of other Jews, had been
arrested and sent to Dachau in November 1938. Overcoming the United Kingdom's defenses—not against Hitler but against fleeing Jews—she finally obtained British
entry visas and with them Levin's release from the concentration camp. They came to London, but in May 1940

Levin, again like thousands of other Jews who had fled from Nazi oppression, was arrested and interned on the Isle of Man until, having being informed that this would get him out from behind the barbed wire, he "volunteered" for service in the Alien Pioneer Corps. Thus Levin gained freedom and the British Army the worst caricature of a soldier it ever had.

Although he was tall and thin, Levin was incapable of ever standing straight. On the command "Atten-shun!" he would shuffle his right boot into some sort of proximity to his left, but his back remained in question-mark posture. He did raise his head, though, to stick forward what he had of a chin, whereupon his forage cap, always worn askew and too far back on his head, would inevitably drop to the ground.

He was the perfect example of what the *Times* special correspondent with the Austrian troops at the Battle of Sadowa meant when he wrote in his newspaper on July 31, 1866:

> I must say that odious as are the contrivances of many military tailors all over the world, nothing can compare in ugliness with a forage cap worn by the Austrians with turned up flaps on the side and put on anyhow, for if a soldier can put on an article of dress the wrong way *he will do so* . . .

In this Levin definitely was the expert. Although he eventually managed not to wear his ever-falling forage cap back to front, his gaiters totally and permanently defeated him. As we only have two legs each we had only two of these and there were only two ways in which one could put them on the wrong way round: inside out or upside down. But not for Levin. He could produce endless variations on the gaiter theme.

This then was the man with whom our section sergeant, the already mentioned Sergeant Lowe, a regular soldier all his adult life, was confronted on parade every morning. But for the war, and I dare say the existence of the Alien Pioneer Corps, Lance Corporal would have been the highest rank this very simple man could ever have attained. But Lowe had been around the world. He had seen India and he had seen Africa, yet nowhere, not in the furthest corners of the British Empire, could our sergeant ever have come across a tribe as exotic to him as those Central Europeans—with Levin the most bizarre of them all—now under his command.

One would have expected an old soldier like Lowe to make life hell for a scarecrow like Levin, drill him, chase him around the barrack square, threaten to make a soldier of him yet. But this he never did. He saw that Levin worked as hard as he could loading and unloading railway trucks for the Royal Engineers, our daily job, and did understand—though he could not have put in into words—that it would not be fair to judge a man like Levin purely by military values. And this sense of fairness and tolerance made the sergeant Levin's protector instead of his persecutor. Before every inspection, for instance, Lowe sneaked into our hut to see if Levin's bed was made up in the regulation manner. It usually was because I did it for him, but if for one reason or another it was not, Lowe would straighten it out. When Levin said to me one day, "You know, there's something very special about the British soul. If you mine deep enough into it, underneath the usual layers of human frailty and stupidity, then you strike a richer lode of fairness and humanity than in any other nation," I knew he had Lowe in mind.

As I have already mentioned, I detested the Pioneer Corps and thought it grotesque that people like us, who hated Nazi Germany more than anybody else, should have to serve in a noncombatant labor unit. Besides, to me it seemed downright inane of the British authorities to forgo so much brain power for so little brawn power because of the outdated importance attached to the accident of one's place of birth. This war was not an old-fashioned conflict between nation states but a civil war between European ideologies.

Yet I liked the British Army. In spite of its red tape and bullshit, in spite of its rules and regulations, which arrogantly assumed the private soldier to be the least intelligent of human beings, it nevertheless respected his individual dignity. It treated its soldiers with strictness but commanded them with fairness and concern for their welfare. Just one example: my battery commander in the Royal Artillery, to which I transferred in 1943 after we were allowed to quit the Pioneer Corps, would make mincemeat of any of his officers when we were out on maneuvers who dared so much as look in the direction of the field kitchens before all the men and NCOs had been fed. And I also liked the British Army because, wearing its uniform, even in the Pioneer Corps, I felt myself closer to achieving my long-term aim of becoming British myself.

I was therefore not the least bit interested when one of the 77 Company's corporals asked me to sign a petition to the War Office requesting the establishment of a "Free Austrian Regiment." It was a remarkably well-drafted document, but then Corporal Laski, the man who approached me and who had written it, was a lawyer. After studying law in Vienna and Heidelberg he joined the legal department of Vienna's municipal administration, where, thanks to his brilliance, he quickly rose to a senior position. He was a rather short, birdlike man in his late thirties. With his small beaky nose, his habit of carrying his head slightly tilted to the right with the garish burgundy and green dress cap of the Pioneers on it—

he was about to go out when he talked to me—he looked like a budgie.

I refused to sign.

"So you want to stay a bloody navvy for the rest of the war," he said.

"Like hell I will," I replied. "As soon as they'll let me I'll join a fighting unit, but a British one. I'm in the British Army and that's where I'm going to stay."

"That," he said, "will not happen. They don't trust us and never will. I joined up in September '39. I was with the BEF in France. We just escaped the Germans when we got through St. Malo and when we got back, some of us carrying the rifles fleeing British soldiers had thrown away, it was touch and go whether or not the British would put us, men who'd taken the loyal oath, behind barbed wire in one of their internment camps. To them you're a bloody foreigner and suspect and you always will be."

But for me the Austrian chapter of my life was closed. Nothing Laski said could convince me otherwise. My future lay in Britain. I can say of myself, as Freud did to H. G. Wells, that it had always been my "wish-fantasy" to live in England and "become an Englishman" and so, after my arrival in England in the autumn of 1938, the initial strangeness of the new country faded within days. I quickly felt at home with the language and its literature and also discovered something not too many of the English-born seem aware of—the attraction, even charm, of Englishness, its history and traditions. I slipped into them as into a familiar and comfortable suit. That it happened to be cut from rough khaki cloth was, under the circumstances, more to my taste than the finest worsted from Savile Row.

So by the time I was posted to Berlin and encountered Schmidt I was—one might say—under the influence of eight years in the British Isles, five of them in His Majesty's Forces. I hated Nazism no less than he did. How could I not, with the fate of my parents a permanent pain? Consciously suppressed and never talked about, it was there just the same. But I would not condemn either the entire nation or someone who, without having been an activist of evil, had, for a variety of reasons, at one time or another believed in National Socialism. For me everybody was innocent unless proved guilty, for Schmidt everyone was guilty unless he could prove he was innocent. Sooner or later he and I were bound to clash.

It happened when we jointly interrogated a fairly prominent film and stage director. With two others he had co-directed *Ohm Krüger*, one of Goebbels's pet film projects, which showed how hypocritical British imperialists, now pretending to fight for freedom and democracy, had subjugated the tiny Boer nation, ruthlessly killing thousands of women and children in the concentration camps that they, not the Nazis, had invented. Sparing no expense for this monster production, the minister for Propaganda and Popular Enlightenment recruited an all-star cast of Germany's most prominent actors and actresses, some eager to participate, others—Gustaf Gründgens for instance refused to accept a fee for playing Joe Chamberlain—who collaborated only when Goebbels's pressure became irresistible.

That this man with all the mannerisms of the Prussian Junker aroused Schmidt's ire I could understand. He had dueling scars on his face, clicked his heels when he came in, sat ramrod straight on his chair, and spoke with the clipped accent of Potsdam officers' mess and barrack square. Another irritant was that, having lost his right arm in World War I, he kept readjusting his prosthesis with his left. Every time he did so its elbow joint squeaked like a knife scratching a plate; the ratchets or whatever of his artificial arm, were either worn or badly oiled. But none of this justified Schmidt's baying at him like a hound at a fox just before the kill. I stopped the interrogation and asked the director to wait outside.

Until then whenever I needed to put the brakes on Schmidt I had been as tactful about it as I could, but now I had had enough.

"You can't carry on like that," I told him. "You're behaving like a Nazi."

I expected a furious rejoinder, but his face, reddened by excitement, suddenly went quite pale.

"That's the worst thing anyone ever said to me. How could you? You, who know what it meant to be persecuted by them?" he replied.

"Yes, I do," I said, "but that's just why we can't be like them. You were. I don't treat them with kid gloves either, when it's necessary, but there's a hell of a difference between being tough and being destructive. I don't like his type any better than you do, but we know he's been honest about his past; he hasn't lied on his *Fragebogen* or tried to gloss over his connection with *Ohm Krüger*. It's the only thing that goes against him. But instead of letting him explain you shout accusations for which you have no proof at all. It's not fair."

"That word was struck from the German vocabulary a long time ago," Schmidt answered.

"Exactly. And it's our job, yours and mine, to put it back again. Let me tell you a little story. It contains the essence of what fairness is all about."

As I told him about Lowe and Levin, I saw on Schmidt's face how he initially rejected it as irrelevant, but little by little his expression changed, and when I finished I knew my tale had made some impact. How effective it was or how long it would last was anyone's guess, but the interrogation—which, incidentally, took place on May 3, 1946—continued in an improved atmosphere. That I know the exact day is no feat of memory. That Prussian Junker and I met for a second time that evening at the Gründgens premiere in the Deutsches Theater, a date easy to verify. When he saw me there, he walked up to me, clicked his heels, bowed, said "Thank you," did an about-face, and disappeared into the crowd.

Grüdgens's first stage appearance since the war, for which he had chosen Sternheim's play *The Snob*, a mild satire on the morals of the Wilhelminian bourgeoisie, was not just a great theatrical occasion. It was an event, the most important by far in early postwar Berlin's social and cultural life. The air inside the theater was positively electric, so highly charged was it with anticipation as the city's artistic and intellectual elite thronged its foyer and corridors, while the ticket touts outside demanded, and got, up to one thousand Reichsmarks for a seat.

At first glance the audience looked rather elegant: most of the men in suits, most of the women in festive gowns. But when I began to single out individuals I saw the shabbiness of the suits and how loosely the dresses hung on bodies with curves flattened and bulges shriveled. But what interested me were faces rather than clothes. So many were good, sensitive, and intelligent. I was sure if I, as I used to at HQ Military Government, had suddenly asked for identity cards I would not have found many photos of arrogant *Herrenvolk* poses or of lapels with party badges on them. The majority were middle-aged or close to it, men and women who had lived through Berlin's Golden Twenties and had preserved not only memories of their city's metropolitan and cosmopolitan heyday, but also something of the spirit of that time, which was not merely a reaction to the horrors of 1914–18 in the newfound freedom from those restraints that had applied in the Kaiser's Germany. Underlying those famous Golden Years were liberal and progressive ideas that had begun to permeate Berlin's intellectual and cultural life during the final decades of the nineteenth century, to the disgust of the conservatives. It was no figment of Bismarck's imagination when he said he felt "encircled by progressives" in Berlin, the very same reason why the Kaiser so disliked his capital. He avoided it whenever he could. Long before Isherwood's time advanced ideas were fermenting in Berlin, but in the city he portrayed they had come to fruition.

How, I asked myself, had those people of "decent mentality," as Bertha Geismar put it, gotten through the Nazi years? The solace of Furtwängler's music? Hardly! So what was it? Luck? Connections? Knowing the loopholes in the totalitarian net? Exploiting conflicts between and corruption among the powerful? Compromise? Of all the stories I know, perhaps the most typical, as it contains all those elements, is that of Else Bongers, a former actress who has now been Berlin's foremost drama teacher for many years. I often saw her visit Sely, and eventually I too got to know, like, and trust her.

13

"What, You Don't Know Else?"

As one of Sely's two backroom sergeants the only contact I had with Else Bongers was when we happened to meet in Schlüterstrasse and exchanged polite "Good mornings" or "Good evenings." That was all. But I became rather curious about this woman who visited Sely so frequently; and one day when he, in my presence, instructed his driver, Herr Gleicher, to take the staff car to Branitzerplatz and fetch Frau Bongers—a German!—I burst out: "Who is this Frau Bongers, sir?"

"What, you don't know Else?" was Sely's astonished and astonishing reply. "But everybody knows her and, what's more important, she knows everybody. Sit down." He fetched out his snuffbox, went through the ritual, and, having dabbed the overflow off his nose, began: "Else was the head of the UFA's drama school for its young actors and actresses . . ."

"So she was a Nazi," I interrupted. How, I thought,

could she otherwise have held such a prominent position in Germany's leading film company?

"Far from it," he replied. "You can take it from me she's absolutely okay. Completely reliable and objective. Her assessment of film and theater people's true political attitudes during the Third Reich is valuable and invariably correct. And she's also the —let's say—'châtelaine' of Branitzerplatz 3. That's a requisitioned villa in Neu Westend, quite close to the HQ Military Government you know so well, where we entertain Germans. Again, mostly those involved with stage and film. Unlike the Russians' 'Möwe' it's not a club and restaurant, just a place where British Information Control officers meet invited Germans socially. That's important. People talk much more freely over a whisky than across an office desk. When we moved into Berlin, Else was already living in that house. A friend of hers, the tenor Franz Völker, owns it. After she'd been bombed out, he suggested she move in and look after it while he pushed off to his bomb-free chalet at some idyllic Austrian lake. We knew who she was and so Major General Bishop, our chief, told her to stay on and run the place for us."

If my boss trusted Else Bongers that was good enough for me, but I was still curious about her. Later, when we had become friends, I asked Else about her life under the Nazis, but apart from mentioning the odd snippet now and then in the course of conversation she always replied, "Look, George, there's nothing special about me. What happened to me also happened to thousands of others who hated that regime. Somehow we muddled through. God knows how, but we did. None of us, least of all I, did anything heroic. For that one's got to be made of sterner stuff than most of us are. So what's there to tell?"

I do not give up easily and repeatedly tried to get her to open up, but she would not. Not, that is, until June 1,

1983, when I was sitting in the lounge of the Hotel Kempinski in Berlin waiting for her. Having last seen Else in 1949 I was of course wondering if I would still recognize her. I need not have worried. The moment she came in I knew it was her. Her hair was gray now, but otherwise she, at seventy-six, was amazingly unchanged. Her features had hardly been touched by the years, nor had her figure—in a superbly tailored silver-gray silk trouser-suit—lost its Dresden shepherdess grace. An apparent miracle, which had, I realized, a perfectly simple explanation: Else had always had an old face on a girlish body. "Rear view: lyceum; front-view: museum," was how she had resignedly described herself during our Schlüter-strasse period. Only thirty-nine then, she had looked fifty with her face, a bit like that of a Pekingese lapdog, as lined and wrinkled as the muzzles of that breed. But now, sitting opposite me in the Kempinski, she still looked no older, as if her genes, deciding long ago that enough was enough, had determined age should wither her no further.

To conclude from this that Else was no beauty would be right and quite wrong at the same time. She always had been and still was much more than that. Her enormous charm and vivacity, combined with a voice of a musical timbre all its own, transformed her into a uniquely interesting, fascinating, attractive, and with that sylphlike body even youthful woman. I am not exaggerating, I think, if I say that she could have acted Juliet on the stage and gotten away with it. Well, almost.

From the few remarks she had made about herself, I knew that she and her elder brother, Hans, came from a well-to-do liberal middle-class family, and that both of them had belonged to those few but fortunate children who know from early age what they want to be when they grow up. Else resolved that her future was in the theater. Hans that his would be in aviation. He achieved his ambition. He joined Lufthansa and after the war, when the German airline was reborn, he was its first chief executive and chairman.

Although that of David was not among Else's stars the arrival of the Hitler regime finished her acting career. It began promisingly enough in 1930 when she, at twenty-three, got an engagement at the Stadt Theater of Dessau, a provincial city but world-renowned as the second home—Weimar was the first—of the revolutionary Bauhaus school of architecture. There Else met, fell in love with, and married a young Bauhaus architect. His surname was Paulik. I do not know his first name because Else never mentioned it. She only talked of him as "Paulik." He came from a prominent Dessau family. His father was the *Regierungspräsident*, or chief administrator, of the region. Although as a conservative he did not share his son's leftish views, he was nevertheless a convinced democrat and loyal servant of the Weimar Republic. The Nazis knew him as an enemy. And Else and her husband never made a secret of their disgust for Hitler either. That much I had always known, but now at the Kempinski I told Else that I wanted her to fill in the details, as I intended to write about postwar Berlin and about the people I had met there.

"Why were you always so reticent?" I asked.

"Well," she smiled, "I didn't talk much about it in those days when everybody claimed to have been anti-Nazi. That was so ridiculous I didn't want to add my story to the many yarns you heard day in and day out. So, where shall we start? Why not at the beginning, January 30, 1933? In Berlin the Nazis were stomping through Wilhelmstrasse celebrating their Führer as the Reich's new chancellor, but on stage in Dessau I knew nothing about it. The performance over, I was taking off my makeup when I was suddenly called to the telephone. A voice I'd never heard before said: 'Your father-in-law is in the hospital.' Click—that was all. It was enough. I knew the Nazis were in power.

"With half my makeup still on my face I ran to the hospital. It wasn't far, but I was so out of breath when I got there I sort of stumbled right into the arms of a young, rather Jewish-looking doctor, who took me to Paulik's bed. My husband was already there. The old man was bandaged all over. 'Take him away now,' the doctor whispered. 'The stormtroopers are combing the hospital and tearing bandages off people they suspect of hiding behind them. Herr Paulik's had a bad beating. He'll recover, but not if they get him a second time.' "

She paused a moment. Then she went on, "You know, the stink of fear that night in the hospital was so overpowering you couldn't smell the antiseptics anymore. It comes back into my nose every time I think of it. Anyway, we managed to get Paulik out through a back door. My husband still had his car—they took it away the next day—and drove the old man to a hiding place, the cottage of an old family servant. He had intended to go there if the Nazis took over, but it all happened so quickly he didn't have the time.

"We got home in the early hours. We were just about to go to bed when there came that knock on the door that became proverbial as not being the milkman's. When I opened it, five SA louts with drawn pistols in their fists stormed in. 'There you are, you communist bastard,' their leader shouted at my husband. 'There's no place in the new Germany for shits like you.'

"They put him against a wall. Facing it, with his hands raised. I thought the man would shoot him at any moment. I don't know whether I saved Paulik's life, but somehow that remark about there being no place for him in Germany registered and I said quite calmly, but believe me that wasn't at all how I felt, 'He was going to leave Germany anyway.'

"Then I went to the writing desk and took out a letter from a Bauhaus colleague who'd settled in Shanghai, was doing well there, and had wanted Paulik to join him. The letter was actually two years old. Paulik had had no intention of going to China and had said so in his reply, but I hoped that SA man would be too exhausted by his long night of triumph to note the date. He didn't.

" 'All right,' he said, 'let him join the slit-eyes. But if he's not gone within six months we'll be back. You can bet on that.'

"When we went to the bank the next day they told us that our accounts had been blocked. Well, Paulik wrote, his friend sent him the ship's ticket and some pocket money and he was off. I was to follow. It never happened. I said good-bye to Paulik at Bremerhaven and the next time I saw him was long after the war. But that's another story."

Else always spoke quickly and with much emphasis, her face and hands expressively underscoring her words. Yet during those last few sentences she stiffened. Her voice sounded bland and lifeless. It was then I noticed her hands and how the veins on their backs standing out in welts of brown-spotted skin gave away her true age.

"When I got back from Bremerhaven," she continued, "—those things always come together, don't they?—I found a letter from the theater saying that 'under the circumstances . . .' Well, you can guess the rest. Then, without job or money, I did a damn foolish thing. The local radio station had a vacancy; I applied and they took me. But I used a false name. God knows why I did it. In Dessau of all places, where everybody knows everybody. After two days they knew who I really was. What a crazy thing to do! I had to get away. Berlin seemed the safest place. Neither Bongers nor Paulik meant anything in that big city.

"I packed my things, went to the railway station and

asked for a single to Berlin. 'Oh, Frau Paulik isn't it?' the ticket clerk said. 'Don't you like our Dessau anymore, now that it's truly German? I don't think you should leave us. Here we know where to find you.' I hadn't looked at that man before. Now I did. He was the SA corporal who'd threatened Paulik with his gun. I panicked, grabbed my two cases, and ran without looking where I was going straight into our local fishmonger, who was loading his van at the station.

" 'Hey, Frau Paulik,' he said, 'what's the rush? Seen a ghost?' I told him. The story just spilled out of me. 'Never mind that idiot,' the fishmonger said. 'Hop in my van, give me your cases. There, there, you're trembling. Don't worry. I'll drive you to the next station down the line. You'll smell a bit fishy,' he added, with a smile, which did me a lot of good, 'but you'll get your ticket there just the same.'

"I felt safer in Berlin. I rented a nice room in a flat that belonged to a Jew, a clothing manufacturer. He'd had the good sense to transfer the title deeds to his girlfriend, an 'Aryan' mannequin. I lived on what little money my brother, a junior Lufthansa employee with a large family, could spare me, enough for my rent and two stale rolls and a daily pint of milk that I sweetened with some chocolate powder. I couldn't work. Certainly not in my profession. I wasn't in the Reichskulturkammer. And I was afraid of trying any other jobs in case the Dessau radio people had reported me to the police. I spent most of the time in my room reading plays and studying roles. That kept me sane.

"I got in touch with a few of my old drama-school friends. None of them were Nazis, I knew that. They moved in Berlin's film and theater circles and persuaded me to come to parties with them. And at one of those I met that treasure Wolfgang Liebeneiner. That was in 1936. Somehow the personal and professional chemistry between him, the famous actor, director, and boss of Berlin Film, and me, the unknown, unemployed, and unemployable provincial actress was right from the word go. We talked and talked and what I said or how I said it so impressed him he invited me to visit his Berlin Film studios, watch the work, and tell him what I thought of it. A few weeks later he asked me to act as his personal advisor on casting problems, not as an employee, but on a generous fee basis. It was then I told him about Dessau, my husband and father-in-law, and about that false name. 'Who cares?' he replied. 'I don't give a damn. Anyway, it's a private arrangement, so don't worry.' That's how I slipped into my real profession, because a little later he asked me to coach Berlin Film's starlets. That's how I began.

"Years later, in '42 it was, Liebeneiner and I were walking home through the Tiergarten after a party. Hitler was winning one victory after another and life in Berlin was still quite normal, except for the blackout. More luxurious actually than ever before with all that loot, especially from France. It was then Liebeneiner told me that Goebbels had decreed—in wartime, would you believe it!—that every film studio had to have its own drama school. 'And I want you, Else, to run the UFA's in Babelsberg,' he said. I thought he'd taken leave of his senses and told him so. 'Not at all,' he replied. 'It hasn't been announced yet, but I'm the new UFA boss. Say yes, please. And don't worry about anything. Either about your past troubles or about not being in the Film and Theater Chamber. Don't give it a thought. I'll fix all that.'

"And so he did. He had influence with Goebbels. And amazingly retained it, in spite of the fact that he openly defied him over the Gottschalk funeral. You remember that sad story?"

I did. The suicide of the popular actor Joachim Gottschalk, his wife, and eight-year-old son in 1941 deeply shocked his colleagues, even some of those who believed in Hitler. Everybody knew that Goebbels's pressure on Gottschalk to divorce his beloved Jewish wife had caused this tragedy.

"Goebbels," Else continued, "had given explicit instructions not to attend the burial, but Liebeneiner went regardless, and yet in 1942 Goebbels made him UFA chief. He knew, as well as you do because you Brits investigated Wolfgang and cleared him, that he was no Nazi. Yet he kept honoring and promoting him." She shook her head. "It was a curious relationship. In a way, but only in a way, it reminds me a little of that between Speer and Hitler. The big difference, however, is that Speer was a believer almost up to the very end while Liebeneiner never was. Still, both seemed to get away with things for which others would have been sent to concentration camps. Even Liebeneiner can't really explain why. But that's how it was. Talk about the mysteries of the human soul . . ."

"Like your relationship with Paulik?" I asked. "You mentioned that you met again but sort of dismissed it in the same breath by adding 'Well, that's another story.' Don't you want to talk about it?"

"Why not? Though I don't really see why I should tell you. I don't think I've ever talked to anyone about it. But then neither have I talked so much about my past to anyone before. First, though, I'd like another sherry, please."

When the waiter had brought it she said, "Paulik and I met again in 1954, twenty-one years after that parting in Bremerhaven, which was supposed to be for a year at most. He wrote that he'd arrived safely but from then on I just waited and waited. Not a line, not a word. Until, not too long before the war, I got a letter asking for a divorce. I consented immediately. What else was there? Besides, I'd gotten used to living on my own. I'd built my own life. So when we had our *Wiedersehen*, Paulik was long remarried and I knew from the newspapers how successful and internationally respected he was in his profession. Yes, I'd followed his career. I didn't know he was coming to Germany until he was in Berlin. He just rang me and suggested we meet. To be honest, it was unsettling. Anyhow I said yes and we did. Right here, actually. Outside the Kempinski Café, around the corner. You won't believe this, but we just walked the streets. He was crying most of the time. I just couldn't respond. I was all frozen up inside. Through and through. Like an icicle. It was terrible. We were not together long. At some street corner, I've no idea where, we shook hands and said good-bye. We had hardly talked at all. Paulik walked away and I stood there on the spot as if I'd been screwed into the pavement. I couldn't move. And then . . . for the first time in my life . . . I fainted."

Else rose. "It's late," she said, a brief kiss and she was gone. It was nearly midnight. As I went up to my room I remembered Sely's "What, you don't know Else?" and was none too sure I knew her even now.

But how that remark had puzzled and astonished me when he had made it! He knew that his sergeants dealt with the Vieks and the Mohrs, he with the Furtwänglers, Gründgens, Liebeneiners, and, of course, Bongers. Neither Toliver nor I resented this. We would have done exactly the same had we sat in his chair. Besides, it lay in the nature of things that NCOs rarely met Berlin's cultural Brahmins. Officers hosted the functions to which they were invited—at Branitzerplatz or wherever; officers mingled with them at the almost daily theater, opera, or film premieres—so many that even Sely, who loved to see and be seen and sometimes managed to attend two in one evening, could not go to all the events for which he received complimentary tickets. Tolliver and I benefited from the overflow.

But why did he say it? The only way to find out was to ask.

"Oh," he said, a boyish grin lighting up the stern face of this huge man with surprising charm, "I must have said that unthinkingly, forgetting I was speaking to my sergeant. Saw you already in your future incarnation as my deputy. Something I wanted to talk to you about next week when you came back from your naturalization board in Hamburg. But why not now? I'd like you to stay with me after your demob. I'm authorized to offer you Control Officer Grade III, equivalent to a captaincy. How about it?"

Much as I appreciated it, Sely's proposal put me in a bit of a quandary.

14

"Erst kommt
das Fressen, dann
kommt die Moral"

—BERTOLT BRECHT

I had already accepted another post with the Control Commission but had not yet told Sely about it—that was my dilemma. It was not my choice, I had been asked not to mention it, but that did not make me feel less uncomfortable toward him. He deserved my loyalty in any case, but also, by standing up for me, he had actually—unwittingly—helped this dream job come my way. It was no less than that because I, too, just like Else Bongers and her brother, had known from childhood what I wanted to be when I grew up. My ideal was a job on a newspaper and that was what I had been offered.

All my freelance writing had earned me until I came to Berlin was a respectable collection of rejection slips, but that was no deterrent. As soon as that city, my work in Schlüterstrasse, and Anita as well had lost the excitement of novelty, I began to write again. My first article, tapped out one evening on Eva Rose's office typewriter, compared the political awareness and common sense of the man on the Clapham omnibus with that of his German counterpart, the man on the Halensee tram. Calling it "John Smith and Johann Schmidt," I sent it to the U.S.-licensed *Der Tagesspiegel*, then as now Berlin's leading newspaper. It not only printed my article, but Erik Reger, its editor, asked me for more. I knew that serving soldiers were not supposed to publish anything anywhere without their superiors' permission—let alone in a German newspaper—but seeing my name in print for the first time was such a marvelous sensation I took the risk. The not unexpected rocket from Lancaster House promptly landed in Schlüterstrasse and it was then that Sely proved himself a perfect brick. Instead of disowning me, he replied that he had seen and approved my article (a fib) and added that it and other features on the British way of life I wanted to write for *Der Tagesspiegel* were not only unobjectionable but also "reeducational," which was true. So, with his blessing, I could carry on.

On August 8, my article, "The History of Britain's Labor Party," my fourth, appeared in *Tagesspiegel*. That afternoon a Mr. Peter de Mendelssohn rang me. After introducing himself as the American Press Officer who had been that daily's founding father, and mentioning that his office was in the same building—the Ullstein house in Tempelhof—he invited me to come and see him there. What about? I asked. That he would rather explain personally than on the phone, de Mendelssohn replied. Off I went wondering whether, for whatever reason, an American rocket was about to follow the one from Lancaster House. Far from it. Coming straight to the point de Mendelssohn asked whether I would be willing to come back to Germany after my demobilization to work for him as a deputy editorial controller on the planned Berlin edition of *Die Welt*. I could hardly believe my luck, nor could I understand how an American could of-

fer me a job on *Die Welt*, the newspaper for the British
Zone published from Hamburg and owned by the British
occupation authorities.

"I'm not a Yank. I'm a British subject. Well, a recently
naturalized one," de Mendelssohn explained, "and I'm
about to change over to the British Control Commission.
I'm going to be the editorial controller of the Berlin edition. So, what do you say, Clare?"

What a question! What an offer! I would have sold my
soul to a Mephisto for this job, but there was nothing
mephistophelian about de Mendelssohn, who had been
a well-known journalist in pre-1933 Berlin. When we met
he was in his late thirties or early forties and at the beginning of a postwar career that was to gain him considerable literary renown as author and translator of
Churchill's memoirs, and reach its climax during his last
years as editor of the Thomas Mann diaries.

We parted on the understanding that he would deal
with the formalities and that I would not talk to anybody about his offer until they were settled. This I promised, albeit with a somewhat troubled conscience toward
Sely.

Now I had to tell him.

"Hm," he said. "That job's very much up your street,
of course. Pity, but tell me, what do you know about de
Mendelssohn?"

"Very little," I replied. "It was the first time I met
him."

"All right," Sely said. "I won't stand in your way, you
can be sure of that. He's a first-rate journalist and could
be a splendid teacher for you, but he's a bit mercurial.
Still, I suppose congratulations are in order. But should
anything go wrong, promise you'll get in touch with me."

Well, something promptly did. One week after that
talk with Sely I left for Hamburg to attend my naturalization board. Now that the wartime ban on naturaliza-

tions had been lifted it was a mere formality. Aliens who had served in His Majesty's Forces were granted British citizenship more or less automatically. I arrived at the appointed place at the appointed time only to be informed that the gentlemen of the board had packed up and gone home the day before. My chances of being demobbed in Germany and of stepping into my new job right away had departed with them.

"Not necessarily," Sely suggested when I reported my misfortune to him. "You can stay on as civilian Control Commission clerk. You don't have to be British for that. That applies to officer grades only. So forget about de Mendelssohn, stay with me, and as soon as you've got your British passport I'll see you get upgraded to CO III."

"No, sir," I replied. "First of all I want that newspaper job and then I know by now how the official mind works. Once you're in one slot it's damn difficult to get out of it again. And I know the CCG snobbery. Once you've been a clerk you stay a clerk in everybody's eyes. I'm going back to the U.K. to get my nationality. I'll come back as a CO III or not at all. De Mendelssohn says there's no hurry and that he doesn't mind waiting a couple of months or so."

"Well then, George," said Sely, using my first name for the first time, "I look forward to seeing you in Berlin again, even if you don't want to work with me."

My departure date, August 31, was a warm and sunny day. As the U.K. train did not leave Charlottenburg station till the evening and my things were packed by lunchtime there was plenty of time for a leisurely farewell stroll through Berlin. Walking from Kaiserdamm to Kurfürstendamm it suddenly struck me that I had long ago stopped taking any notice of the city. During the eight months I had lived there it had become so familiar that I had moved through it almost unseeingly. Now, as

I looked and listened consciously, I became aware that instead of January's eerie silence—broken only by an occasional clatter, as if unspeakable ghosts were rattling their chains—a steady hum rose from the crowded streets. Not the melody of a bustling city yet, by any means, more like the buzz of electric current flowing through a high-voltage cable and, like it, denoting the presence of an energy dormant but alive. Sunlit spaces lay open to the eye where mountains of rubble had obscured one's vision; Berlin's hard-working *Trümmerfrauen* had wrested some order out of chaos. This, not just the sunshine, made the bombed, shelled, holed, and bullet-riddled ruins no longer appear as on my arrival day as apocalyptic monuments to a malignant zealotry, but simply as buildings that would be restored, rebuilt, or replaced. If not tomorrow then the day after—man the wrecker was a builder too.

I passed the house in Wilmersdorferstrasse where Manya and Rösl had lived and, thinking of them, I wondered whether habituation had blunted my perception not just of Berlin but of the Germans, too. Daily contact with this extraordinary people, who had come so perilously close to fulfilling the ambitions of an evil, dynamic, and unbending will, inclined one to see them as such an ordinary lot. One had to strain one's imagination to visualize those downtrodden men in Nazi or Wehrmacht uniforms again, or remember that some of those emaciated women queuing for scarce rations outside the shops could well be the same I had seen hailing their Führer with such orgasmic frenzy, not only in newsreels or the films of Leni Riefenstahl, but with my own eyes too. But more than those memories it was their constant whining about the injustice of their fate and their inexhaustible self-pity in defeat that ensured that one could not forget how pitiless they had been in victory. A nation bearing the mark of Cain pretending it was composed of Abels. Oh, they cursed Hitler all right, but not for the crimes he had committed in their name (and with the willing help of many). They cursed him for betraying their trust and their loyalty by giving them in return for the lives they had given him a truncated Germany, its soil drenched in German blood.

There were no Nazis now. It was grotesque, but Hitler had denazified the German masses more thoroughly than any Control Council Directive. Nazism was dead, but the mentality that had helped it rise was not. That is how the world at large, not just I, saw the Germans of and at that time. A harsh judgment and not unfair, but—fortunately—premature. Only a very wise man gifted with almost prophetic insight, certainly not I, could have understood then that a nation that had suffered a defeat unparalleled in all history needed time to come to terms with itself. Also, that Brecht's laconic *"Erst kommt das Fressen, dann kommt die Moral"* ("Grub comes before morality") reveals a truth that does not apply to Germans alone.

Yet if the masses felt neither guilt not shame, there was also a minority, and a not insubstantial one, of people who, instead of grieving for themselves, grieved for the victims of Germany's extermination and execution squads. Composed mostly, but not exclusively, of men and women who never held illusions about the Hitler regime, they worked for the rebirth of that Germany, now buried deep beneath the moral debris of National Socialism, where not an outlaw but the law had ruled. They knew that their country would have to bear the burden of the short-lived Third Reich for many generations yet, if not, perhaps, for all of a thousand years. Working on *Die Welt*, which was well on its way to becoming one of the biggest and most successful newspapers published in Germany, would enable me to work with those people and to help them.

What better reason for returning to Berlin, I thought as the U.K. train moved out of Charlottenburg station. That there were other reasons less noble or altruistic as well, I knew, but strangely, or perhaps not so strangely, I became fully aware of those only after I had arrived in Britain.

15

"Carpetbaggers of the Twentieth Century"

Did Brecht's words *"Erst kommt das Fressen, dann kommt die Moral"* state a universal truth, or were they valid only for the Germany of his time? An open question, but—turned around—they were true for the Britain to which I had returned. Grub there—rationed and dull though it was—was enough for morality to have priority. Fair shares for all, the redistribution of wealth, was the country's moral imperative. Thus out of step with other Western democracies, all of which put wealth creation first, Britain—losing at home the war it had won in Germany—followed the flag of austerity toward economic and political decline. An outcome that would have been pretty much the same whether Tories or Labor were in power, for both parties were still in the psychological straitjacket of consensus politics. A necessity in war, in peace they were a denial of choice—the essence of democracy. Few seemed to care. Slumbering in the cradle warmth of an intellectually sterile and illusory national unity was popular.

At the time I, the freshly minted neo-Brit, was all for Labor and equality but, lacking the native puritanical streak, I was none too keen on austerity. I had to admit to myself that I was eager to return to Berlin also for reasons other than pure idealism or a fascination with Germany. There, as an occupation official, one knew who had won the war, led a more interesting and comfortable life, and was given responsibilities and powers well beyond anything a twenty-six-year-old could expect in the U.K. But after a few weeks I began to wonder whether I would ever get back there at all. Having had a five-minute interview with a very pleasant gentleman at the Home Office and having subsequently sworn allegiance to the Crown before a commissioner of oaths I informed de Mendelssohn that I had been naturalized. There was no reply to this or to my follow-up letters, but after *Der Tagesspiegel* published in November my "Thinking about a Dream," which caused quite a stir in Berlin, I hoped I would at last hear from him.

Its highly controversial subject was the arrival in Germany of the families of CCG and army personnel. The British were not the first to reunite what officialese termed "Married Elements" with their "Dependents." As already mentioned, the Soviets allowed the wives of SMA officers, but not those of Other Ranks, to join their husbands within a few months of the end of the fighting. The French were also quick off the mark. With Gallic sangfroid they included in their family scheme—entirely financed out of German occupation costs—not only wives and children, but *grandmère et grandpère,* and occasionally *frère* Jacques and *tante* Odile as well. The Americans brought out their families, accompanied by huge gasoline-guzzling limousines instead of grandma and grandpop, at about the same time as the British. Naturally, the requisitioning of scarce undamaged properties for Allied families caused much hardship for the Germans ordered to get out. There were protests. The strongest, however, came not from Germans but from leading British personalities, whose letters were published in *The Times*, the most noteworthy being one jointly signed by Mrs. Clementine Churchill and the Duchess of Atholl. It gave me the idea for my story.

"During one of these dark November nights," I wrote, "I dreamed I was reading a copy of the *Völkischer Beobachter*, the Nazi party's own newspaper, published in 1942. Going through its pages I saw a letter from Emmy Göring and Magda Goebbels in which the Third Reich's two 'leading ladies' had this to say:

> The undersigned wish to protest against the policy of allowing the wives of German officers and officials to join their husbands serving in the occupied countries. This enables many of them to lead lives of luxury that are in crass contrast not only to what the occupied peoples have to bear, but also to the wartime austerity of our lives in the Fatherland. In cities like Warsaw or Rotterdam, to name but two heavily bombed by our Luftwaffe, scarcity of accommodation has led to terrible overcrowding. Many families have to share flats too small for one. Nevertheless every day people are forced to leave their homes so that one German officer's wife can enjoy the luxury of a four- or five-room apartment. We ask our government to put a stop to this.

Ending my article by stressing once more that this was only a dream, I pointed out that the many letters in *The Times* were nothing of the kind and that any Berliner could look up Clementine Churchill's letter, of which my Emmy Göring/Magda Goebbels fantasy was an almost verbatim translation, in that newspaper that was available in all British Military Government reading rooms.

Many *Tagesspiegel* readers wrote to me, except of course de Mendelssohn. Most letters expressed admiration for Mrs. Churchill, yet a surprising number of Berliners, as opposed to other Germans, disagreed with her. Feeling the first quivers of the Cold War they were so afraid that the West might abandon them to the Soviets they wanted British, American, and French families in their midst.

Berlin's first free election had been held in October. The result was as disastrous for the Russians and their Socialist Unity party as the earlier Social-Democrats-only ballot had been. With a miserable 19.8 percent of the vote it obtained a mere 26 out of 130 City Council seats—63 went to the victorious Social Democrats, the rest to the other democratic parties. After this the Soviets knew that unless they managed to squeeze the West out, Berlin would never again be theirs alone. The angst of the population that Soviet pressure could succeed was grist to the mill of communist propagandists, who invented new canards about the Western powers' imminent exit daily. Hence the sight of newly arrived Joan from Putney pushing her pram through Grunewald, of Jean from Connecticut shopping at the Dahlem PX, or of Jeanette from Neuilly walking her dog in Frohnau tranquillized Berliners' nerves.

Mine, however, were fraying. Having used up most of my army gratuity I tried to find a job. But as I honestly mentioned at every interview that I intended to return to Germany eventually nobody wanted me. Thanks to a recommendation from David Astor, the editor of *Observer*, the *Manchester Evening News* took me on as a temporary junior reporter, but that was only for five weeks and by the middle of December I was unemployed again and back in London. Then on the morning of my twenty-sixth birthday a Post Office messenger delivered a telegram. Kind wishes from my relatives in Australia, I thought, but no, it was from Sely. "Report immediately Norman Cumming, 48 Prince's Gardens, regards Kaye," was all it said, but that was enough. The address was that of the CCG's London HQ where my school chum Oppenheimer had wangled my posting to Germany the year before. After that cable the letter from de Mendelssohn that arrived in that morning's mail was merely a confusing anticlimax. "Dear Clare," I read, "I have now completed arrangements for you to join me at *Die Welt*. Go and see a Mr. Norman Cumming at 48, Prince's Gardens in Kensington. He is au fait with everything."

Well, Norman Cumming was nothing of the kind and I was spared a difficult decision. I gave him de Mendelssohn's letter. "That's the first I've heard of that," he said, going through my file. "There's not a word here about *Die Welt*, or de Mendelssohn. PR/ISC Intelligence is where you're going or Sely will have my guts for garters."

I signed on the dotted line, was given a clothing allowance of £25 for which Messrs. Alkit of Cambridge Circus provided a smartly tailored blue-serge officer's uniform, and was sent on a four-day course to Bletchley. There we attended fairly superficial lectures on German history, learned how four-power control was supposed to function and how the Control Commission for Germany (British Element) was organized. As was to be expected, the people I met at Bletchley were a mixed bunch, ranging from those, a high percentage of them women, who spoke excellent German, knew the country and its history, to middle-aged middle-class former officers, who saw the CCG as their last refuge from a Britain so changed they felt strangers in their own country. At that time the Control Commission employed twenty-six thousand British personnel, of which only a minority, approximately six thousand, actually dealt with Ger-

many. The others made up its swollen bureaucracy, a
happy hunting ground for those former majors and half-
colonels, some of them of that grand colonial manner so
worrying to Kurt Schumacher, the leader of the German
Social Democrats. He was only half-joking when he said
that the one reason he feared India's coming independence was that her unemployed pukka sahibs might be
dispatched to Germany to civilize the natives. Schumacher need not have worried, for by August 1947, when
they lowered the Union Jack in New Delhi, not only the
Indian Civil Service but also the Control Commission
was running down. Too late, however, for it to rid itself
of its largely undeserved "carpetbaggers of the twentieth
century" image in Britain, which it owed to overstaffing,
the much-publicized black-market activities of some, the
easy "fraternizing" with German women, and last but
not least to the British public's envy of anyone materially or sexually better off, often fueled by exaggerated
reports about the misdeeds of the CCG by British newspaper correspondents in Germany—not all of them angels either, by any means. Knowing all this, however, did
not lessen my joy in having a job at last, or my pleasure
in the sleeping and dining-car comfort to which I was
now entitled on the army train from Ostend.

We crossed into Germany on February 12 of that dreadful
1947 winter, when coal merchants in Britain weighed out
the rationed lumps, like potatoes, by the pound. Near
lunchtime the train stopped in Hamm again. Taking
some things I had prepared for its railway children I went
out into the corridor. The windows were so frozen over
I could neither pull them down nor see through them. I
opened the carriage door. There were no children, the
station was deserted. Gray clouds, heavily snow-laden
but too icy to shed their load, hung like a dirty shroud
over this desolate scene. The only visible human being

was a railwayman checking the brakes. It needed no great flight of fancy to hear in the ringing of his hammer against their metal casings Coleridge's "matin bell ... knelling us back to a world of death."

At Charlottenburg station Sely's driver, Herr Gleicher, was waiting for me. He took my luggage and, as I followed him down the stairs and saw the soldiers from the train struggling with their kit bags, I felt unashamedly good about not being one of them anymore. Gleicher drove the square, squat staff car, which skidded easily, with great care over the iced slush on the unsanded streets. I had left a sunlit Berlin and returned to a freezing "world of death." Yet it was amazing how quickly eye and mind got accustomed again to surroundings that, shocking to every new arrival, were too familiar to an old Berlin hand like myself to have any real emotional impact.

Gleicher stopped outside a modern apartment building in Dillenburger Strasse and handed me the keys to flat No. 6. I walked up three flights of stairs and unlocked the door. Compared to how I had lived in London it was paradise. Two of the four rooms of the flat were mine. The bedroom—my name already on its door—was to the left of the corridor and my study with its little balcony overlooking the street was opposite. Both rooms were sparsely but adequately furnished with "officers, for the use of" standard items; simple, chintzy, and bright. The long inventory list with its bold print warning that the cost of anything lost or damaged would be deducted from my pay, which I had to check and sign, was on my desk. Bathroom and kitchen I shared with the other tenant, a Mr. Mackintosh. By the time I had unpacked and stored my things, washed and shaved, I was ready for lunch. The mess I had been assigned to was the so-called 400 Club on Breitenbach Platz, a couple of minutes' walk from the flat. Being the biggest British officers' mess in

Berlin it was considered rather inferior, a sort of Lyon's Corner House. Never mind the cachet, I thought, as I walked up a thickly carpeted staircase, passed the crowded bar, looked into the comfortable coffee lounge, and then sat down at one of the neatly laid tables in the large dining room where a German waitress, prim in white-aproned black dress, presented the day's menu.

After coffee I phoned the British car pool for transport to Schlüterstrasse; nothing to pay, one just signed the driver's duty sheet and tipped him with a couple of cigarettes. When the gray-haired little porter in Schlüterstrasse, who always called me "Herr Mr. Clare," saw me he rushed to get the elevator, but I, wanting to savor the moment of my return, walked up the stairs. Nothing had changed. Johannes R. Becher's Deutscher Kulturbund was still in the building. There had been much talk about ordering this communist front organization out of the British Sector, but it was only done the following November when relations with the Russians had reached a low and American pressure for action a high point. The British Film Section, mockingly called "J. Arthur Rank's Own" by those suspecting that his interests rather than official ones were paramount to its work, was on the second and third floor as before.

When I finally reached the fourth floor I thought I was home, but on entering our waiting room I was none too sure of that. Like a circus ring it was swarming with midgets. Tiny men and women standing on the chairs around the big table were bending over it filling in their *Fragebogens;* another group in the middle of the room agitatedly discussed in squeaky voices whether such questions as "Did you serve in the general or Waffen SS?" or "What was the last rank you held in the Wehrmacht?" needed to be answered by them at all; two little chaps, obviously fed up with this nonsense, practiced handstands in a corner and as there were not enough chairs for so many—there must have been about thirty of them—some were reading their questionnaires lying comfortably on their tummies on the carpet. Carefully tiptoeing over them I fled to our offices.

"Oh, welcome back, Mr. Clare," Eva Rose greeted me, "you've arrived at the right moment. The major's still at lunch and knows nothing about what's going on out there. But if the Lilliputians from Karli Schäfer's Circus are still here when he comes back there'll either be an explosion or he'll laugh himself to death. They've been told that they must be checked out before they can hop back into the arena. Can you imagine!"

"Get me Schmidt on the phone, please," I said.

Having exchanged the appropriate courtesies I pointed out to the Spruchkammer secretary that circus dwarfs were definitely none of our business, so would he please tell them to get out right away. I added that there had been quite enough talk about the "Denazification Circus" anyway, so we had better not prove it to be literally true. If this story got into the newspapers we would be the laughingstock not only of Berlin but of Fleet Street, too. That convinced him.

This settled, I was about to open the door that led to my old office when Rose stopped me. "You're going the wrong way," she said, getting up and opening the door to Sely's room. "Your desk is in here now. The major had it brought in yesterday."

And there it was next to Sely's. Without doubt this was the biggest surprise of my return. Standing there contemplating with pleasure how things had changed for me I let a few minutes pass before taking off my greatcoat. I was about to hang it up when I heard Sely saying:

"My, don't we look smart in that ritzy uniform, George? But you'd better keep that greatcoat on. Heating in British offices is minimal at the best of times, and on some days it's switched off altogether. Scarcity of coal, but it also shows the Germans that we're doing our share saving fuel. Now sit down, Rose is making us some coffee, and I'll fill you in on what's been happening while you were away. And, by the way, I'm of course 'Kaye' now."

Taking out his snuffbox, he went through the well-known ceremonial, so much more stylish than lighting a cigarette, of sending a pinch up his nostrils. He acknowledged my words of thanks as well as the refreshing sensation of the snuff in his brain with a gentle "Ahhh" and then he began to talk.

16

"Only
the Women!"

"While you were away," Sely said, "the U.S. Documents Center became fully operational. That's the big news. What with their records and our own files, no one now gets away with a falsified *Fragebogen*. Until, that is, the case comes up in one of our Military Government courts. Then it's the old story of judges wanting confessions on top of documentary evidence. Now, I shan't brief you about the Docs Center. You've got to go and see for yourself. They're in Zehlendorf. Their commanding officer, Lieutenant Colonel Helm, is a tough German-American warhorse, a professional soldier in the Weimar Republic's Reichswehr before he emigrated to the States in the twenties. He's very cooperative and so is his deputy, Kurt Rosenow, the chap who's done all the real work. When we're through I'll ring Helm and make an appointment for you.

"Now—as for our own duties. They haven't changed, though our priorities have. We're taking a fine-tooth

comb to the people on *Die Welt*, North-West German
Radio, and the German News Service. Let me put it this
way: ISC, like a virgin waking up one morning and finding herself with child, suddenly discovered itself a major
employer of German journalists. Only an immaculate
conception it wasn't. These outfits were staffed in a
hurry, there was no Docs Center yet, and some ex-Nazis
with falsified *Fragebogen*s slipped in, a few into leading
positions. The press dug up a couple of cases and there
was one hell of a fuss. As they all, *Die Welt*, NWDR,
and GNS, are in Hamburg, we've now got our own office
there. Leo Felix is in charge. You don't know him, I
think. He comes from Censorship. He's sound enough,
but doesn't always have the right touch. Tends to upset
people; our own, I mean. You and I will have to have one
leg in Hamburg and deal with the more sensitive cases
ourselves, which reminds me . . ."

He unlocked his desk, took out a letter, and gave it to
me. Addressed to Colonel Edwards, PR/ISC's deputy
chief, it was from Public Safety, the CCG's police division. Couched in somewhat more diplomatic language
than my summary of it, its author, a public safety commander, accused our section of denazifying with—in his
words—"excessive zeal." Was PR/ISC Group aware of
this, he inquired, or—and there was the sting—of the
fact that the officer in charge, a Major Sely, his Hamburg
representative a Mr. Felix, as well as his man in Hanover, one Staff Sergeant Ormond, were all of German-
Jewish extraction, which might well incline them to act
in a spirit of revenge? Did PR/ISC consider it advisable
that such a delicate task should be entrusted to people
of such background?

"Well, " I said, having read it, "do I pack my bags and
take the next train back to London?"

"No," Kaye laughed, "that journey won't be necessary.
Ted Edwards called me over to Lancaster House and dic-

tated his reply with me there. We're supposed to be excitable Continentals, but compared to a raging Welshman that's nothing, I can tell you. 'Bloody ignorant jumped-up bobbies ... should have stayed home pounding their fucking beats ... treat Nazis like naughty boys who'll be fine once they've been given a good talking to' was one of his milder references to Public Safety. Anyway, he told them that he was responsible for the recruitment of his intelligence staff and needed nobody to tell him who they were or where they came from. And as they had his full confidence he had to refute the commander's aspersions on their integrity with the same determination with which Public Safety had refuted reports that it allowed former Gestapo officers to seep back into the German police. That did it. No more's been heard from Public Safety. Mind you, their letter actually did some good. Here, in this new memo to our immediate boss, Michael Balfour, our functions are set out more clearly than they ever were before. It's the result of that Public Safety letter."

Taking his copy from the "pending" tray, Sely read out to me: " 'The duty of the Intelligence Section is to collect information on personalities and institutions active in the German information service and cultural world and to supervise denazification and licensing in that sphere. The former activity will presumably continue, whereas the latter is likely to diminish in importance, being ultimately confined to the task of ensuring that PR/ISC-operated media remain pure and license applicants acceptable.' "

"Certainly precise," I said. "Did the chief write it?"

"Oh no," Kaye replied, "not him. It's from Ted. Cecil Sprigge, who took over from General Bishop in October, is a nice enough chap, but a nonentity, harmless, useless, clueless—you can add as many 'lesses' as you can think of. God only knows why they picked the former Rome correspondent of the *Manchester Guardian* for the job. The deputy military governor, General Robertson, has no time for him at all. He listens to Ted, though. There you are, then. In the proverbial nutshell that's what happened while you were enjoying yourself in London."

"Remember that Furtwängler file I did for you, Kaye?" I said. "I got quite involved in that affair. I know he was cleared, but how did it actually go?"

"Biggest circus we ever had here when his case came up in December. The outcome of course was a foregone conclusion, in spite of the old boy behaving like a bull in a china shop. His arrogance, that godlike condescension with which he treated the Spruchkammer, put their backs up. Mind you, Alex Vogel in the chair was pretty silly, too. He concentrated on the van der Nuell case. The music critic, remember, whom Furtwängler never forgave for describing von Karajan as a 'musical miracle.' Vogel tried to pin the blame for van der Nuell's eventual call-up and death at the front on Furtwängler. A harebrained idea. Far more important issues were at stake, but with the fuss Vogel made about that scribbler they never got round to them. Incidentally, the Spruchkammer clearance has not yet been confirmed by the Allies. The Yanks are still dragging their feet. And the great man's fallen for Schmidt's secretary, our Eva Rose's sister. He asked her to come and see him some time. Here, look at the copy of his letter."

It said: "Herr Peppermüller of the Philharmonic Orchestra will see to it that you get this letter. Perhaps you could let me know, through him, whether it would be possible for us to have a long chat. I should like you to tell me something about what the last one and a half years were like in Berlin. Maybe you could come and visit me here in Potsdam? My apartment is warm and completely undamaged. And I could arrange for you (on a Sunday perhaps) to be driven home by car in the evening. Nowadays distances have become so gigantic."

"Did she go?" I asked.

"No. She thought it wiser not to. But you see how human great men can be."

And so could Kaye. I would have done better not to ask my next question, "How d'you want to divide our duties?" I ought to have known that he was no friend of clearly defined responsibilities. I promptly got my come-uppance.

"That we'd best play by ear," he replied somewhat sharply. "You leave that to me. And now you'd best go and say hello to the staff. You'll like Sergeant Wildman. He's replaced Tolliver." And then, to take me down a peg or two, he added: "There's of course no replacement for you. After all, you're back." That was meant and understood as a reminder to his new deputy, the former Sergeant Clare, not to forget to whom he owed his recent rise in the world.

My appointment at the U.S. Documents Center was made for the following Wednesday. I was to get there at midday, lunch with Helm and his senior staff, and have my guided tour through the archives afterward. I had expected to find a big barracks of a place but what I actually saw when I arrived at Wasserkäfersteig was a largish suburban villa, like so many in Zehlendorf. However, the high barbed-wire double fence around the periphery of its extensive grounds, the floodlights, and the armed, steel-helmeted sentries told me I had come to the right spot.

The story of the U.S. Documents Center—still in Berlin today—might well be included in Ripley's Believe It or Not series. It owes its existence to the owner of a Bavarian paper mill where, shortly before the end of the war, a closely guarded truck convoy delivered for immediate pulping the central membership register of the Nazi Party—the *Zentralkartei* of the NSDAP—and lots of other top-secret Nazi files. But the mill owner procrastinated. First he claimed not to have enough coal to do the job, and when that was brought up he pretended his machines were breaking down for lack of spare parts. Delay after delay, excuse after excuse, a dangerous game. He won it the day the tanks of the Seventh U.S. Army came clanking up the road to his factory. Believing they had found a great Nazi treasure, which indeed they had, jubilant GIs began emptying the sacks. But their euphoria quickly evaporated when—instead of gold bars or banknotes—eight and a half million index cards tumbled out of them.

Sorting the material, transporting it to Berlin, storing it in the cellars of what had been a major telephone exchange and listening post for Göring's own agents, installing sophisticated safety equipment, and getting the villa that was to house the administration into shape took well over a year.

"As a matter of fact, we've not yet quite finished sifting what after all is the biggest . . . and nastiest 'Who's Who' in the world," Sergeant Major Warren, the British representative at the Documents Center, told me when we went down to the vaults after lunch.

"There they all are, our friends, every one of them," he said, pointing at the big filing cabinets holding the *Zentralkartei*. "Every little and every big Nazi of the Grossdeutsche Reich is here. It doesn't matter where he lived, whether local records were destroyed, or whether the Russkies got hold of them, we've got the lot. Whenever a new member joined, a duplicate record card was automatically sent to the *Zentralkartei* in Munich. Few people know that. That's why many Nazis who fled from, say, East Prussia, the Sudetenland, the territories now held by the Poles, or the Soviet Zone, think they can get away with lying. Not a hope. You give us the name, place, and date of birth, and we'll find your chappie."

"But what about those, and we've had quite a few of them, who claim they never knew they were in the party?" I asked.

"No problem," said Warren, a slight, slim, rather good-looking man who had been attached to the Yanks for many months. "Just come along."

He led me to another vault.

"There," he said, pulling open a random drawer, "you've got the membership application forms. Nobody, but nobody, ever became a party member without knowing it. Party membership was strictly personal. In other words nobody could obtain it on somebody else's behalf. Every application had to be signed by the applicant himself. Now come next door. That's where we have the files of the Nazi party's own court, which disciplined and punished wayward members. I'm sure you've come across people who admit having joined the party but claim they got so disillusioned with Nazism that they resigned. Now sometimes it's true, but most of the time they were kicked out for petty crimes, intrigues—all sorts of offenses against good Nazi order and discipline. Most of them fought, and hard, to stay in the party. It's all here in these files: declarations of loyalty, denunciations of so-called enemies of the state . . . for listening to the BBC, for being 'Jew-lovers' or defeatists, even for just telling a joke about a Nazi leader. But now for a special treat. How would you like to see Hitler's own membership card? It's in our safe."

"No thanks," I said. "He never got around to falsifying his *Fragebogen*."

Warren smiled. "True enough. Let me show you our

Chamber of Horrors instead. That's where we keep the SS files, including Himmler's personal ones."

The rooms we had walked through so far had all been interconnected, the fireproof doors between them standing open. Now we went back into the main passage until we came to an all-metal door, which Warren unlocked. It was my first glimpse of the vaults where I, later that year, spent the bigger part of my annual leave doing research for a biography of the Third Reich's SS and police chief. It was Warren who gave me the idea when he took a folder marked FÜHRERBESPRECHUNGEN from its shelf and suggested I look through it. It was a perfectly ordinary *"Leitz-Ordner"* of the kind one finds in every German office, but speared on the metal spikes between its gray cardboard covers were the strips of paper on which Himmler, in his own spidery handwriting, noted down the agenda for his next meeting with Hitler. I still have in my notes the verbatim text of two Himmler wrote in September 1939. The first one says: "380 Jews to be shot in Ostrowo." The second: "Archbishop of Lublin and 13 priests to be brought to Germany for execution." Each of the points Himmler submitted to Hitler for his decision is ticked off and underneath, again in his own hand, the SS chief always records the words: *"Führer sagt Ja"* *(Führer says yes").*

I came to think of that file again years later, when the writer David Irving argued in one of his books that Hitler knew nothing about the mass murder of the Jews. According to him, Himmler alone was responsible for the Final Solution. As if the man who did not dare to order the shooting of a "mere" 380 Jews in Ostrowo without Hitler's prior consent would have dared to order the killing of millions without the Führer first having said *ja!*

It was a relief to return to daylight and breathe fresh

air again. But, provided Sely and Helm agreed, I wanted to return to Wasserkäfersteig again as soon as possible with a party of German journalists. The only publicity the Docs Center had had so far, Warren told me, had been the brief press release issued when it became operational. Not enough, I thought. The more the German public knew about it the better. In spite of Public Safety's suspicions about our "excessive zeal," we took no pleasure in catching out *Fragebogen* falsifiers, nor did we prosecute them in a "spirit of revenge." People should know that this game was no longer worth the candle. Once the articles had appeared in German newspapers I intended to have them cut out, mounted on cardboard, and displayed in our waiting room. Nobody could then, like Viek, say he had not been warned.

By the time I had thought all this through I was back in Schlüterstrasse. Full of my bright idea I rushed up the stairs and into our office, but as Sely had a visitor I had to rein in my eagerness to tell him about it.

The stranger, a tall and handsome man I guessed to be in his early thirties, got up; Sely introduced us, we shook hands. I did not understand the name but was too shy to say so. I sat down behind my desk and they resumed their conversation. I took a closer look at the caller. His very fair hair was combed straight back from his forehead; his nose, without being too fleshy, was strong and straight; his lips were generous and sensuous; his chin firmly boned, longish, and somewhat pointed; but his eyes struck me most. Of lightish, almost watery, blue and slightly veiled, they were like two-way mirrors; he, looking out, took in everything, but no one looking into them could penetrate his thoughts. By type he seemed to me more Scandinavian than German and, though Sely and he spoke in that language, I wondered which he was.

His self-assurance, obvious joie-de-vivre, quick, apt, and humorous repartee were qualities not generally associated with either Danes or Swedes. For Germans, at least those I had come across, they were even more exceptional. And so was the free, easy, and natural way in which he chatted with Sely. They conversed as equals—not at all the norm in encounters between British occupation officers and Germans. If that impressed me, then the man's knowledge of the British press, and in particular his understanding of the importance of human interest, which he and Sely were then discussing, impressed me even more.

Eventually they started gossiping about our PR/ISC colleagues. As I had so far met only a few of them, most were just names to me. Nick Huijsman, for instance. According to our apparently very well-informed visitor this reputedly brilliant Lancaster House press supremo was a gifted artist with a somewhat morbid penchant for painting bleeding hands. Next they discussed the new and highly controversial German magazine *Der Spiegel*, originally started as *Diese Woche (This Week)* by twenty-one-year-old Major Chaloner of Hanover Information Control. Its outspokenness so upset Whitehall and Lancaster House that the British authorities washed their hands of it and transferred it to German licensees. Finally, having gossiped their way through most of the PR/ISC establishment, they got around to Ken Kirkness, the head of the Book Section. Him I had met. Sely seemed puzzled by his guest's keen interest in that retired colonel.

"Why are you so fascinated by Kirkness?" he asked. "You don't have much to do with him."

"No, very little, but, you know, thinking about the future," the visitor smiled, "I'd like to get the name and address of his tailor. He's the British Empire's best-dressed representative in the whole of Germany. Now that you must admit. He's a picture-book English gentleman from top to toe; the cut of his trousers is simply . . . breathtaking."

True enough, but for the fact that Kirkness was of course a Scotsman, too fine a distinction even for someone from Hamburg, from where I had meanwhile learned our visitor came—a city said to be so Anglophile that they unfurl their umbrellas there whenever it rains in London. But the suits, mostly tweeds, in which trimly moustachioed Ken Kirkness, every inch the former cavalry officer, clad his slim six-foot frame, were indeed cut by the very best scissors of Savile Row. And those drainpipe trousers that encased his long legs were not only wonders of bespoke tailoring, but so skintight that putting them on and taking them off had to be a twice-daily triumph of mind over matter.

"Wouldn't you like to know how he gets in and out of them?" I said.

"You're absolutely right," he laughed. "I've been wondering about it for quite some time. Do you know?"

I shook my head. But that little joke, the first words I had spoken, had somehow established a rapport between us. And as I noticed how well dressed our—as I now knew—German visitor was, he immediately read my thoughts. Pointing to his sports jacket—he wore it English fashion with gray slacks and well-polished brown brogues—he said, "No, Mr. Clare. Not black market. All from Fritz Simon, an old schoolfriend of mine who emigrated to London."

When he had left I said to Kaye, "You know, in all that time I didn't get his name. I gathered he's German and a magazine publisher, but who is he?"

"Axel Springer, the Hamburg publisher. Don't tell me you haven't heard of him."

"No, never."

"Well, don't worry, you will—and plenty," Kaye said.

What I would then have described as Axel Springer's overwhelming charm—*charisma*, the more appropriate word, was not yet part of everyday language—made a strong impact on me, as with a few exceptions it did on everybody. For instance, on the Major Barnetson who gave Springer his first license. Later, as Lord Barnetson, chairman of Reuters and United Newspapers, he liked to tell the story of his first meeting with, as he put it, a "charmingly hard-headed" license applicant, "the most successful and one of the most agreeable of my protégés." That was in 1946 and Major Barnetson, having spent a long, hot summer day listening to license applicants, all of whom had bored him with stories about their— true or fictitious—dislike for the Third Reich, about their—true or fictitious—sufferings under the Nazi regime, was tired and longing for a cool drink in his mess when the last candidate entered his office. To cut short the expected long story about his Nazi experiences Barnetson greeted him with the question: "Now tell me, who's been persecuting you?" He never forgot Axel Springer's reply: "To tell you the truth, Major, only the women."

One of the exceptions not bowled over by Axel Springer's charm was Nick Huijsman. When in the autumn of 1947 Springer talked to him about a license to publish a Hamburg evening paper, Huijsman, saying, "I'm not in the business of creating German press lords, Herr Springer," refused it.

I, captivated by him, wanted his friendship and hoped he liked me too. He did, and he told me so: thirty-two years after our first meeting, in a letter he sent me on the twenty-fifth anniversary of my joining his publishing group. When it came to revealing his personal feelings Axel Springer was never overhasty.

Yet in early March 1947 the thought that this, or any other, German could one day be my boss would not have occurred to me in my wildest dreams, not even had I known that PR/ISC's high-ups were planning major staff reductions.

When I rejoined the group in February it employed 500 British personnel—130 in PR, 370 in ISC. This total was to be cut to 400 by April 1, another 100 were to go by the beginning of October, and by April 1948 the group was intended to have a strength of 250. Such a rapid rundown required a thorough reassessment of PR/ISC's functions and organization. The most active of the reorganizers was the director of PR and (temporary) full colonel J.D.A. Lamont, the bane of Pat Lynch's early life in the Berlin Information Control Unit. He buried HQ under an avalanche of planning papers, a keenness possibly motivated by the point he made in the final paragraph of each of his submissions. It was that he as a military officer was paid £20 less per month than the equivalent civilian grade and was, therefore, thinking of resigning. His higher-paid opposite number—Michael Balfour, the civilian director of Information Services Control—eventually put a stop to Lamont's laments with a memo he sent the chief. Expressing himself with the elegance of the professional historian, which he was, Balfour wrote:

> The plethora of plans for the reorganization or disorganization of the group are a tribute equally to the fecundity of my colleagues' imagination and to the leisure they enjoy. . . . I have been acting on the assumption that we are in Germany not just to prevent the singing of the "Horst Wessel Lied," etc., but to drive some ideas into German heads . . .

This was not what concerned Lamont and his PR crew, who were in Germany to drive ideas about the sagacity of British policy into the heads of British journalists. Balfour's words highlighted the Pushmi-Pullyou character of that curious two-headed animal that PR/ISC was.

17

"We Are Not in Germany Forever!"

This PR/ISC Pushmi-Pullyou, unlike dear Dr. Dolittle's, was no gentle beastie. In their futile quarrel over which of them deserved to be in front, its two heads, PR and ISC, kept growling and snapping at each other.

PR's job was to gloss over the fact that Whitehall's policies for Germany, so vacillating and supine in Hitler's days that—*pace* Clausewitz—war was the only possible other means *not* to continue them, were once again confused, uncoordinated, and often contradictory, not least because too many cooks were stirring its German broth. Nominally John Hynd, the minister for Germany, was the chef, but in truth this third-rank Labor politician was little more than a kitchen help. With the secretary of state for war as his superior and without a seat in the Cabinet poor Hynd was a prime example of responsibility without power. In a Commons debate on Germany a fellow MP, summing up Hynd's character and position, remarked: "The Honorable Gentleman must, I am sure, have something of the sensation of a minnow floating among the whales." Painful but true, because Labor's leviathans, Attlee, Bevin, and Cripps, paid scant attention to his views and Hynd fared no better with the several senior British officers in Germany, who were out of sympathy with the policies of the socialist government.

A German historian writing in 1980 about the obscurity of British decision making for Germany observed:

> On present knowledge it is difficult to ascertain which persons or institutions determined British occupation policies. Most influential were: Bevin; his deputy McNeil in the Foreign Office, the secretary of state for war; the head of the Control Office for Germany and Austria, John Hynd followed by Lord Pakenham; the military governors: Viscount Montgomery, Sir Sholto Douglas, Sir Brian Robertson. Bevin, presumably, laid down the basic guidelines, but how far he could influence important single decisions is uncertain, and one can only make assumptions as to how closely the military governors followed War or Foreign Office directives.*

To the skeptical British correspondents accredited to the Control Commission, PR had to present this maze—albeit with checkered success—as a rectilinear channel for the smooth flow of wise and determined policies. Whitehall, fixated by the effect of press power on political and civil-service careers, saw this as the group's foremost mission and so PR, favored by the powers-that-be and a bumptious creature by nature, believed itself to be the forehead of PR/ISC.

Information Services Control rightly and sharply dis-

---

*Hans-Peter Schwartz, *Vom Reich zur Bundesrepublik* (Stuttgart: Klett-Cotta, 1980).

puted this. And its task—to change permanently (as far as possible together with Britain's allies) the mentality of the defeated but in every respect highly sophisticated German nation—was not only without precedent in all history but of vital importance to the future not just of a few Whitehall panjandrums. Though a seemingly Herculean chore, it was not as impossible as it sounds. The poison of Nazism, through the metamorphosis of its devastating failure, had changed into its own antidote. Beyond that, in all walks of life and in every field of activity, there were Germans, those of the previously silenced minority, who remembered and wanted to restore a Germany where not one man but the law ruled supreme. With their help the much ridiculed concept of "re-education" was made to work, all the better the further the victors stepped back to allow time and the Germans themselves to complete what they had begun. Hence ISC's most urgent job—Michael Balfour said as early as August 1946: "We are in Germany for a limited time, not forever"—was to find those Germans to whom it could gradually transfer its own responsibilities, mindful of Balfour's other warning: "The trouble is that it is always the wrong Germans who make capital of the actions of the good Germans."

Views similar to those expressed by Hugh Carleton Greene—another high PR/ISC official who made a lasting contribution to postwar Germany—after he took over as broadcasting controller for the British Zone from one Rex Palmer, whose reign over Nord-West-Deutscher-Rundfunk, Germany's biggest radio station, had been nothing short of disastrous. Palmer's ignorance of broadcasting—his professional qualification was that he had been the BBC's pre-war *Children's Hour* "Uncle Rex"—was only exceeded by his ignorance of Germany. Carleton Greene was an expert on both. The *Daily Telegraph*'s Berlin correspondent before the war and during it the head of the BBC's German Service, his name and voice were familiar to the millions of Germans who had secretly listened to his broadcasts during the war. In October 1946, in his first address to his staff, he summed up his policy in one startling sentence. "I am here to make myself superfluous," he said, convinced, as he explained many years later in his essay "The Rebuilding of German Broadcasting," that "the future lay with the Germans." But, like Balfour, he too had to ensure that he put it into the hands of the right Germans. "I had to deal with some awkward staff problems," he—by then Sir Hugh Greene and BBC Director-General—wrote in that paper, "because the availability of documentation showed that some senior members of the staff had falsified the questionnaires they had to fill up and had a past in the Nazi party. There had to be some painful surgery."

Kaye and I were his scalpel-wielding consultants.

Junior reporters, writers, and executives, I interviewed on my own at the Nord-West-Deutscher-Rundfunk HQ in Hamburg's Rothenbaumchaussee. Those who had been in the Hitler Youth and had said so on their *Fragebogen* got immediate clearance. But the young man who came in wearing the uniform of a tram conductor—he was doing a broadcast on what it was like to work on Hamburg's overcrowded public transport—presented me with a problem I had not come across before. My impression of him was of high intelligence and patent honesty, yet there it was: according to the U.S. Docs Center he had not only been in the Hitler Youth, as he had stated, but in the party too. Genuine surprise, even horror registered on his face when I showed him the copy of his NSDAP central register index card.

"There's no way I can explain this," he said. "I swear I know nothing about it and never applied. The date given here for the start of my membership is that of my eighteenth birthday. I can tell you exactly what happened on that day. I was conscripted into the army and was a soldier until British troops took me prisoner just outside Hamburg. I never paid any membership dues. Believe me, if I had known anything about it I would have said so."

I did not doubt he was speaking the truth, especially as the Docs Center—in spite of Sergeant Major Warren's remark that no one ever unknowingly became a party member—had been unable to trace his application form. I told him to carry on pending further inquiries, but where or with whom I could make those I had no idea.

Senior staff Kaye and I interviewed jointly, always in Hugh Greene's office and always in his presence. His then still slim over-six-foot frame comfortably curled up on a settee at the back of the room, he just listened without ever interfering or saying a word either during or after an interrogation. I felt much too junior to ask him why he—unlike all other high British officials—did this, but guessed, correctly as Hugh confirmed in 1983 at our last meeting before his death, that his motive was to look after his staff and also to ensure that no one we interviewed could later claim he had been roughly handled.

The toughest case we ever had to crack was that of Hans Zielinski, one of Hugh's leading employees. He was an editor in the politically sensitive news department, but thanks to a strong personality and keen intellect his influence in NWDR went well beyond that function. Kaye and I had first met him socially over coffee in the office of Major Rolf James, one of Hugh's deputies. Although his looks—thinning blond hair, pale bluish eyes, sharp nose, longish face with dueling scars—were those of a Heydrich-type Nazi intellectual, one quickly forgot his unappealing appearance in conversation with him. His political and professional views sounded neither recently acquired nor superficial and were refreshingly free of democratic Newspeak clichés or the usual self-pitying laments. His frank and constructive criticism not so much of the policies but of some of the practices of the occupying power further enhanced his image as a man of courage, a man one could trust.

Then came the shock of the Documents Center check. An active functionary of the National Socialist Students' League at university, Zielinski had joined the NSDAP in 1931 and from early 1932 till the summer of 1933 he was also a brownshirt stormtrooper. He resigned his party membership in 1936. None of this was stated on his *Fragebogen*, where the only membership mentioned was that of a Catholic Student Fraternity.

Hugh on his settee, Kaye and I behind his desk, we waited for Zielinski to come in. Ignoring his outstretched hand Kaye ordered rather than told him to sit down. Then, without any further ado, he read out every single question on Zielinski's *Fragebogen* together with his reply. That over, we remained silent, a standard ploy, which unsettled most people, but not Zielinski. After a little while he said: "Would you mind telling me, Herr Major, what this is all about. My memory's quite good, you know, and I remember perfectly what I wrote on my questionnaire."

Giving him a dark and piercing Torquemada look Kaye replied: "I'm glad to hear it. We'll now go through each question once more and you answer it verbally. Mr. Carleton Greene, Mr. Clare, and I want to hear the truth, I repeat . . . the truth, from your own mouth."

Zielinski, sounding completely self-assured, answered each question exactly as he had done in writing. There were no hesitations, no circular replies, no "howevers." At the end Kaye said: "Would it surprise you, Herr Zielinski, if I called you the most accomplished liar I've ever come across?"

"Yes," he said, "it would. I am and have been an anti-Nazi. I have protected and helped Jews, and though I hate to mention this and only do so now because of what you've just said, my wife is half-Jewish. That, Herr Major, is the truth."

We showed him the copy of his NSDAP membership entry. "I'm sorry," he said, "but this has nothing to do with me. God knows why or how my name and dates got in there. I repeat I was not a Nazi. If you give me time I can bring you written testimonials about my behavior during the Nazi years. From Germans whose democratic past is beyond doubt and from Jewish refugees abroad as well. Will you give me the time to do this?"

He looked to Hugh Greene for support, but he, pointing at Kaye and me, indicated that the decision was ours.

"All right, let's do it your way," Sely agreed. "You get those papers and we'll meet again."

After Zielinski had left he turned to Hugh Greene. "I did not show him all the documents," he said. "They'll have more impact if we come out with them one by one. Slowly, slowly catchee this monkey. So let's keep our ammunition dry. In any case I think that calm of his is a sham. He's been shaken."

Kaye underestimated Zielinski. Generally we dismissed the so-called *Persilscheine*, washing "Whiter-than-White" certificates, with contempt. Nearly every Nazi produced some saying what a good human being he was, and many, almost right the way up the party hierarchy, somehow managed to find pet Jews abroad willing to testify that they had been decent, even helpful. But Zielinski's *Persilscheine* could not be disregarded so easily. They were from German politicians, academics, and artists of impeccable reputation; and the Jewish refugees in the United States and Britain who vouched for him

were men whose names meant something in pre-Hitler
Germany.

At each subsequent interrogation, we confronted Zielinski with a new document, but he steadfastly stuck to
his lies. We tried to unnerve him by letting him believe,
though we never explicitly said so, that we were about
to give up. Then we suddenly recalled him. It did make
him more insecure, yet he never contradicted himself
during cross-examination and seemed to have near total
recall of every question we had asked and of his reply:
no, he had never been a member of the party; no, he had
never knowingly signed an application form; no, he
had not been a brownshirt; no, no, no! Eventually, con-
ceding that our documentary evidence was impressive,
he stressed that it was no more than circumstantial and
as British law did not require him to prove his innocence
but us to prove his guilt why, he asked, did we not bring
him before a Military Government court so that a judge
could decide. That, of course, was the one thing we did
not want to risk without a signed confession. Told somewhat sharply that it was not for him to tell us our business, he apologized.

Our views on Zielinski differed. Kaye saw him purely
as a liar who had fraudulently wormed himself into an
important job with the occupying power. This was true,
yet though I of course agreed that he had to be removed,
I thought that the motive for this dishonesty lay deeper
and was more complex. That he had atoned for the errors
of his youth long ago and worked against the Nazis had
been confirmed by all those who had vouched for him,
by the fact that he had left the SA almost immediately
after the anti-Jewish boycott of 1933 and had resigned
from the party in 1936, the year of the Rhineland occupation and the Olympic Games, when Hitler's star was
rising fast. I, being younger and more idealistic than
Kaye, felt some sympathy for this man and regretted that

he should have got himself into such a mess. I think Zielinski sensed it and this may have influenced the outcome of his fifth and final interrogation.

Sely being on leave, I was alone, except of course for Hugh in his corner. I started by going over all the old ground once more. What else was there to do? But when we got around to that signature on his membership application he admitted for the first time that it could be his. He had thought a lot about it, he explained, and a vague recollection—like a scene in a dream—of a fraternity evening after a dueling session had come back.

"We were all drunk," he said, "and I think I passed out in the end. But before that I seem to remember somebody pushing a pen into my hand and telling me to sign something. I had no idea what it was at the time but thinking about it now it does seem likely to have been that application. So, there it is. I heard no more about it and forgot the whole thing."

He was, I thought, halfway there and it occurred to me that we had never yet confronted him with all our documents at the same time. Like a poker player putting his hand on the table I laid them all out on the desktop, one next to the other: his index card from the Central Register, his NSDAP membership pass with his photo showing the swastika badge in his buttonhole, his application form, his SA and National Socialist Students' League identity cards.

"There you are," I said, "just look at this display. Look at your photo. I'm not saying you are a Nazi—you were and you changed your views—but you did get your job here by false pretenses. That's what all this is about. We didn't use voodoo to conjure up these documents and you know it, but if you want to go on playing games . . ."

He interrupted me by raising his right hand as if to

swear an oath, and then dropped it in a gesture of dejection.

"No, I won't ," he said. "Give me a piece of paper and I'll write out my confession."

I turned around. Hugh was sitting stiffly upright, shaking his head in disbelief. Nothing was said. We watched Zielinski writing and when he finished Hugh came over and witnessed his signature.

"Why now?" I asked Zielinski.

"Time to make an end of it," he said. "I've had enough." That was all. I did not press him any further.

Including Zielinski, twelve former Nazis were eliminated from Hugh's staff. Zielinski got a six-month sentence but eventually returned to journalism.

"There is no reason," Sir Hugh Greene wrote, looking back on his two years in Germany, "for those of us who worked in broadcasting in the British Zone after the war to feel that we wasted our time. We did not attain our ideal, or, if we did, only for a fleeting moment. But we did wrench German broadcasting away from both its Weimar and its Nazi roots and we did provide a new structure, even if some things we cherished were later abandoned, much to the regret, I may say, of many Germans . . . if one thinks in terms of 're-education' it was not in every way an unsuccessful operation."

And Germany acknowledged the role he had played. After his death German television broadcast a one-and-a-half-hour documentary on Hugh's life and work.

Although Hugh spoke specifically—and in nicely understated terms—of the British contribution to German broadcasting, the very same words could be used to sum up what Information Services Control as a whole achieved in postwar Germany. It did provide new structures, it did introduce new ideas, it did place good Germans into important functions and as far as possible prevented bad Germans from "making capital of them." But though it could keep them out for a time it could not keep them out forever; and the transfer of responsibilities, including denazification, to the newly established German authorities produced some unfortunate results.

At this point, even though it means jumping twelve months forward in my story's chronology, it is relevant, especially in the context of the Zielinski case, to mention the denazification of one of those big Nazi fish who kept swimming around the net while the Allies had direct control and then surfaced after German panels had taken over. I am talking about the lawyer Dr. Rolf Rienhardt.

Rienhardt joined the Nazi Party in 1923, when he was a twenty-year-old law, economics, and history student at Berlin University. After graduation he quickly made a name for himself as an outstandingly able lawyer and when he was twenty-five he became legal adviser to Franz Eher Verlag, the NSDAP-owned publishing enterprise. He also defended Hitler in a number of court cases, but his rapid climb to the top branches of the Nazi tree only began after Hitler's World War I sergeant major, Reichsleiter Max Amann, party member No. 2, boss of Eher Verlag and one of the very few men who were on close personal terms with the Führer, appointed Rienhardt his chief of staff, or *Stabsleiter*. In some cases the holders of that rank were just glorified butlers who helped their bosses into their overcoats and sent flowers to their mistresses; in others, as in Rienhardt's, they wielded real power. Without him Amann, a brutal, brainless, and uncouth drunkard, could never, not even after 1933, have made Eher Verlag into the biggest publishing empire in all German history. But his *Stabsleiter*, employing methods that varied from plain but always elegantly phrased blackmail to shrewd, sometimes well-hidden, political, financial, and legal manipulations, acquired for Eher, in addition to giants like Ullstein, also hundreds of newspaper publishers big and small up and down the country. After ten years Amann headed a group publishing 350 titles with a combined circulation of twenty million. Yet all the while the former sergeant major's jealousy of his able assistant grew in proportion to his empire, and in 1943 he used his influence with Hitler to remove Rienhardt. Struck off the list of men excused military service, the newspaper takeover genius was called up. Still a staunch Nazi he volunteered for the Waffen-SS and was given a commission in Himmler's elite corps.

This, in brief, was the history of the man who appeared before a Bielefeld denazification court in March 1948 and was acquitted. The comment of the Berlin daily *Der Morgen* on this astonishing verdict is representative of the view of most German newspapers.

> Rienhardt [that paper wrote] was not only the grave-digger but the hangman of the German press. That Amann kicked him out in 1943, when he had completed his mission, does not excuse him. That sort of behavior was normal among the bigwigs of the Third Reich. Rienhardt's defense that he was merely Amann's legal adviser was believed by the judges. Just as they believed his claim that he was conscripted against his will into the Waffen-SS, when in fact he volunteered for service with the Leibstandarte Adolf Hitler, Hitler's personal SS Regiment. Rienhardt's acquittal merely proves the inadequacy of these proceedings. If this man is allowed to go unpunished then the fate of thousands of small-time

> Nazi fellow travelers who were dealt with much
> more harshly is inexcusably unjust.

Such words of censure Rienhardt took in his stride—all
the way up the ladder of a successful postwar career.
Bielefeld having been so good to him he stayed there as
managing director of *Westfälische Zeitung*, a local newspaper, until he joined the much bigger South German
magazine publishing house of Burda in the same capacity. Leaving in 1958 he became a director of the Frankfurt
advertising agency William Heumann and after Heumann was taken over by Mather & Crowther—today
Ogilvy & Mather—in 1963 he retained his seat on the
board. Indeed, in terms of recent German history, Rienhardt was a man for all its seasons.

Of course others of his ilk came crawling out of the
scorched timbers of their Nazi past. Their reappearance
and the leniency with which they were treated—our old
friend Hans Hinkel, one of the vilest of the breed, was
eventually categorized a "minor criminal"—caused
much concern among Allies and Germans alike, but
none of these Nazis—even had they wanted to—could
have turned back the wheels of history. By 1948, after
two and a half years of occupation, Anglo-American policies had taken root, especially in the media field, where
the carefully selected publishers and journalists who
were now in the saddle had a vested interest in keeping
out yesterday's men. But over and above that, the ideal
of press freedom was neither foreign nor a novelty for
Germany, even if it emerged in that country rather by
order from above than by struggle from below. That the
press should be free Frederick II ordained in 1740. Five
days after he had ascended the Prussian throne he told
his—no doubt stunned—chef du cabinet, Count Pode-
wils, that "The gazettes, if they are to be interesting,
must not be interfered with!"

Now, there's many a slip betwixt the cup filled with the heady draft of press freedom and a prince's lip service to it, a rule to which Prussia's enlightened autocrat was no exception. Of course Frederick the Great interfered with the "gazettes" whenever it suited him, but, being ahead of his time in this as in so many things, he on the whole preferred manipulation through disinformation to censorship. The resulting ambivalent relationship between state and fourth estate continued for another two centuries, but from then on, whenever authority and press collided, the latter quoted the old king's immortal sentence as defense of free speech—sometimes, but by no means always, to good effect. Eventually German newspapers protected themselves not only with such august sentiments but also with the ingenious invention of a novel editorial function—that of the *Sitzredakteur*. Responsible for editorial content, this gentleman wrote no line and edited no copy, but it was he who sat in the dock if the paper was taken to court and—if unlucky—finally in a prison cell. Everybody of course knew what a farce this was, and by and by it became so embarrassing that even the most powerful thought twice before invoking the law against an obstreperous journal; Bismarck, for instance, did nothing when Leopold Ullstein denounced the chancellor's policies in his newspaper in 1878. "We want constitutional government," the founding father of Germany's greatest publishing dynasty wrote, "not chancellor absolutism. We demand that Germans be treated as a free people and not as a vanquished nation!"

Strong stuff, but the uncannily prophetic leader written for a Berlin newspaper on the eve of World War I was even more outspoken. "In a few days," it said,

> tension will have turned into catastrophe ... the saber-rattlers sniff glory and once our military open

their mouths our politicians will do as they are told
... hence, before it is too late: the warmongers' cal-
culations are wrong. The Triple Alliance is nothing.
Italy is not going to get into this war, and if it does
it will not be on our side. Britain is not going to
remain neutral ... she will not permit our armies to
march through Belgium. If Britain fights us then the
whole English-speaking world, particularly the
United States, will join the battle. Britain is respected, if not loved, everywhere. Something that
cannot be said about ourselves. Japan is not going to
attack Russia, more likely us, and the Habsburg empire does not have the military strength to deal with
Serbia, never mind anybody else. Whether we shall
be the victors at the end of this most terrible of all
wars must remain an open question. But even if we
do we shall have won nothing. The only victor will
be Britain. We will have one million corpses, two
million cripples, and a debt of fifty billion. That and
nothing else will be the final balance sheet of this
war.

Actually this article was never published. By the time it
went to the printers on July, 30, 1914, the military had
opened their mouths and imposed military censorship
throughout the Reich. But that is not the point. That it
would have been printed had it been ready twenty-four
hours earlier, that is. Germans knew what press freedom
meant and from 1918 to 1933, the fifteen years of the Weimar Republic, they enjoyed (or abhorred) the freest in the
world. Men like Goebbels, Amann, and Rienhardt could
"interfere with the gazettes," could put them in chains,
but what they could not do was to eradicate the memory
of what a free press was like.

But even if the Rienhardts were no danger, should they
have been allowed so soon to obtain positions of some
influence again? Of course not, in an ideal world, but in

the real world the Western powers by then had no choice, because the rules of the German game had changed. In the struggle between East and West, in the struggle for Germany, the defeated had become the potential allies. The West was about to bury the past, while the East decided to disinter and use what it mistakenly considered to be politically still potent for its own purposes. This was the theme of Colonel Tulpanov's address to senior staff of the Socialist Unity Party's political academy in the spring of 1948

> The Soviet Military Administration [he explained] recently reexamined its attitude toward former members and functionaries of the Nazi Party. We concluded that there are useful people among them, although they would not easily fit into the existing political organizations. After some extensive talks with former Nazi functionaries we felt that they ought to play an active part again and we, therefore, have suggested to them that they should found a new party. Collected and united in it, these people could make a worthwhile contribution to the development of the Soviet Zone. This new party, which will probably be called the National Democratic Party, will be given a chance to share in the political development of our Zone.

18

"Cabaret"

Back in Berlin on the evening of the day after the Zielinski breakthrough, I found myself sitting right behind bull-necked-and-shouldered Tulpanov at the Ulenspiegel cabaret in Nürnberger Strasse. Returning in style—one to which I was not at all accustomed—I had motored in from Hamburg that afternoon with Hugh Greene in a dream automobile, the super-smart red-leather-upholstered black Maibach tourer he had "inherited" from SS General Karl Wolff, Himmler's court favorite and onetime chief of staff.

Chatting during the journey we discovered a shared affection for the cabaret, and Hugh, who was going to the Ulenspiegel that evening, invited me to come along. What we meant by "cabaret" were not the erotic/neurotic nightclub revues so much the rage in Isherwood's Berlin of the twenties and early thirties, decadent, vulgar rather than comic, even depressing—

like the contemporary drawings and paintings of a George Grosz, which, intending to denounce a corrupt world, merely added yet another dimension to it—but the political, satirical, and musical one à la Ulenspiegel, the best in Berlin. Its sketches were written and its music composed or adapted by Günter Neumann, a wizard of wit and irony, a word- and tunesmith of genius. With a few pithy lines of verse, often sung to old popular tunes, which brought back memories of better days, he drowned in waves of laughter floating on a sea of unwept tears: pain, hunger, cold, prostitution, and the black market—the life one lived in Berlin. In the "Little Piccolina" sketch, for instance, of his *Blackmarket Fair* revue that Hugh and I had come to see.

Piccolina, supposed to be of tender age, was pushed on stage in a broken-down pram, climbed out of it, toddled to the footlights, took a pacifier out of her mouth, and sang:

How I hate this misery!
Mummy what have you for me?
Mummy doesn't have a bean
Friend, starvation makes you keen.

Evening came and out I went
Stood about till heaven-sent,
Came an Ami pleasure-bent.

Me, outside the coffeehouse,
Wriggled bum to arouse.
I will not a ninny be
So let's forget my puberty

Oh, oh my dear! Oh, oh my Johnny
One-two-three I was his honey.
Never criticize the Allies
That would be oh, so unwise.

Johnny took me like a lady
And we traded—nothing shady,
Two pounds coffee so I'd do it,

Fruit-juice cans so I'd renew it.
Hot we got with burning skins
For a couple corned-beef tins
But for chocolate—Hershey bar,
I went further much than far.

Mummy, Mummy, oh, my tummy!
I want herrings, sour pickle
In my womb I feel a tickle.
Life is really rather rummy
I, myself, shall be a mummy.

There was no trace of German self-pity in Neumann's texts. On the contrary, he was sharply though wittily critical of his fellow countrymen, but also had the courage to laugh at the Allies. Caricaturing the Americans and their fear of offending Soviet sensibilities—at least in the cultural field they then still handled the Russians with kid gloves—Neumann had on stage a Major Gagson as an American Theater officer and a Major Tolpatschoff as his Soviet opposite. Both talk about the cultural joys each of them imports for "his" Berliners, but the film version of *Ninotchka* will not be among them. Gagson explains why:

Films we send in endless flow
Ninotchka with Garbo though
We keep back in Hollywood.
Wouldn't have been "charasho"
To upset dear "Uncle Joe."

Tulpanov loved this. He fell about laughing, slapped his thighs in delight, and finally stood up, a one-man ovation. Some Germans began to move uneasily in their seats, wondering what was the wiser course—to be or not to be on their feet with Tulpanov. But before they had made up their minds the colonel sat down, having first shaken the hand of the American officer nearest to him, the last gesture of Soviet-American amity I witnessed in Berlin.

Ulenspiegel's triumphant success added much to the luster of Berlin's Golden Hunger Years. But then this city, so racked by fear and uncertainty, was naturally fertile soil for the political cabaret, which flourishes best in times of upheaval. Born in the atmosphere of intellectual unease that existed in Germany just before the outbreak of World War I, it flowered—albeit with cautiously forked-tongue double-speak—in the Berlin nightclub Katakombe during the early Hitler years and reached new heights in the perplexed pre-Anschluss Vienna of my teenage years. Significantly it did not transplant to insular and self-assured Britain until an awareness of painful and unsettling decline seeped into public consciousness in the early 1960s, the time of *Beyond the Fringe* and *That Was the Week That Was*, the latter the baby and pride of the BBC's then Director-General Sir Hugh Greene, who, as a young *Daily Telegraph* correspondent, fell in love with the Katakombe, and—incidentally—also with Tatyana Sais, its most famous diseuse, the widow of Günter Neumann and later Lady Greene.

Friedrich Luft, now the doyen of Berlin's critics, then a young journalist at the beginning of a distinguished career, described with great perspicacity what the Ulenspiegel meant to his fellow Berliners in 1947:

> Freedom in Berlin, carefully supervised as it was by the four occupying powers, was not all that free. Anyone who, like Günter Neumann, wanted to direct the searchlight beam of satire on to the prob-

lems of that time and make people not only laugh at his jokes but also think, had to tread very carefully. He was dancing on raw eggs. How easily could he have stepped on the landmine of Allied displeasure. The uniformed controllers had a somewhat limited sense of humor. Why should it have been otherwise?

But even so Neumann knew how to knock the new ideologues and the humorless prophets of a new one-sidedness. He showed us how poor we were, how hungry, how we longed for hope. But in such a way that we could laugh about it. He spelled out the truth without pity and yet he gave us consolation and new hope. And we guffawed our pleasure and agreement.

I remember clearly that I went to the premiere in a pair of borrowed shoes because I only possessed a pair of worn sneakers. When I returned the shoes to the friend who had lent them to me I tried to convey to him something of the sensational success of that first performance. I summed it up by saying that Neumann had given us new insights into deadly serious topics and by never falling into the trap of maudlin silliness he had cheered us all up. It was a theatrical miracle.

Cheering up was what Berlin needed. Every day I saw weedy men with hollow-cheeked bony faces and sunken eyes bent between the shafts of wheeled pushcarts—rickshaws for the terminal journey of the corpse in the wooden crate on them—shuffle toward cemeteries where, all too often, their load had to be dumped to await burial till the granite-frozen earth had softened. Close on sixty thousand people, mostly the elderly and the very young, died of cold and hunger during that winter of 1947. And all the time, even after the frost had gone and a warming sun shone from a blue sky, fear, fear of the Soviets, hung like a black thundercloud over the city. Now that was a feeling I understood. Fear has been ingrained in the Jewish race-memory at least since Roman legionaries shouting "Hep, hep, hep!" *("Hyronimo est perdita"*— Jerusalem is destroyed") drove my far-distant ancestors to the four corners of the earth. And I had a thorough refresher course in it when the "Perish Judah!"–screaming Nazi columns marched through Vienna. So I observed as something of a connoisseur how the Soviets used fear to further their aims in Berlin and how their techniques differed from those of the Nazis.

The Russians were cleverer. Cruelty for them was not an end in itself nor brutality its own purpose—and, therefore, purposeless. Torture, though they used it, did not give them master-race orgasms. It was a tool to achieve an end. Twice defeated in elections but still determined to bring the whole city under their control, they used fear to undermine the population's inner powers of resistance. Their message was not that it was better to be red than dead with a bullet in the neck, but that it was wiser to collaborate than to be kidnapped. So they began to "take out" political and human-rights activists who opposed them. It was all over in seconds. A car screeched to a sudden halt, hefty men jumped out, grabbed their victim, bundled him into their vehicle, and before those who witnessed it could even begin to comprehend what had happened, they were racing off in the direction of the Soviet Sector. There, of course, such dramatics were unnecessary—people just disappeared.

After every kidnapping in the Western sectors their commandants sent protest notes to their Russian counterpart, General Kotikov, which he promptly rebutted. The Soviet administration had heard no evil, seen no evil, and committed no evil, and—adding insult to injury—he usually pointed out to his colleagues that it was their and not his responsibility to prevent "banditry," the term he used, in their sectors. In one respect, though, these "bandits" showed considerable caution: they never kidnapped a leading Berlin politician whose sudden removal might have aroused world opinion.

These Soviet tactics set off—just as snowdrifts sliding off a mountaintop start avalanches—the mass emigration from Berlin to West Germany. Still a trickle in 1947 it widened, as Russian pressure grew, into a stream that drained the German capital of much of its vitality and also of many of its industries, thereby helping along the German economic miracle. It was hardly what Stalin had intended, but decentralization from Berlin removed managements from the isolating and self-absorbed atmosphere of a great metropolis, and bringing them closer to their markets made them more responsive to their demands.

On the other hand the exodus of artists and intellectuals from Berlin had a painful consequence: provincialization, not just of the cultural life of the capital but of the whole of Germany. Contrary to folklore, the natural habitat of the creative genius is not the solitary garret. Originality sparks brightest when hammered by controversy and argument; the fires of the imagination are often kindled by the shavings of ideas littering the cafés, restaurants, pubs, and clubs of the big city where writers, publishers, painters, actors, their critics, directors, collectors and producers, sellers, and buyers, meet. Away from Berlin and living, often very well, in a diaspora stretching from Hamburg to Munich, Germany's creative community lost much cohesion and productive friction and this—together with the disappearance of the Jews and their extraordinarily fruitful symbiosis with German culture—made the country, once in the forefront of artistic and intellectual achievement, slide down to second rank.

Though we were in no danger, we too began to feel the hardening of Soviet policy. It became noticeable at every level of four-power cooperation, even at such a low one as Kaye's and mine. The first indication of change came when we proposed dinner at the Embassy Club to Brown, Bouquet, and Gouliga. Previously Gouliga always accepted such invitations with pleasure, but this time he mumbled something about his car being in dock for a complete overhaul. Neither Kaye nor I realized then that Gouliga's problem was not mechanical but diplomatic. Kaye, in his usual determined way saying "Fiddlesticks" or words to that effect, told Gouliga we would pick him up at the Soviet HQ in Karlshorst and that Gleicher would drive him back. Gouliga hemmed and hawed a bit, but eventually he said he would come.

Arriving punctually at the Soviet HQ we were directed to the building where Gouliga had his office. In my best Russian—I had started lessons three months earlier—I told the sentry guarding it to let the captain know that we were there. After a few minutes a German-speaking Red Army lieutenant came out to say that Gouliga was in conference and regretted being unable to join us. We did not know it, but it was the beginning of the end of an era.

At our next committee meeting, in the last week of April, Gouliga appeared accompanied by a dark, stocky, and rather unprepossessing sublieutenant. Unlike the captain in his smartly tailored walking-out uniform, this chap wore the Red Army's battledress, a rather shabby high-necked olive-green blouse with breeches of the same color stuck in unpolished black kneeboots.

"Gentlemen," Gouliga said, "I want to introduce Sublieutenant Levin. As from today he is the Soviet representative on the committee. I'm truly sorry to leave, and you know how much I enjoyed working with you, but they've made me deputy director of our new House of Soviet Culture. It'll still be a couple of months or so till the builders are out, but once it's officially opened I want you to come and see it and have lunch with me there. So thank you for your hospitality and friendship and I'll be in touch." He rose and left.

There was a moment of silence. We had received a slap in the face, that much was obvious. What else was the appointment of a sublieutenant, the lowest of the Red Army commissioned ranks, to a committee that had one major, two civilians who ranked as majors, and one who ranked as captain, as its members? Then Kaye, who was in the chair that month, said a few polite words of welcome to Levin and asked if there was anything he would like to say.

Levin nodded. *"Nix Daitsh—Porusski,"* he said.

We understood this to mean that he spoke Russian only and Michel Bouquet asked him in that language whether that was so.

Levin's reply, which Michel translated, was that his own linguistic abilities were neither here nor there. We were an official body, a Kommandatura subcommittee, and each of us should, therefore, speak in his own language, but most certainly not in German. Whether or not the Western representatives used official interpreters was none of his business, but he would certainly do so in future. Furthermore as a Kommandatura committee the only proper place for our meetings was the Kommandatura building. He, therefore, proposed that this meeting be adjourned and reconvened at the Kommandatura. He would make the arrangements and let us know when, at what time and in which committee room we were to meet.

No more was to be said. According to the book he was right. So we all nodded and this meeting, the shortest we ever had, was over.

"At least you don't have to worry about being late for lunch," Bouquet teased Brown.

"I suppose we might as well go to the club now," Sely

said. "Michel, please ask the lieutenant"—he politely dropped the "sub"—"whether he'd like to join us."

Of course the reply was *nyet*, but then Levin, thinking this was a little too blunt, added, "but thank you all the same."

At our Kommandatura sessions Levin proved himself an abominable *nyeti*, saying it with Molotovian frequency and fervor. He did relax a little over lunch in the Kommandatura mess and after he had downed three tumblers of vodka there was even an occasional smile.

I had been officially recognized as Kaye's substitute, but though I occasionally added my ha'penny worth to the discussions my main job was still to take the minutes, to which—strangely—Levin had not objected. But he always took copious notes of his own. If Kaye was on leave I was the British representative, and at the first meeting with me in that role I nearly caused a diplomatic, or rather undiplomatic, incident.

We were discussing the case of an actor from Hamburg, a popular comedian, who was due to appear in a British Sector theater. He had been in the party, but a Hamburg denazification panel, deciding he had been only a nominal member, had cleared him. The whole thing was routine, but Levin was not having any of it.

"The man was a Nazi and if he wants to appear in Berlin he must be cleared by the Schlüterstrasse people first," he said.

I protested.

"What happens in the British Zone does not concern me," Levin replied, "what happens in Berlin does. This city is under four-power control. Your man must be examined by the proper authorities established by the Berlin magistrate and recognized by the Kommandatura."

"But, Lieutenant, nobody has to be denazified twice," I objected, "unless there's new evidence. Do you have such evidence?"

"Nyet."

"So you withdraw your last remark?"

"Nyet."

"Would you please have a look at the regulations, Lieutenant," I said, taking the papers from my file.

"Nyet."

Brown and Bouquet backed me up, but that made no impression on Levin.

I decided to get tough and threw at Levin the names of several actors who had been party members but were appearing in Soviet Sector theaters without prior clearance from the Schlüterstrasse tribunal.

"Irrelevant. Not comparable," was Levin's reply.

I saw, but chose to overlook, Brown's warning glance and said with some vehemence, "That's just too damn silly for words. You in your sector do as you damn well please and here I am sticking to the regulations, something you're so fond of to the last dot on every 'i,' and what do I get from you? One bloody *nyet* after another!"

As the interpreter translated I could see Levin's face begin to redden underneath that permanent five-o'clock shadow of his, but before he could reply Brown stood up and announced it was time for coffee break. Levin nodded agreement.

As we walked down the stairs to the canteen Brown said to me, "No coffee for us, George. We're going out into the fresh air for a little walk. What you need is cooling down."

It was a very pleasant late-spring day and once we were outside in the street, he said, "You're right, of course. One hundred percent. But that's not the point."

"So what is?" I responded. "That bloody man's impossible. Gouliga never behaved like this."

"Now then, why d'you think they shifted Gouliga?" Brown said. "One reason we all know is that they want to downgrade us. There are others. With Gouliga we were still all playing good guys together, and within limits he was allowed to have a mind of his own. He's got good connections and up to a point he could be cooperative. In their terms he's a white man, a party member, educated, a Russian, a Soviet Wasp if you like, and at twenty-eight he's a full captain. Now look at that poor sod Levin. He's a Jew, must be in his latish forties, and he's a sublieutenant. He's scared of putting a foot wrong and so he's exactly what they want—a robot dancing on a tightrope. Gouliga could afford to make a mistake. But not Levin. It's always safer to say *nyet* than *da*, because it's easier to change a no into a yes than the other way around. Levin is a poor shmuck. Don't be tough on him. Let that actor come and if Levin makes a fuss we'll appeal to the cultural affairs committee. But I bet you he'll look the other way. He doesn't really want to know, but if you tell him then you get your *nyet*."

When we resumed the conference I apologized to Levin for having lost my temper. Brown suggested that my heated remarks be struck off the record and Levin said—he really did—*da.*

Gouliga kept his promise and invited us to the House of Soviet Culture. For once we had beaten the Russians to it, because our equivalents, the British Die Brücke reading rooms and the U.S. Amerika House libraries, had opened well ahead of their place. But when we, Ralph Brown, Michel Bouquet, Kaye, and I—Levin of course was not invited—got there we realized why. Our information centers were adequate but functional, but their House of Soviet Culture was what it had always been—a palace. Restored by the Russians to its full eighteenth-century elegance, its fresh coat of light ochre paint gleamed in the June sunlight, its flawless façade was a dazzling contrast to the soot-blackened, burned-out, and bullet-riddled buildings that lined Unter den Linden, once Berlin's most stylish boulevard.

Gouliga met us in the foyer, showed us around the downstairs exhibition halls, and, when we had duly admired everything, led us up a wide, gracefully curving staircase to the first floor. There we entered a circular room where his director and their chief interpreter were awaiting us. The director was stoutish and rather nondescript, but the black-haired and incredibly thin interpreter lady's sharply intelligent face was impressive. The introductions over, two old German waiters in immaculate white jackets shambled in offering on silver trays goblets filled with Crimean champagne. With little gray Hitler moustaches on their pinched and wrinkled faces, that curious pair looked like a couple of former Gauleiters recently released from a Russian internment camp.

The room itself, with white wood-paneling and a big French center window opening on to a balcony surrounded by a black-and-gold-painted wrought-iron balustrade, had the refinement of Frederician-Prussian simplicity. But the round table in the middle with its gold-damask cloth and napkins, valuable antique gold-rimmed white china from the Berliner Porzellan Manufaktur—while the others were busily chatting I had quickly turned over a bread plate and seen the famous mark—a confusing array of silver and a whole regiment of cut-crystal glasses of various shapes and sizes, all of this dwarfed by a big silver bowl with fruit as the centerpiece, was of such over-ornate opulence it was far more Romanov than Hohenzollern. For one moment I wondered whether all this magnificence was an illusion—like believing that communism is about equality—and had the director, raising his glass in the first toast of the day—far too many were to follow—said "Gentlemen, the

Tsar" instead of, as he did, "Gentlemen, to Allied friendship," I would not have been at all surprised.

We sat down. I had Brown on my right and Kaye on
my left. The interpreter lady, whom I had meanwhile
heard speaking French, German, and English with equal
fluency and without a trace of accent, sat between Kaye
and her boss. Michel was next to him on the other side
and Gouliga closed the circle. One waiter put two big
jugs of foaming beer on the table while the other filled
our glasses with vodka. Baskets with bread and rolls,
from the whitest white to darkest brown, were handed
around. The waiters went back into the pantry and returned with bowls of salads: beetroot, potato, tomato,
cucumber, lettuce; jars of various pickles were already
on the table. Then they left to fetch huge platters laden
with everything that swims in sea and river: herrings
smoked and herrings soused, oily tuna and sardines, hal-
ibut in sauce tartare, golden sprats, anchovies brown, jel-
lied carp, and garnished trout. An iced bowl filled to the
brim with caviar was in the center of the platter and
around its edges were slices of salmon and sturgeon
smoked. Good, I thought, a lavish fishy cold lunch, and
I filled my plate. When we had finished the plates were
cleared, new ones brought, and I expected some exciting
Russian pudding to follow.

But instead of dessert new platters were brought in.
On them, bedded on golden aspic and ringed by stuffed
eggs à la Russe, were sliced cold meats and sausages,
hams boiled and cured, roast chicken, supercalorific jel-
lied pig's heads and pâtés.

It all looked so tempting I could not resist, but when
I had emptied my plate I said to Kaye, "I can't eat another bite now. How are you doing?"

Overhearing us the interpreter lady said, "I hope that
isn't true, Mr. Clare. All you've had so far was *Zakuski*,

our traditional Russian hors d'oeuvres. We're only starting. You can't opt out. You'd hurt your host's feelings.
Really! And think of your empire. That wasn't built by
weaklings, now was it?"

I should have had the courage to say, "Nor by me either, dear lady, but though my spirit's willing my stom-
ach isn't," but of course I did not. And so—with stiff
upper lip—I spooned up some of the borsch, battled
through the creamy Boeuf Stroganoff with rice, nibbled
at the orange cream, sipped at the wines, and, woozy in
head and queasy in tummy, finally revolted when they
offered us chocolate cake with the coffee. But in this I
was not alone. Our host the director, Michel, Kaye, and
Gouliga also passed, but that anorexic-looking woman
and the not at all anorexic-looking Ralph Brown demol-
ished a big slice each.

Our table conversation was stilted. Kaye and Ralph
Brown tried to keep it light and jocular, but got little
response from the Russians. Singing for their dinner, I
suppose, they lectured us on the glories of Soviet culture
under the guidance of that great musician, writer, philosopher, and choreographer in the Kremlin. Eventually
Gouliga and his director concentrated on the Russian-
speaking Michel while Kaye and Ralph chatted with the
lady interpreter. She was brilliant. Though talking to
them she did not miss a single one of her boss's words
and every now and then she interrupted to translate what
he had said. After that she smoothly took up their talk
again, unfailingly at the exact point where she had left
it.

Throughout this orgy of gluttony I was always aware
of the waiters. When not serving they stood by the pantry door, their faces expressionless masks. But what went
on in their heads as they watched each of us consume
more calories than they and their families got in a
month? Most of what we ate was German food, their

food, because the Soviets, unlike the British and Americans who imported everything their troops and officials needed, provisioned themselves from the German economy. Would the waiters be allowed to take the leftovers? Afterward I asked our Russian expert Michel. "Oh no," he said, "our three Russian friends will grab them. They don't live like that every day either, you know."

In the setting of Berlin this feast, a truly Potemkinish cook-up, was obscene. What would a Günter Neumann have made of it?

Or of me, for that matter? I had said very little, acting, in spite of Joanna Cantrell's warning never to be more British than the British, the respectful young "Anyone for tennis?" type. Instead of letting the new identity I was in search of grow slowly and naturally I, wanting to be accepted as one of the boys by the PR/ISC establishment, rather forced it—until Mlle. Ganeval, the daughter of Berlin's French commandant, shocked me back into reality.

19

"British!"

Bluntness ran in the Ganeval family, and the general's daughter, that damsel who caused me such distress, had plenty of it, the father's earning him the distinction of having a Berlin bridge named after him. This, the General Ganeval Bridge, spans a section of the motorway to Tegel, the city's principal airport, which but for him might not be there today.

In 1948, when the Western Allies countered the Soviet blockade with the airlift, Berlin's two airfields, Tempelhof in the U.S. and Gatow in the British sectors, became dangerously congested; to have a third one was imperative. There was a landing strip at Tegel in the French Sector, but it was too short for the big, heavily laden planes. And slap in the middle of the ground needed for a runway extension stood two extraterritorial obstacles—the broadcasting masts of Soviet-controlled Radio Berlin. What could be done about them? While the diplomats dithered Ganeval had his sappers blow up the transmitters. When the deed was done the livid General Kotikov, demanding to know how on earth Ganeval could have done such a thing, got the reply: "Why, with dynamite of course, mon cher!"

In the summer of 1947 the general gave a gala dinner at the French Officers' Club in Frohnau for the famous Italian film director Roberto Rossellini, who was in Berlin shooting his *Germany—Anno Zero*. I was delighted when the elegant French officer with golden adjutant's aiguillettes, who showed me to my table, informed me that Mlle. Ganeval would be my vis-à-vis. She, a plump, pleasant-looking young woman of about my own age, was already seated when I arrived. I introduced myself and we began to chat. After I apologized for my labored French and asked whether she spoke English, she readily switched to it. Then she suddenly asked: "Tell me, what's that uniform you're wearing? I've never seen it before."

"It's British. I'm a British civilian officer," I replied.

"What, you're British?" she exclaimed in loud surprise. "Why, you don't look it at all!"

People close to us stopped talking and began to listen.

"But I am," I said, bending over my plate to hide my embarrassment.

"You can't be! You're much too dark! I thought you were Spanish," she went on relentlessly.

"Zz . . . Zz . . . ," I stammered, my t-aitches sounding terribly foreign in my own ears. When I am agitated my carefully nurtured English accent always goes down the drain. Taking a deep breath and forcing that damn tongue of mine against my upper teeth I told her: "There's a fact, you know, that not everyone British is blue-eyed and fair-haired. Quite a few French, for instance, came over in 1066."

She smiled, shrugged her shoulders, and changed

the subject. For her that was the end of it, but not for me.

She had challenged what was most precious to me: my new roots in the country, culture, and civilization I admired above all others and to which I wanted to belong. Besides, Anglophilia went back a long way in my family; the story of how I was given my first name, often told me by my mother when I was a boy, made it seem almost in the order of things that Britain should have become my home.

It was my mother's father, a rather stern and determined gentleman, who decided I should be called Georg, and, modesty not being his strongest suit, he explained why, saying, "One only has to add an 'e' to it and it's English. Maybe one day my first male grandchild will be an Englishman. What could be better? Perhaps even prime minister. After all, he wouldn't be the first Jew in Downing Street," and with these words he so to speak put Disraeli instead of a teddy into my cradle.

But since that time of innocence I had learned that there was more to becoming an Englishman than putting an "e" after "Georg" and, with occasional lapses, I had taken in Joanna Cantrell's warning that neither uniform nor bowler hat and pencil-slim umbrella, nor even plummy speech, would get me the acceptance I craved in a country where "manners," and not as the Germans have it, "clothes," "maketh man." But though I had soaked up not only English forms of behavior but also those other and inner values that are of the essence, my new identity was still too insecure to tell that young French woman the truth about my origins. Crying out "What, you're British?" she made me feel naked and exposed, an overreaction partly also from vanity. The former refugee underdog hated the thought that he would not be taken for one of the topdogs, which was how the British, at least those in Germany, saw themselves. But what I wanted to be and how our colleagues and superiors actually felt about people like Kaye and myself were not one and the same thing.

Unlike the Americans, who had many former refugees among their Military Government officials, the British Control Commission employed relatively few people of our background. Why this was so Michael Balfour explained in his essay "Reforming the German Press, 1945–1949," which was published in the *Journal of European Studies* in 1973.

"We were more easygoing than the Americans," he wrote in the paragraph dealing with the licensing of German newspapers,

> in the rigor with which we controlled our licensees. This was only partly due to broadmindedness; it arose just as much from a shortage of staff who could speak German, had journalistic experience, and possessed political awareness. The Americans used a number of anti-Nazi refugees who had become American citizens; we had fewer such people available and more qualms about their qualifications to represent the British point of view.

Neither he nor I could ever have imagined then that a Viennese refugee, who arrived in Britain in 1938 aged twelve and is now Sir John Burgh, KCMG, would one day, as director-general of the British Council, become the Chief Apostle of the British way of life. Yet why not? Had not Isocrates, the Athenian orator and statesman, declared four hundred years before the birth of Christ that the designation of Hellene was not a matter of descent but of attitude!

One way in which we "neo-Hellenes" certainly differed from most of the British-born Control Commission officials was that we had no language problem. We, therefore, had more contacts with Germans not only in the line of duty but also socially, while the others, particularly after the arrival of the U.K. families, lived in closed ghettolike communities with their own clubs, cinemas, and NAAFI shops—a privileged existence where one never had to queue or wait. It was a way of life well illustrated by the anecdote—*si non e vero e bene trovato*—about the English boy back in Britain after some years in occupied Germany, who, walking past the line of people waiting for admission outside a suburban swimming pool, proudly proclaims at the ticket counter the magic password: "British!"

Overall there was—understandably—little fondness for the Germans among the British, sometimes intermingled with traces of a *Herrenvolk* attitude usually mellowed by the century-old collective experience of dealing with the lesser breeds. An example of a more inflexible type was the half-colonel commanding our Düsseldorf Information Control Unit, who put me in an extremely awkward situation. I had been sent to Düsseldorf to discuss with the local authorities there Gustav Gründgens's intention to take up their offer of the directorship of its municipal theaters. Germany's great actor-director was tired of Berlin, or rather of the Russian pressure to direct or appear in plays of their choice, and, besides, Düsseldorf was also his native city. I was staying at the officers' mess where Karl Arnold, the lord mayor of Düsseldorf, was to pick me up. Despite my protests he had insisted on doing this personally. We were then to go to the town hall for a conference, which was to be followed by a visit to the opera and a dinner with him and other leading citizens. Now, Arnold was not just a local worthy. He was the most prominent Christian Democratic Union politician after Adenauer and had come close to beating him for the party leadership. Furthermore he was the minister-president designate of North-

Rhine/Westphalia, the biggest and economically the most important of the *Länder* of the future Federal Republic. When the mess butler came to tell me that Herr Arnold had arrived I told him to show him in so I could offer him some refreshment before we left. "Sorry, sir," he replied. "Germans are not allowed in the mess. Colonel's strict orders, sir." I jumped up and rushed out into the hall to welcome the *Oberbürgermeister*, but there was nobody there. They had left him standing outside the door in the cold. That happened in March 1947, eighteen months or so after the end of the nonfraternization rule.

A small but not insignificant group—some press correspondents belonged to it—among the British hated and despised Germans while, at the other end of the scale, there were those who rather admired some of the tenets of the Nazi creed. Harmless, though pretty ridiculous, were the snobs courting Germany's aristocratic high society to gain, in return for favors, acceptance as huntin', shootin', fishin', boozin', and sleepin' partners. There were wide-boys and carpetbaggers as well as lazy mediocrities, who hung on to their jobs by the silk threads of their old-school or regimental ties. Yes, of course there were misfits, but they never endangered what the majority was striving for: laying down a fundament on which the Germans could build a viable democracy.

In 1983 I asked the leading Berlin art critic Friedrich Luft how Germans had seen the British in those postwar days. "Without question as the soundest, most responsible, and fairest of the victors," he replied. And three years later, in 1986, Dr. Gerd Bucerius, least known but probably most successful of German press tycoons, wrote in his *Die Zeit:* "In 1946 the great London publisher Victor Gollancz visited Hamburg and I led him through the ruins. He kept on moaning about the Royal Air Force and apologizing for his country. 'Occupation never succeeds,' he said—but that was not true. It is impossible to think of a better and more humane occupation regime. We did not in those days thank the victor-powers enough."

It is only right that a German should introduce Gollancz into this story. To them he was a saint, a British saint whose halo shone all the brighter for his Judaism. Many German towns honored his memory by naming streets after him, but for the British dealing with Germany the left-wing publisher was often a thorn in the flesh. Half-admiringly, half-mockingly nicknamed the "Archrabbi of Canterbury," Gollancz, through his "Save Europe Now" movement, worked for Germany's sick and undernourished, particularly its women and children, whose distress he vividly—if one-sidedly—described in his books. His efforts on their behalf were not without nobility, but what that true rabbi, Leo Baeck, has defined as rectitude escaped him. A sense of proportion balancing guilt and innocence, cause and effect, was not in Gollancz's character. For that he was too egocentric, too self-publicizing, too unconscious of how his biblical zealotry damaged his own case—for example, with the reader's letter attacking his lifelong political friends in the Labor Party, which he published in the *News Chronicle* shortly before Christmas 1946. It caused a sensation in Germany and much embarrassment to the Control Commission. "The shamelessness of our government," Gollancz wrote, "is reaching new dimensions. Mr. Strachey, the food minister, has stated that turkeys, chicken, and extra rations of meat, sweets, and sugar will be available this Christmas. Have our Christian statesmen no idea of what is presently happening in Germany? Obviously not, or they would not make such idiotic announcements."

To decry such meager rewards for a people who, by standing alone against Hitler, had prevented his ultimate victory, and thereby—if only as a by-product—saved Gollancz and his fellow Jews from the gas chambers was hardly the best way to win British sympathy for Germans. Like the German Social Democratic Party leader Kurt Schumacher, who lectured the Allies that "Total victory means total responsibility," Gollancz also ignored the fact that the total war unleashed by Hitler's Reich had preceded total defeat and its inevitable consequences. Without any regard for cause and effect both men wanted the scales of justice weighted in their favor.

Despite war and destruction, however, need Germany have been quite as destitute as it was? Was there not more wealth, were there not more goods stashed away than one would have thought possible? If not, how else can one explain the miracle that occurred the day after the new Deutschmark replaced the valueless Reichsmark? Here is Walter Wallich's economist brother Henry's eyewitness description:

> Currency reform transformed the German scene from one day to the next. On June 21st, 1948, goods reappeared in the stores, money resumed its normal function, the black and gray markets reverted to a minor role, foraging trips to the country ceased, labor productivity increased, and output took off on its great upward surge. The spirit of the country changed overnight. The gray, hungry, dead-looking figures wandering about the streets in their everlasting search for food came to life as, pocketing their 40 DM, they went out on their first spending spree.

That is how it was. I too saw it happen and shops rapidly fill with goods that could not possibly have been produced from one day to the next.

Gollancz's campaign—and in this he had effective support from some of the British press—also contrasted the life-style of the Control Commission with that of Britons at home. It was true that we enjoyed a comfortable existence: free accommodation, free servants and transport, luxurious messes and clubs with unrationed food at low prices, duty-free alcohol and cigarettes. Yet life in Germany was not one unending "Tom Collins"–sodden orgy. Accused of living like drones, we were, in one respect. "Life expectancy" in the Control Commission could be very short, and the word *redundancy* hung, like the sword of Damocles, constantly over our heads. Those material blessings were one compensation; the other was that the work most of us did was exciting and satisfying. Mine certainly was. It put me in touch with people in Berlin, men and women, willing and eager to bridge that chasm between German and Western thought that had widened and deepened so disastrously under Nazi rule; people without self-pity, people who had experienced defeat not as an end but as a beginning; people who knew that the occupation was but a necessary prelude to a freedom that their own country's victory would have denied them forever.

That young reporter I had interviewed at Nord-West-Deutscher-Rundfunk in Hamburg, whose party membership had been so puzzling, belonged to this group. We had only talked for an hour, but that was long enough to convince me that he, and those like him, would play an important role in shaping Germany's future. That, however, was not the only reason I had remembered him. We had found similar cases since then. Young men who, according to Documents Center evidence, had been party members, but claimed that this, if true, happened without their knowledge or consent. One of them gave me a clue when he told me that the Hitler Youth leadership's annual April 20 birthday present for the Führer was always a list of those of its members who, having reached eighteen the previous year, had joined the party.

✠ 248 ✠

When I heard that, the penny dropped. I now knew who could solve this problem for us—Baldur von Schirach, of course, the former Hitler Youth leader and later *Gauleiter* of Vienna. And I knew exactly where to find him. He was right there in Berlin at Spandau—a few kilometers from Schlüterstrasse—together with the other Third Reich leaders who had escaped the death sentence at Nuremberg. Getting there, however, was not just a question of distance. Applications to interview a Spandau prisoner had to go through channels, and those stretched from Lancaster House via the Allied Kommandatura all the way up to the Allied Control Council, the highest authority in Germany. Our PR/ISC seniors thought it a good idea, but doubted that permission would ever be granted. It was easier for the proverbial camel to pass through the eye of the needle, I was assured, than for me to get through the gates of Spandau prison. And Kaye and I were warned that it would take months to get a decision. We applied, just the same.

20

A Man Without Qualities

Not in Germany—or anywhere else for that matter—is there another small provincial town like Weimar, where the mere mention of the name brings to mind some of the loftiest manifestations of the human spirit and also one of its most tragic failures. In the late eighteenth and early nineteenth century this modest grand-ducal residence was the mecca not only of Germany's but of Europe's intellectual elite and a must for any high-minded young Englishman on the Grand Tour. They all came to Weimar to bask in the aura of Johann Wolfgang von Goethe and Friedrich Schiller and to sit at their feet, a privilege granted to but a chosen few. Others had to make do with a glimpse of the great men passing by, on foot or in their carriages, yet if devout greetings were acknowledged by gracious nod it was sheer bliss to be alive. And no Weimar pilgrimage was complete without at least one visit to the theater over which Herr von Goethe presided and where, some two centuries later in

1919, the ill-starred National Assembly of the first German Republic conceived a constitution of such thoroughly immaculate democratic perfection it could not but be impotent in face of its enemies.

In the 1920s Goethe's—in every way far distant—successor as director of Weimar's theater was one Karl Friedrich von Schirach, a muddleheadedly romantic German-Wagnerian nationalist. Although his wife came from a distinguished American family—with two of the signatories of the Declaration of Independence among her forebears—so infected was she by her husband's Teutomania that she let their son be called Baldur, after the god of light—fruit of the loins of Odin, the master of winds and battle, and Frigg, his goddess consort. According to the Edda, the ancient Nordic saga, Loki, the fire-demon out to annihilate the world, destroyed Baldur the god, but Baldur the young man willingly threw himself into the arms of the new Loki, who was arising in Germany.

During his self-proclaimed "Years of Struggle" Adolf Hitler always looked up the von Schirachs whenever he came to Weimar. He felt good in the bosom of that family, which shared his views. And as a master-class student of political melodrama he took a keen interest in the theater. A visit to von Schirach's playhouse became part of Hitler's Weimar pilgrimages, occasions when he liked the handsome teenager Baldur to be his companion. With that family background and such close exposure to the Führer's magnetism, the boy—unsurprisingly—became a fanatical Nazi, and in 1928, when he was twenty-one and studying at Munich University, Hitler made him the head of the National Socialist Students' League. In that task young von Schirach showed considerable organizational talent, although to fail in it would actually have been more difficult than to succeed. As it was, the seeds he planted fell on already fertile ground, richly manured with the drug of chauvinism; the stab-in-the-back legend and its innate anti-Semitism; the Versailles Treaty and its war-guilt clause; anti-capitalist anti-Jew propaganda, anti-Bolshevist anti-Jew propaganda, and that quasi-"green" anti-civilization posturing, which hyped alleged peasant purity over so-called city debauchery. But what appealed most of all to that intelligentsia demimonde at the universities was—as always—mindless radicalism, something at which the Nazis were second to none. By 1931, the very year when Hitler rewarded Schirach with the leadership of the Hitler Youth, Nazism was proportionately twice as strong among university students as among the general population.

After Hitler became chancellor he promoted von Schirach to *Reichsjugendführer*. Aged twenty-six he was now the master of German youth, one of the top functionaries of the Third Reich, and also—not for nothing had he imbibed the Weimar spirit—its foremost poet and lyricist. Wreathing Germany's "Man of Destiny" in glorifying verse he created works like the "Song of the Hitler Youth."

> Our flag a-flutter in front,
> Man for man toward the future we throng,
> We march for Hitler through night and dread
> With the flag of youth for freedom and bread
> Our flag a-fluttering leads,
> Our flag to new times us speeds,
> And the flag that guides us to eternity,
> Yes, this flag means more than mortality.

Reichsjugendführer and "poet laureate" von Schirach further strengthened his place at the top by his "dynastic" marriage to Henriette Hoffmann, daughter of Heinrich Hoffmann, Hitler's court photographer and close confidant. Now the young man really had everything, everything, that is, except inner strength and character, a lack he compensated for with growing arrogance and vanity. After 1940, when he became Reich's-Governor and *Gauleiter* of Vienna, his megalomania was such that his intimates referred to him behind his back as the "Pompadour of Vienna"—a vile and ignorant slur on a noble and cultured lady.

But as Hitler's viceroy in the old imperial capital, von Schirach did fancy himself the anointed successor to the Habsburg crown, a folie-de-grandeur well illustrated by a story Albert Speer tells in his memoirs. Planning in 1942 to visit Vienna for talks with local industrialists, Speer sent von Schirach a message suggesting they meet at the airport and save time discussing productivity problems while driving to Vienna. Although Speer, as *Reichsminister* for armament and the Führer's favorite, was the far more powerful personage, the reply he received from one of Emperor Baldur's minions pointed out that the privilege of being personally welcomed on arrival by the governor and *Gauleiter* was only granted to visiting heads of state. The *Herr Gauleiter*, therefore, looked forward to seeing the *Herr Reichsminister* at his office in the old Austrian parliament. Speer responded that he in turn would be happy to receive Herr von Schirach in his suite at the Hotel Imperial. Alas, Speer does not record who came to whom, or, indeed, whether the twain met at all. But they had plenty of opportunity for more informal personal contacts later on during their twenty years together in the Spandau prison fortress, the portals of which actually opened to me more quickly than I had expected.

Four weeks after we had submitted our application to interview von Schirach the Control Council authorized my visit. And so, together with a lady interpreter and shorthand writer whose job was to record my talk with the prisoner, I drove to Spandau on the appointed day. A British half-colonel, "our" prison commandant, awaited us at the main gate. He took us to a conference room where the other three commandants and their interpreters were already assembled. Coffee was served and I was asked to explain once more, and in detail please, why I wanted to interrogate the prisoner. As the British were in control that month, the British commandant was in the chair and it was he who briefed me about the prison rules. Most important, he said, was that I did not say a single word to Schirach not strictly relevant to the subject of Hitler Youth transfers to party membership. The Russian and French interpreters whispered their translations to their bosses and they and the U.S. commandant nodded their heads in affirmation. If I slipped up, he further warned me, the prisoner would be marched back to his cell and I ordered to leave, with possible disciplinary consequences. The prisoner was to be addressed by name only—the designation "Herr" or the aristocratic prefix "von" were not to be used. Clear?

I confirmed it was, but asked what would happen if Schirach strayed from the subject? That, I was told, was impossible. The prisoner knew full well what punishment would follow. Besides, the American commandant added, Schirach was the most docile and servile of the lot. Then the lady from the Interpreters' Pool and I each had to sign a document, acknowledging with our signatures that we had been told the rules and would on no account communicate to the press anything we had seen at Spandau.

When all this was settled we followed the commandants out of the office, up a staircase and along a corridor patrolled by armed British soldiers until we came to a steel-barred gate that a sergeant warder unlocked for us. He then guided us through the inner prison until we reached a steel door in the left wall. Opening it, he showed us into a fair-sized room, cut in half by a floor-to-ceiling steel grille with two adjoining prison cages behind it. Benches for the guards ran along the walls, and centered behind the grille stood one wooden chair. Two equally plain chairs and a table were on our side. The sergeant moved them in front of the right-hand cage and asked us to sit down. Then he, the commandants, and their staffs trooped out.

As I heard the warder's key turn in the lock and its ratchets click home I had the sensation of being incarcerated myself. My hands went cold, my breathing became slightly labored. I was afraid. Sure, with my brain I knew that I was perfectly safe, yet in my soul I had an inkling, it could not be more, of what it must have felt like to be a Viennese Jew rounded up on the orders of the man I was about to encounter. In his eagerness to report Vienna cleansed of Jews to Hitler before Goebbels, as *Gauleiter* of Berlin, could announce a similar triumph, the servile Schirach initiated deportations so prematurely that trainloads of women, children, sick, and elderly men arrived in Poland before the death camps were ready for them. Kept in open-air corrals, like animals, they were exposed to indescribable suffering. It was this act that got Schirach his twenty-year sentence for "crimes against humanity" at Nuremberg.

I was jerked out of my thoughts when the door of the left-hand cage suddenly opened. The four commandants with their assistants came in and sat down. Then two soldiers led a prisoner into the other cage. He looked at me, I looked at him. He was an old man, still big, but not as big as he must once have been. The prison garb hung loosely on his body; everything about him seemed slack and sagging: the bent back, the fallen-in chest, the flabbily protruding belly. Slowly, like an old bull-elephant searching for a place to lie down and die, he shuffled toward the chair behind the grille and slumped into it.

This wasn't the forty-year-old Schirach! It couldn't be! But for a few moments I was too stunned to say anything. I simply could not believe that the world's most costly prison administration, with only seven prisoners to look after, could make such a grotesque mistake, but there was no doubt: the man looking at me through lifeless eyes was the seventy-four-year-old Konstantin von Neurath, until 1938 Hitler's foreign minister and, after Reinhard Heydrich's assassination in 1942, *Reichsprotektor* of Bohemia and Moravia.

"Colonel," I gasped, "this isn't Schirach, it's Neurath!"

"Well, I'll be damned," he exclaimed, looking over. "Why, so it is!" And his three colleagues nodded their agreement.

"Get him out! At the double! And get it right the next time," he shouted at the soldiers. They tapped Neurath on the back, he rose, turned, and tottered out.

When they returned, they were escorting Schirach, or rather the ghost of the Emperor Baldur, whose photos I had looked at that morning before going out to Spandau. No longer running to fat, as in his heyday, the puffiness that had destroyed his youthful good looks and brought out the petulant effeminacy of his features had given way to deeply drawn lines in a face with the pasty pallor of a waxworks puppet.

He sat down and asked me in a soft and monotonous voice: "May I know why I've been brought here?"

I was about to tell him, when the Soviet commandant snapped out a few angry-sounding words. His interpreter translated: "The prisoner will only speak when he is spoken to."

Like a recruit on a Prussian parade ground Schirach called out: *"Jawoll, Herr Oberst!"*

"I want information from you," I said, "about the procedures used to enroll Hitler Youth members into the party after their eighteenth birthday."

I had spoken in German but Schirach asked: "Should I reply in German or English? I'm bilingual."

"Deutsch!" the British commandant said.

Again: *"Jawoll, Herr Oberst!"*

"Did you have to use pressure," I asked, "to get those young men to apply for party membership or did they volunteer?"

At that Schirach became a bit more alive. With a sardonic grin he replied: "Pressure? That's what they tell you now. They would! Pressure? Good God, they all rushed to get into the party! A proper stampede it was. Had it been necessary to queue to get in, those in the rear would have trampled the ones in front to death. That's what it was like. Believe me, sir."

Until that moment I had been perfectly calm, but when Schirach, unexpectedly and deferentially, used the English "sir" to address me—the Jewish vermin he would not even have spat at in Vienna—I felt as if he had emptied a bucket of slime and vomit all over me.

I had to struggle to keep my anger under control. "Tell me, then, how the system worked," I asked.

"It was very simple," he said. "On becoming eighteen they filled in membership application forms. With the appropriate recommendations, or otherwise, these then went up through channels to the *Reichsjugendführung,* my office, and when approved they were sent to party HQ in Munich. That was all."

"And each year on Hitler's birthday you presented him with a list of boys who had joined the party?"

"Yes. That was my idea," he said, "and Hitler liked it."

"Why?"

"Well, it showed that young Germans were dedicated to him."

"And that you had trained them to be ardent Nazis?"

"Yes, that's right," he said.

"So it would have been in your own interest to push as many boys as possible into the party, even those who had not applied and did not want to be members."

"It might, had it been necessary. It never was. As I told you, they were dead keen. The numbers went up year by year."

"Were any changes made after you went to Vienna?"

"I don't think so. Axmann, who took over from me, just continued what I'd started."

"Right. Are you saying, Schirach, that no Hitler Youth could ever have become a party member without his knowledge?"

"Most certainly not while I was in charge. Nor would I think at any time before 1943."

"Why do you say that?"

"Because one can't really be sure about what happened once the devastating air-raids started. Communications broke down all over the place. It was chaotic. Another point, but now I'm guessing, is that applications may well have fallen off as some of the chaps realized where we were heading. Presenting Hitler with shortening lists wouldn't have done Axmann's career much good. So he might well simply have nominated eighteen-year-olds for party membership. I can't say for sure, but it's a possibility."

"But, surely, the young men would have gotten to know about it? The party must have sent them membership cards and would have insisted on its dues."

"It would have tried. But, as I said, things were in chaos. How were they to get hold of young soldiers fighting at the front? Who knew where their units were? The army had other worries than playing postman for the party. They would have gotten hold of some of the chaps, but never all of them."

There it was, the simple explanation of the problem that had so baffled us. I turned to the commandants and said I had finished with the prisoner.

Von Schirach was taken back to his cell and we all went down to the administrative offices where my interpreter typed out her shorthand notes. They were then translated into French, Russian, and English by the commandants' interpreters, read and approved. After that we all went back to the interrogation room, Schirach was brought in again, told to read the protocol, check it, and, if he was satisfied it was a true record, initial each paragraph before finally signing the document.

Why, I wondered, as we silently watched Schirach do that, had I, except for the reaction to his first "sir," not felt an all-consuming hatred for this man? Was it because he seemed such a cipher? I suddenly remembered Robert Musil, an author my father had greatly admired, and his work *The Man Without Qualities*— a title that just about summed up the former master of my native city.

The Schirach interrogation and also La Ganeval's unforgotten hurtful remark had forced my past into my present. What would it be like to see Vienna again, to walk through the familiar streets and avenues of my childhood and youth, and to talk—not without some *Schadenfreude* to be sure—to my former compatriots and find out how they now felt about that frenzied ardor with which they had thrown themselves, like young Baldur, into Hitler's arms? I wanted to go. Making this decision, however, was easier than finding a reason to justify a duty trip. But sometimes things have a curious way of working out. The—as it were—unknowing and indirect sponsor of my first postwar visit to Vienna turned out to be no less a personality than Herbert von Karajan.

21

"Tu Felix
Austria . . ."

A few days after I had been to Spandau, Walter Legge, artistic director of EMI Records, founder of the London Philharmonic Orchestra and Britain's leading impresario of classical music, came to see us in Schlüterstrasse to talk about his protégé Herbert von Karajan. Defying the ban of the Allied authorities in Austria on the former Nazi Party member, EMI had already made recordings with the conductor in Vienna in September 1946. However, cutting discs was one thing, selling them another. Although von Karajan had meanwhile been denazified in his native Salzburg, Legge was worried about his two principal European markets—Britain and Germany. Would we, he asked, continue to prevent the sale of von Karajan's records in Germany, or raise objections if he gave concerts in London and made further recordings there?

At this Kaye laughed out loud. "We're not, Mr. Legge," he said, "denazifying the U.K. But as far as Germany is concerned—not a hope. Neither we nor the Americans nor the French accept the Austrian denazification. You know just as well as I do what happened with Furtwängler and, unlike Herr von Karajan, he wasn't even a party member."

Legge did not like this, but he was excellent at public relations and so, for the sake of future goodwill, he stayed for a while, regaling us with anecdotes about the jealousies, backbiting, and intrigues in the world of music and opera. Listening to him I suddenly realized that he had given me my cue. Turning to Kaye, after Legge had left, I said: "You know we always discount Austrian denazification, but we don't really know what goes on there."

Kaye was never slow on the uptake. "True," he said, "but what exactly are you getting at?"

"Simply that we ought to know more. After all, there's a continuous exchange of artists between Austria and Germany."

"I don't need a von Karajan to hear your leitmotiv," Kaye smiled. "So you think somebody ought to go to Vienna to find out on the spot. And I bet you know who, don't you?"

I nodded.

"Hm. Still, it's not a bad idea. You know the place, you know the people, and having served in 77 company, you, of course, also know Schnabel, the British Theater and Music Officer."

I did indeed. Schnabel, also known as "MacSchnabel" for reasons to which we shall come in a moment, had been the second "alien" commissioned officer in my Pioneer Corps company. But I had already met him earlier. Shortly after I joined up at the Pioneer Corps Training Center in Ilfracombe I was sent to pick up a Sergeant Schnabel at the railway station and take him to our tent camp on a hill site near the town. I worried how I should recognize him. I knew that he too was from Vienna, but that was hardly enough to identify a total stranger. It was no problem. Instead of a kit bag he carried a beautiful and well-traveled leather case with a mystifying "Major P. Schnabel" in big white letters stenciled on it. And, yes, even in battledress there was an air of the Viennese dandy about him. His had none of the usual bagginess and fitted like the proverbial glove. Only a good bespoke tailor, no quartermaster store, could have provided it.

He saw me staring at the lettering on his trunk. "Does that puzzle you, dear boy?" he asked in German, speaking with the twangily nasal intonation of the Austrian aristocracy. "It's easily explained; I was a major in the Heimwehr, don't you know."

At this I ought to have taken an instant dislike to him, but could not. One simply had to admire the sheer chutzpah of a man who traveled through a Britain fighting for democracy with his old rank in the Austrian fascist militia painted on his luggage. It was impossible not to like this nice and easygoing man, and, later, when Schnabel came to 77 Company as a newly minted second lieutenant, even former Austrian lefties grew fond of him in spite of his political past. He had a light touch that our other officers, including the non-British natives we got, by and by, lacked. Schnabel was conscientious and did his duty, but when that had been seen to, he liked to sit down and entertain us with stories of Count Bobby and Count Rudi, the two imaginary Austrian chinless wonders about whose droll adventures Vienna has been laughing for longer than anyone can remember. After a few months Schnabel left us on "temporary" secondment as chief ski instructor to the Cameron Highlanders, from which he, of course, never returned. We missed him and the daily joke sessions with that Viennese original, who from then on, naturally, was only spoken of as "MacSchnabel."

Although the names of his friends among Austria's high aristocracy dropped from his lips like the rain from heaven, he, though a bit of a snob, was never pretentious, nor did he ever claim that blue blood ran in his veins; on the contrary, he readily admitted that he was liberally sprinkled with Jewish corpuscles. After the war he remained in Vienna but so great was his pride in having served the Crown that even death was not allowed to part him from Britain's royalty. The obituary notice in the Viennese newspapers was pure Schnabel. "Died in Vienna on February 17, 1983, Peter Joseph Schnabel, aged 82, Royal British Major ret.," it said.

Anyhow, in 1947, when the proposal for my visit, my "super-swan," as Kaye liked to call it, had been approved by PR/ISC and by Colonel Beauclerk (the late duke of St. Albans), controller of British Information Services in Austria, I set off, equipped with all the necessary bumf, railway warrants, travel permits, frontier passes, and what-have-you on the U.S. military train to Frankfurt/Main. There I had to stay overnight before catching the next U.S. train to the border, and finally, having passed the controls, I boarded another U.S. military train for Vienna. That last lap of the journey took ages. We stood for hours on the bridge over the Enns, where the Soviet Zone of Austria began, while Russian soldiers, checking that no unauthorized persons were aboard, took their time going through the coaches. When I finally arrived at the "officers only" Park Hotel in Hietzing, close to the British HQ in Schönbrunn Castle, where a room had been booked for me, I was rather travel-weary. Although I had never stayed there I knew the hotel well. I may even have been conceived in the Park Hotel, where my parents had spent their honeymoon. And when I was a boy they often took me with them for a treat when they dined there with their closest friends, who lived in that rather select Vienna district.

As I walked into the dining room at breakfast time I immediately noticed that nothing but the clientele—assorted captains and majors putting away their bacon and eggs—had changed. Everything was exactly as I remembered it, including my father's favorite corner table where I had so often gorged myself on my best Park Hotel pudding: creamy cold rice with lots of raspberry sauce poured over it. Standing there I could taste all the favorite dishes of my childhood—Wiener Schnitzel as crisp and as dry as it is served only in Vienna, *gulyas,* boiled and boiled again till its red paprika gravy had just the right flavor, and with it *Nockerln,* those thumb-thick flour dumplings that go so well with it; *Zwiebelrost-braten,* a pot roast, usually accompanied by *Semmel-knödel,* big round dumplings made from old rolls cut into small squares and soaked in milk.

Ah, *Knödel!* What about those made from potatoes and filled with either cherries, plums, or apricots, brought to the table with roast breadcrumbs and melted butter poured over them? What delights! Yet for all of them the English language has but one word, *dumplings,* so plump and heavy it is enough to give one indigestion. The Austrian cuisine is so good and varied because it took most of its tastiest dishes from the many countries of the old Empire: *Nockerln,* for example, are germanized Italian *gnocchi; gulyas*—beef, veal, or *Szegedin* cooked with sauerkraut—come from Hungary; the famous Wiener Schnitzel is a close relative of the *Costoletto Milanese; Reisfleisch* is Serbian, and liver is usually served in the Venetian style.

Of course nothing I ate in Vienna either on that or on subsequent visits, in simple inns or luxury restaurants, ever quite tasted as it used to when I was a child. Nor did Vienna, although little has changed, look the same. I had expected no less, yet it was a shock to find streets remembered as wide and long so short and narrow, and huge squares so shrunk one could almost spit across them. Vienna had been bombed, there had been fighting in the streets, yet compared to Berlin or Hamburg it had suffered little. The opera was burned out, the Burgtheater too was an empty shell, but so many of Vienna's famous landmarks—churches, museums, monuments, the grand houses along the Ringstrasse, and the baroque palaces of the inner city—had hardly been scratched. I would not have wanted it to be otherwise. The destruction of this beautiful city would have given me no vengeful satisfaction. All the same, to find so little changed, so much familiar, was a harrowing experience. It brought home—sharply and painfully—the frailty and brevity of human life measured against the timeless endurance of stone.

I thought of my parents. How often had we walked together past those buildings while my father, who loved his Vienna and knew its history so well, had told me when they had been built, who had lived in them, who it was the monuments commemorated. There they all were, standing as firm as ever, but where was he?

I crossed the very curbstone in Währingerstrasse over which my mother in her shortsightedness had stumbled when I was, what—four or five? Seeing her suddenly sprawled on the pavement was so terrifying for the little boy that I dirtied myself and we had to go back and change my clothes. That curbstone was there, but where was she?

That was what I felt as I walked to my first appointment, but I also fought against those feelings and memories. They were too dangerous, too threatening; repressing them, I willed them from my mind. Not altogether successfully, for they came back, sometimes in daydreams, more often in nightmares.

That first appointment was of course with Mac-Schnabel. I had phoned him to ask when I could come to his office for a talk.

"Not at the office, dear boy, surely," he exclaimed in horror. "It's the sort of thing you do in your Prussia, but not in Vienna! You ought to know. Let's meet for coffee at eleven."

"Where?" I said.

"How can you ask? Really! There's only one place in this town where gentlemen take their morning coffee, don't you know. At Demel's, of course."

Overpunctual, as always, I sat well before eleven at a table in the famous *confiserie* founded by an erstwhile court-confectioner in the Kohlmarkt, a few steps from the Imperial Palace. At Demel's it seemed time had stood still. Although most of the waitresses in their long, black dresses and frilly white aprons looked old enough, they probably were not the same ones who had served coffee and cakes to archdukes, princes, and counts, but the marble-topped tables with the bentwood chairs on which so many top bottoms had rested certainly were. I had ample time to take it all in because in Vienna punctuality does not mean on the dot, but fifteen to twenty minutes after it. I had forgotten, but Peter Joseph Schnabel—*ci-devant* Heimwehr major, former Pioneer Corps sergeant, and now major in the Cameron Highlanders—obviously had not. But to be there before him was the best thing I could have done; not for all the coffee and the cakes at Demel's today (in 1947 there was not much choice) would I have missed his entrée. As he came through the door the waitresses curtsied and welcomed him with a chorused *"Grüss Gott, Herr Major."* He, in Glengarry, black-buttoned khaki doublet, silver-buckled

Sam Browne and Douglas tartan close-fitting trousers, graciously raised his silver-topped swagger cane in response. He saw me and waved, but it took a while before he finally reached my table. MacSchnabel clearly was a local celebrity, knew everybody who was anybody, and quite a few of Vienna's male and female somebodies were having their morning coffee at Demel's. Slowly, with many a *"Küss-die-Hand"* to the ladies and many a drawled *"Ja, Servus"* to the gentlemen, he progressed through the room, proving with his every gesture that his native Highlands were the Vienna Woods and Hofmannsthal his Robbie Burns. Had the Cameronians worn the kilt instead of trews, this performance would have been even more wondrous.

Schnabel, as always, was delightful company, the perfect raconteur. I could have listened to him for hours. Eventually I felt duty-bound to remind him that we were meeting for a purpose.

"Tell you what, dear boy," he said, "you don't want me to give you a boring lecture on what I do or how our four-power committee works. Best you come and see for yourself. You timed your visit perfectly. Our next committee meeting is the day after tomorrow. Ten-thirty at my office. You just come and sit in and if you have any questions you just ask them."

"In front of your Soviet member?"

"Why not? I mean, be a bit careful what you say, but this isn't Berlin, don't you know? Things are different here. We're in Vienna."

I was to hear those last two sentences repeated quite often during my visit.

Schnabel's office was at Rechte Wienzeile 97. The first to arrive after me was a gentleman in French uniform. The moment I heard him say *"Servus, Peter"* to Schnabel I knew his cradle had stood closer to the Danube than to the Seine. He became rather formal when he was introduced to me, till Schnabel explained, "George is one of us, too."

Also "one of us" was U.S. Captain Ernst Häussermann, head of the American film section. The son of a distinguished Burgtheater actor and director, he later stayed in Vienna and followed in his father's footsteps. For the record: Haüssermann was deputizing at that meeting for Captain Ernst Lothar, the U.S. Theater and Music Officer, who, before the Anschluss, had been Max Reinhardt's successor as chief of Vienna's Theater in der Josefstadt. As the man had said: "Things are different here. We're in Vienna."

How very different I was yet to discover.

We sat around drinking coffee, chatting and waiting for the Soviet committee member. Häussermann was getting impatient.

"Why is she always late?" he grumbled. "I wonder what excuse she'll have today?"

"A sweet one you'll like, Ernst," a woman's voice said in unmistakable Viennese.

Looking up I saw a slim, dark-haired woman of about thirty in the uniform of a Red Army captain. She put a little parcel on the table, unwrapped it, and out came a Sacher torte.

"I had to go and fetch it," she said, "that's why I'm late. So let's have it with our coffee."

I could just see Sublieutenant Levin turning up at the Kommandatura bearing gifts!

Schnabel introduced us. Her name was Lilly Wichmann. "Well, isn't the world full of old Viennese?" she commented, instead of saying, as Levin would undoubtedly have done, *"Nyet,* not possible. No visitors."

But as I listened to their discussion I realized that not only the atmosphere between them, but also their functions were not comparable with ours in Berlin. The four agreed on by no means everything, but *nyet* was not the most important word in Lilly Wichmann's vocabulary. Underlying everything that was said was the Viennese belief that talking gets people together, that conciliation is better than altercation, and that a compromise badly fudged is preferable to a crystal-clear rupture. It was all very *gemütlich* but also rather provincial. Whatever happened in Vienna, I thought, was not of great consequence, but what happened in Berlin was.

Denazification did not figure much in their deliberations. That, they explained, was because Austria, unlike Germany, had its own central government. Although the Allies had the final say, they largely restricted themselves to a supervisory role. We did not discuss the subject for any length of time, but I learned enough to write my report. They did not say it in so many words, but my impression was that in their particular field they found the whole thing a bit of a nuisance. They wanted good music, good opera, good theater, and if an artist had blotted his political copybook—well, what did it matter in dear little Austria?

When the meeting was over Schnabel said: "I mustn't forget, Laski wants to hear from you. Give him a ring, will you?"

"Laski, our corporal? Is he here?"

"Very much so. And he's no corporal either. When you ring ask for Lieutenant Colonel Laski."

He then told me the story of the "irresistible rise and rise" of the former corporal to his present rank, which is also told—albeit indirectly—in the paper Lord Schuster, in spite of his name a true-blue Britisher, published in 1947 in the *Journal of the Society of Public Teachers of Law*:

> At an early stage of the occupation of Austria, when I headed the Legal Division of the British Adminis-

tration in Austria, it was apparent that, as the Legal
Division would be concerned with Austrian and German law, it would be desirable to recruit Austrian or
German lawyers for the service. There were many
Austrian and German refugees with legal qualifications serving in the British army, some in the Pioneer Corps, but some also in the actual fighting
forces.

But we were met by the determined refusal of
higher authority to allow us to recruit any enemy
alien, even if his "hostile" character might have been
supposed to be purged by the fact that he had borne
arms for this country, and actually held His Majesty's commission. This problem might have been got
under by naturalizing people who had rendered service of this kind to the country, but this simple solution was rejected.

We got over it by the English process of supposing
that you change the nature of an action by calling it
by a different name. Although we were not allowed
to employ former Austrian or German lawyers in the
Legal Division we were allowed to establish a British-
Austrian Legal Unit, in which these gentlemen were
allowed to serve . . .

Laski, whose petition for a separate Austrian fighting
unit attached to the British Army I had refused to sign,
was posted to Austria, still a corporal, in 1945. There the
former legal whizkid of the Vienna Municipality was recruited for Lord Schuster's Legal Unit and commissioned. Powered by a first-class legal brain instead of an
umbrella, he flew past captains and majors like a sort of
military Mary Poppins until, as a half-colonel, he landed
in the commanding officer's chair.

I phoned him. He asked me to come to his flat in
Hietzing for a drink before taking me out to dinner
at the British Officers' Club in the Kinsky Palace.

The lieutenant colonel was a much nicer man than the corporal had been. Laski was more relaxed and the cynical bitterness with which he had regarded the British in our Pioneer Corps days had gone. No doubt the ingenious and very English manner in which Lord Schuster, by calling them by another name, had made those awful alien lawyer-weeds smell like roses in Whitehall noses had something to do with it, though probably not as much as Laski's second and obviously happy marriage to a genuine English rose, whose presence made our evening together the great success it was.

But I did not spend all my time in Vienna in British offices, clubs, or messes. Far from it. I met and talked to people in cafés and restaurants, visited our old neighborhood and its shops and chatted with their owners. Some of them recognized me, most did not. I never wore uniform on those occasions, nor said who I was, so those I spoke to talked freely.

I found that selfsame self-pity in Vienna so familiar to me from Germany, but with the added dimension of lamblike Austrian innocence. Although most Germans trotted out all kinds of excuses for their own involvement with the Nazi regime, they were slowly becoming uneasily aware of a kind of impersonal national responsibility for their country's past. Not so the majority of Austrians. Having mentally mislaid the Hitler years they filled the void with Austrian patriotism—so rare in March 1938 when Führer and Anschluss received their rapturous welcome. Austria was in fashion now, as symbolized by the ubiquitous peasant hats few would have worn in Vienna before the war. They sprouted on many heads that, not long ago, had sported the brown or black caps of SA or SS. Everything German was out, even the way the Viennese now spoke the language. Because it was more akin to Hochdeutsch, the soft Viennese which was my mother tongue had been replaced, even among the educated, by the rough indigenous dialect of the city's less savory districts.

And in 1947 no one, at least no one I spoke to, doubted for one moment that Austria had been the first country overrun by the Germans. After all, the victors themselves had said so in a much quoted passage from the Moscow Declaration of 1943. Quite true. Yet that declaration also had another passage, which somehow had not entered public consciousness. It said: "We remind Austria that it cannot escape either the responsibility or the consequences of having fought side by side with Hitler-Germany in this war. The final settlement must, therefore, depend on the part the Austrians themselves will play in the liberation of their country." And that, politely expressed, turned out to be less than overwhelming.

The Austrians, living up to their historic maxim *"Bella gerant alii—tu felix Austria nube!"* which commemorates the Habsburgs' felicitous policy of extending their realm by shrewd dynastic marriage rather than war, wooed the Americans, French, and British with some fervor. The recent matrimonial experiment with Germany, so eagerly consummated, having proved a mésalliance— had she not lost the war, what a happy union it would have been!—the country opened its arms to its semiliberators. And not in vain. British, French, and Americans responded readily to the romance of Vienna, its glamorous history, its music, its people—so polite and so seductively winsome, so apparently different from the Germans—and readily danced to and swallowed "Tales from the Vienna Woods." It was not yet a honeymoon, but an engagement between the Austrians and their Allied "guests" seemed on the cards; proof that one can have one's Sacher torte and eat it at the same time.

Was my judgment too harsh and influenced by resentment? I thought not. I had not looked for breastbeating and sackcloth and ashes. What I had looked for, and not found, was some self-doubt, some self-questioning. It did exist in Germany. In private conversations and in the media, more and more often, it was asked: "How was it possible?"—the very question that had made me go to Germany in the first place. Had I, had anybody, found the answer? There would be time—plenty of it—to think about it on my return journey.

For the second time in my life, but with very different feelings, I boarded a train to Berlin at a Vienna railway station. In 1938 it had meant parting from my home; now all it meant was departing from an uncannily familiar foreign city.

Epilogue

Where in happier times Goethe and Schiller used to stroll, in the beechwoods of the Etterberg close to Weimar, the SS implanted the hell it called Buchenwald in 1937. Seven years later the German communist leader Ernest Thälmann was murdered in that concentration camp, and—as I write this—its former chief clerk, the SS Staff-Sergeant-Major Wolfgang Otto, is being tried in Düsseldorf for alleged complicity in that killing. Coming across Otto's photo in a German newspaper I saw not a face of evil but that of a very ordinary, gray-haired, bespectacled, tired old man with liverish and wrinkled skin, thin lips, dark eyes, flabbily jowled chin. However, what really astonished me was his strong resemblance to M. Quinkal of St. Pierreville in the Ardèche, a member of the local Resistance, whose plan to hide my parents on a lonely mountain farm from Vichy's gendarmes and—ultimately—from men like SS Hauptscharführer Otto, so tragically miscarried.

Two near-Doppelgänger: one, the simple French villager, a man of courage and compassion, the other, educated and a teacher in civilian life, a man without pity, who routinely logged the names of those who died at Buchenwald each day on its gallows or with bullets in their necks, from starvation or the cholera; who drowned the screams of the tortured and dying in German marching Muzak relayed over the camp's public-address system; and who, as he admits, sometimes also acted as executioner. Now, aged seventy-six, Otto cannot fathom what the courts want of him. It all happened so long ago. He only did what he was told and now and then, yes—he acted on his own initiative.

What explains the difference, the vast divide as human beings, between those two look-alikes? Nationality? Were Germans more callous and cruel by nature than other peoples? Was that why the overwhelming majority served Hitler without revolting against his ends or being revolted by his means? Is this the answer to the question "How was it possible?"

But what, then, about Stalin's Soviet Union where among Gulag guards and Katyn executioners Wolfgang Otto had so many Russian "brothers"? In his book, *The Drowned and the Saved*, the great Italian author and Auschwitz survivor Primo Levi wrote: "The true crime, the collective, general crime of almost all Germans of that time was that of lacking the courage to speak." The very same could be said about almost all Russians of Stalin's time. They did not speak on behalf of the kulaks or the Archipelago slaves, yet the Russian people were never condemned as the Germans were. Why?

Germany, but not Russia, had always been seen, and for many centuries saw herself, as part of the mainstream of Western civilization. Hence the shock caused by the horror, the ferocity, and above all the irrationality of the crimes that were committed in her name was infinitely greater than that of the sufferings Stalin inflicted on his subjects. Further, German aggression unleashing the dogs of war made Russia the ally of the West, where in any case the opiate word *socialism* had numbed the critical faculties of so many opinion makers ever since the October revolution. Last but not least, the Russian peoples went to Bolshevist rule straight from Cossack knout and Tsarist autocracy. They never had a choice between totalitarian and democratic rule, but the Germans living in the pluralist Weimar Republic had that option. And they chose Hitler.

In fact, as the records of Weimar Germany's last four general elections show, they never did. Up to and including 1928 neither the Nazis' brilliant propaganda nor the violence of their stormtroopers, neither the constant denunciation of the "Shame of Versailles" nor their rabid anti-Semitism got them more than 2.6 percent of the vote, a figure Hitler would have never reached—never mind exceeding it—had he ever openly said: "Give me power and I shall order the slaughter of all Jews—men, women and children." Some commentators claim that anyone reading the chapter "Nation and Race" in *Mein Kampf* ought to have foreseen this outcome. Post-Auschwitz one may read this into his words, but pre-Auschwitz such a thought would not have occurred in a million light-years to any of the few, including myself, who actually went through *Mein Kampf* from cover to cover. And that its author himself, as he dictated the relevant passage to Hess in Landsberg prison in 1925, could have had the Final Solution in his conscious mind is, at the very least, open to doubt.

At the next German general election, held after the Wall Street Crash and the beginning of mass unemployment in September 1930, the Nazi vote increased to 18.3 percent, and at the following, in July 1932, when nearly six million were on the dole, it shot up to 37.4 percent. This was the best result Hitler ever achieved in a truly free ballot. Four months later, in November of the same year, when Germans were called to the polls once again, his share of the vote declined to 33.1 percent—one percentage point more than Labor got at the British general election of 1987. True, his party was still the biggest in Germany, but the overall majority Hitler wanted in order to achieve power legitimately eluded him. And yet a mere two months later he headed the government of the Reich, thanks to the machinations of former chancellor Franz von Papen, who, like most politicians of the time— German or non-German—had no idea what kind of man it was he was dealing with. Confident that the vulgar rabble-rouser would quickly prove himself incompetent for high office and thus pave the way for his own comeback, von Papen assured the near-senile President Hindenburg that Hitler's certain failure would exorcise the Nazi devil once and for all. Trusting the scheming Catholic politico, the initially reluctant old man appointed Hitler, who thus was handed power on the proverbial platter exactly at that point in history when the impact on the German electorate of the singular concatenation of national and international political and economic forces that had favored his rise was beginning to weaken and his fortunes were on the decline.

On January 30, 1933, Hitler moved into the Wilhelmstrasse, and four weeks later, on February 27, that divine providence he so often appealed to gave him the gift of the Reichstag fire—almost certainly not the work of the Nazis but that of Dutch anarchist Marinus van der Lubbe alone. But Hitler immediately saw his opportunity and seized it. Within twenty-four hours all basic human rights guaranteed by the Weimar constitution had been suspended, and the entire communist leadership and others Hitler wanted out of the way were arrested and put into the newly erected Oranienburg concentration camp. Then, to show that he had public support for his actions, Hitler called a snap election for March 5, 1933.

It was the last still partially free poll held in Germany, although by then many aspects of the media, especially broadcasting, were already under Goebbels's control. Even so, with 43.9 percent of the vote and 288 out of the 647 seats of the Reichstag, the absolute majority escaped Hitler again, but now, with 107 opposition members imprisoned, he could do without it. On March 23, 1933, Göring observing the MPs through binoculars from his elevated seat as Reichstags-President, the emasculated parliament passed the Law to Remedy the Distress of the People and the Reich, the harmless, even beneficent-sounding title of the Enabling Act conferring near-dictatorial powers on Adolf Hitler. The transformation of the party politician into the idolized leader of the German nation was beginning.

Watching him on old newsreels it seems incomprehensible that a sophisticated and cultured people could have surrendered itself to that man. Strutting, ranting, and wildly gesticulating, he looks like a jungle-tribe witch doctor performing his juju. But what appears so ridiculous now worked like magic then. And not just on the evil or simpleminded. In his memoirs Professor Golo Mann, the historian and son of Thomas Mann, describes the impression Hitler made on him and a friend when they attended a Nazi rally in 1928. "I did have to defend myself," Golo Mann writes, "against the dynamism and persuasive power of the speaker, but my friend, a Jew, succumbed. 'You know,' he whispered, 'he's right after all.' How often I was to hear those words!"

The reason why even a staunch anti-Nazi like Golo Mann had to will himself to resist the seductive force of at least some of Hitler's arguments, even long before he was invested with the aura of the "Führer and Chancellor," was that Hitler—in what he was and in what he stood for—personified those aspirations, convictions, and detestations funneled into the German psyche during the Napoleonic wars. It was a time when virulent nationalism, supplanting the romantic patriotism of young Germany's early resistance to Bonaparte, swept aside the classical Western humanism that had inspired German thought in Goethe's, Schiller's, and Lessing's days. Arndt, Jahn, Hegel, Fichte, and von Treitschke were Germany's new spiritual leaders; no one born and bred in Germany could totally escape their influence. Imbued with contempt for the pragmatism, humanism, and liberalism that pillared Western thought, they, the most celebrated German philosophers, poets, and historians of their time, considered nationalism the highest goal to which all Germans had to devote all their energies. They proclaimed it to be the mythical mission of the Teutonic race to spread its *Kultur* among the nations, if need be by force, and postulated the absolute supremacy over the individual of the state, which in Schiller's view, "was only a result of human forces, only a work of our thoughts, but man is the source of the force itself and the creator of the thought . . . [hence] the first law of decency is to preserve the liberty of others; the second to show one's own freedom."

Curiously and dangerously paired with this *"über alles"* and "unique mission" mentality went a belief that the German was too innocent and good-natured to withstand the wicked designs, hidden behind noble sentiments, of the hypocritical and decadent West. This pure, poor chap was symbolized in thousands of newspaper cartoons by the figure of *"Der deutsche Michel,"* a rolypoly, kindhearted, sleepy simpleton with a nightcap on his head who, never noticing how they take advantage of him, lets France bedevil the world with libertarian licentiousness and Britain (object of von Treitschke's "fi-

nal reckoning") spread herself all over the globe with the
help of her "Jewish Manchesterites' " evil capitalism—
hated no less by Treitschkean conservatives than by
Marx and his disciples. What else but their vile machinations could explain why Germany was the Johnny-
come-lately junior among the great nations of the world?

But now Germany's savior and avenger, the Führer—
Hegel's *Zwingherr*, or tyrant, who imposes unity and
greatness on the Germans—had arrived. Shrewdly exploiting the nation's vacillation between angst and megalomania he won her soul, as Mephistopheles won
Faust's, by promising, "No bounds are set to your desires."

So Michel wakes up, gets out of his nightwear, and
dons the Nazi uniform. But of course not all Germans
were Michels. Thousands of those who would not abandon human values populated the concentration camps.
Indeed, during the early stage of the Third Reich some
skeptics and Cassandras still spoke their minds, but as
Hitler's rapid and spectacular internal and external suc-
cesses belied them, their warnings found little echo. As
far as the average German was concerned he performed
miracles. Thanks to him, Germans could once again hold
their heads up in pride. Their soldiers marched into the
Rhineland, the Versailles Treaty was a discarded scrap
of paper, Austria came "home into the Reich" and so did
the Sudeten Germans. So dazzled were most Germans
by the glitter and the glory, they did not see how their
rulers, and they with them, were sliding deeper and
deeper into criminality with every passing day. The Führer *was* the state and neither could do wrong. And if acts
of injustice and brutality were committed right under
their very noses, then they averted their eyes and said
their "Lord's Prayer": "If only the Führer knew, if
only the Führer knew, if only. . . ." (By the way, David
Irving, the British writer who maintains that Hitler nei-

ther ordered nor knew of the Final Solution, is still saying it.)

That is how it was. When Primo Levi wrote, "the collective, general crime of almost all Germans of the time was that they lacked the courage to speak," he overlooked the fact that they lacked any desire to do so in the first place. But was that a crime or the collective failure as human beings of a people that had never learned—either under the Kaiser or under Weimar—to strike the right balance between liberty and authority that is the hallmark of democracy? Conditioned from childhood to cherish and obey authority, most Germans enthusiastically embraced Hitler's apparently invincible totalitarian regime. And once such a regime is established, as Primo Levi also says in *The Drowned and the Saved*, "The pressures it can exercise over the individual are frightful. Its weapons are substantially three: direct propaganda or propaganda camouflaged as upbringing, instruction, and popular culture; the barriers erected against pluralism and information; and terror . . ."

Here is the answer to "How was it possible?" Any totalitarian regime will always find the murderers and torturers to do its bidding, be it in the extermination camps and killing woods of Poland or in Cambodia's killing fields. The Ottos, few of them sadists by nature, are always and everywhere among us. In societies ruled by the law they lead ordinary lives and can do no harm. But under lawless and inhuman regimes—Hitler's Germany, Stalinist Russia, Batista's or Castro's Cuba, the Argentine of the generals, the France of Pétain and Laval, Franco's Spain, fascist Italy, Rakoczy's Hungary, Gottwald's Czechoslovakia (the list is endless)—there is never a shortage of butchers who do the gruesome work, if not always with that same thoroughness and efficiency with which the Germans, from Heinrich Himmler to Wolfgang Otto, did theirs.

Yet, but for Hitler, Himmler would have remained a chicken-farmer and Otto a schoolmaster. What was it about this egomaniac Austrian that made him who he was? There can be no conclusive answer. His most impressionable years coincided with the last two decades of a multinational empire torn asunder by the hatreds its peoples felt for each other. There the youth soaked up not only those doctrines that divided Germany from the mainstream of Western civilization but also the contempt of Austria's Pan-Germans for the "subhuman" Slavs together with the anti-Semitism of Schönerer, Liebenfels, and Lueger. So of course did others, but in his incomprehensible mind those ideas were magnified and transmogrified far beyond anything their originators ever had intended. He could think the unthinkable right through to its logical conclusion. If the mission of the Teutonic race was to spread its culture to other nations by force, then wanting war was logical. If one believed Slavs subhuman, then it was the logic of their destiny that they should become Germany's slaves; and if, as Treitschke said, "the Jews are Germany's misfortune," then Auschwitz was the final and logical solution for the Jewish problem. In the last analysis Hitler was the ultimate executor—in both senses of the word—of all the aspirations, convictions, and detestations that had split the German from the Western mind. His end was their end.

One might have expected a spiritual vacuum to follow the collapse of the Third Reich and of the ideologies that had spawned it, but this did not happen. The other Germany, though buried under the pressures of the totalitarian regime, had not fossilized. Freed from the deadweight of the past, it surfaced again in 1945; slowly at first, but then, with the support of the Western Allies, at ever-increasing pace. That was the true postwar "German miracle" and it first came to pass in the Berlin of the Golden Hunger Years. In Berlin, still Germany's capital, still its intellectual and artistic center, the links between the German and the Western mind were reforged. Berlin was not only the city of the *Luftbrücke*, the airlift, but also the *Kulturbrücke*, the "cultural bridge" between Germany and the West, the crucial place at a crucial time. The Federal Republic, the best Germany Germans and the world have ever known, was not born in Bonn but in Berlin. The story of that city and of that time, however incompletely, is what I have been trying to tell.

Dalham, Suffolk
June 1988

Acknowledgments

None of the people mentioned in this book is fictional, but in some cases names have been changed.

I should like to record my sincere gratitude to the following:

—Alan Maclean for being such a wonderful literary signalman. He knows exactly which switches to pull in the mind of a derailed author to get him back on track again.

—Professor Michael Balfour, former director, Information Services Control, Control Commission for Germany (BE), for reading my manuscript and making most helpful suggestions.

—Eva Meyer, the former Fräulein Rose of ISC Intelligence Section, for her great help with documentation.

—The Günter Neumann–Stiftung, Berlin, and Frau M. Grindel, for permission to translate and print two of

the songs from *Schwarzer Jahrmarkt (Blackmarket Fair)*.
—The late Sir Hugh Greene for his valuable help.
—Kurt Rosenow, former chief of U.S. Documents Center, Berlin, for checking the relevant chapter.
—Finally Christel, my wife, for her constant insistence on clarity.

Lest any reader wonder why she, to whom this book is dedicated, does not figure in my story, I must explain that she was exactly nine years and seven months old when I arrived in that city in January 1946. And so, for the sake of discretion, we postponed our first meeting—incidentally not in Berlin but in the *Daily Telegraph* building in Fleet Street—for another fourteen years.

Recommended Reading

BALFOUR, MICHAEL. *West Germany.* London: Ernest Benn, 1968.

BARLOG, BOLESLAV. *Theater Lebenslänglich.* Munich: Drömer, 1981.

BORGELT, HANS. *Das war der Frühling in Berlin.* Berlin: Schneekluth, 1980.

DREWNIAK, BOGUSLAW. *Das Theater im NS Staat.* Düsseldorf: Droste, 1983.

EVANS, RUTH DUDLEY. *Victor Gollancz.* London: Gollancz, 1987.

GRUNBERGER, RICHARD. *A Social History of the Third Reich.* London: Weidenfeld & Nicolson, 1971.

HAFFNER, SEBASTIAN. *Anmerkungen zu Hitler.* Munich: Kindler, 1978.

HURWITZ, HAROLD. *Demokratie und Antikommunismus in Berlin nach 1945.* Cologne: Nottbeck, 1983.

KOHN, HANS. *The Mind of Germany.* London: Macmillan, 1961.

BEFORE THE WALL

LEONHARD, WOLFGANG. *Die Revolution entlässt ihre Kinder.* Berlin: Ullstein, 1961.

LEVI, PRIMO. *The Drowned and the Saved.* London: Michael Joseph, 1988.

——*The Periodic Table.* London: Michael Joseph, 1985.

MANN, THOMAS. *Die Tagebücher.* Frankfurt: Berman/Fischer, 1977.

NELSON, WALTER HENRY. *The Berliners.* London: Longmans, 1969.

SCHEWE, HEINZ. *Gesucht Berlin.* Hamburg: Christians, 1978.

SCHWARZ, HANS-P. *Vom Reich zur Bundesrepublik.* Stuttgart: Klett-Cotta, 1980.

STERN, FRITZ. *Dreams and Delusions.* London: Weidenfeld & Nicolson, 1988.

TAYLOR, SIMON. *Prelude to Genocide: Nazi Ideology and the Struggle for Power.* London: Duckworth, 1985.

VISHNEVSKAYA, GALINA. *Galina.* London: Hodder & Stoughton, 1984.

WESSLING, B. W. *Furtwängler.* Stuttgart: Deutsche Verlags-Anstalt, 1985.

INDEX